Also by David Shobin
The Unborn

The
SEEDING

by David Shobin

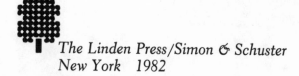

The Linden Press/Simon & Schuster
New York   1982

For
Sharyn

Copyright © 1982 by David Shobin
All rights reserved
including the right of reproduction
in whole or in part in any form

Published by The Linden Press/Simon & Schuster
A Simon & Schuster Division of Gulf & Western Corporation
Simon & Schuster Building
1230 Avenue of the Americas
New York, New York 10020
THE LINDEN PRESS/SIMON & SCHUSTER and colophon
are trademarks of Simon & Schuster
Designed by Irving Perkins Associates
Manufactured in the United States of America
10 9 8 7 6 5 4 3 2 1

Library of Congress Cataloging in Publication Data

Shobin, David.
   The seeding.

   I. Title.
PS3569.H567S4   813'.54   82-3243
ISBN 0-671-43176-5   AACR2

The
SEEDING

Prologue
February

IT WAS BITTERLY cold, and the snow that fell was dry and powdery. The dark-skinned man huddled in his navy greatcoat, keeping to the building's shadows. Across the wide boulevard, a score of passersby had already gathered around to gape, horrified, at the twisted body of the young woman. A widening circle of crimson seeped from her lifeless form onto the snow-covered sidewalk where she had fallen from six stories above. The sound of the crowd's hushed murmuring was carried away by a gust of wind whose intense chill added to the grayness of the morning.

A swirl of snowflakes dotted the man's face, flecks of white crystal that settled on his cheeks without melting. He heard the shrill, distant sirens and glided unseen into a nearby telephone booth. The fog of his breath misted the icy glass, concealing him further, hiding the determined cast of his face. He knew they had committed a costly blunder and could not make that mistake again: this setback alone would take them months to overcome. His chilled fingers leafed with surprising deftness through the pages of the telephone directory, searching for the address of the last alternative, the only other woman who possessed the qualities that, once they were ready, would enable them to succeed. Finding it, he stole from the booth and rejoined the shadows.

July

Chapter 1

"I DON'T BELIEVE—"

"Not now!" snapped the doctor, keeping his admonishment to a whisper. He glared at the technician for emphasis, then peered at the patient. Good. She didn't appear to have heard. She seemed to be drifting into and out of consciousness, quiet and unconcerned, barely aware of her surroundings, or of the testing she was undergoing.

"Is that enough?"

"Get another longitudinal scan."

The ultrasound technician applied more oil to the patient's belly and gently eased the transducer up and down her abdomen. The sonar-generated images that appeared on the oscilloscope were vividly ominous. Abnormal masses were everywhere. Large and small, the lumps filled her pelvis and abdomen. They could mean only one thing.

"That's it," said the doctor with a nod, speaking softly. He had seen enough. "Call Patient Transport and send her back."

The physician slipped out of the sonography room and breathed deeply as he returned to his office. Never in his dozen years in radiology had he seen anything like it. It was frightening. There came an unnecessary rap on the door frame, for the door was open.

9

"Got a minute?" asked the white-coated visitor.

"Yeah."

"Did you finish Flanagan?"

"Just now."

"You still have your mask on."

"Hmmm," grunted the radiologist, slipping off the green surgical mask. Since Mrs. Flanagan's unknown disease was considered potentially contagious, all personnel coming into contact with her were required to wear protective masks.

"You don't look too happy."

"I can't understand it," said the radiologist. "I did her IVP five, maybe six days ago. There was nothing. Bupkis. Normal renal function, clean pelvis."

"And now?"

"She's loaded with masses. Nodes or mets, I don't know. Not that it matters now."

"I thought so."

"Why?"

"We tapped her bone marrow yesterday. The slides came through this morning. Her marrow is nearly gone, wiped out. Overrun, I should say."

"With what?"

"Whole clusters of blastic cells—sheets and sheets of them."

"Leukemia?"

"No, I don't think so. The pattern doesn't fit. It might be some kind of bizarre lymphoma."

"It didn't show up on her peripheral blood smear?"

"No, that's the clunker. She still has a high white count, but what do you expect with a fever like that?"

"Did you tell Clements?"

"Did *you*?"

"Thanks a lot," sighed the radiologist, not relishing the thought of bearing bad tidings to the short-tempered Chief of Obstetrics and Gynecology. He picked up the phone and dialed the department's extension. Clements came onto the line with a roar audible across the room. The radiologist winced. As succinctly as possible, he related his findings and those of the hematologist. His summary was interrupted by a voluble ranting that continued for at least a minute. There was silence, and a click. The radiologist hung up.

"Sounds like he's in fine form today."

"Did you hear?"

"Just the tone, not the substance."

"Clements wanted to know what kind of jackass I think he is. Before I could respond with my true sentiments, he asked if I was trying to tell him that a young, healthy woman could get admitted to this hospital with a mysterious illness that now appears to be well-nigh incurable. And before I could say 'You betcha,' he announced that we'll be conferring outside Flanagan's room in half an hour. Want more?"

"There goes the golf game."

Precisely thirty minutes later, in a classroom several doors away from Annie Flanagan, an anxious group of residents and students awaited the entrance of Dr. Ridley Clements. He stormed in within seconds, white coattails flying. Tall, square-jawed, he had a commanding presence. His knitted brow betrayed his fury. His voice boomed.

"I won't spare you my feelings," he began. "This case is an outrage. If I find any negligence here, I won't hesitate to recommend that that person be suspended from the staff. I don't give a damn whose toes are stepped on, or whose careers are endangered. I simply can't allow things like this to happen on my service! In a moment, we'll go to see the patient. Then we'll reassemble here. For those of you who have been so preoccupied elsewhere that you don't know the pertinent facts in this case, I'll briefly summarize. Five weeks from now the patient, Mrs. Flanagan, is due to give birth to her second child. We anticipated a normal vaginal delivery, without complications. Until recently, Mrs. Flanagan was a healthy, intelligent individual, eager to participate in natural childbirth.

"Exactly one week ago she was readmitted to the Obstetrical service delirious, with a high fever. The working diagnosis was an infectious process, probably uterine. Appropriate cultures were taken, and antibiotics were begun. Interestingly, all the cultures were negative. And so was every single laboratory test! I was assured time and time again, by my own physicians and numerous consultants, that nothing at all could be found. And yet the patient didn't improve. In fact, her condition has steadily worsened, and we lost the fetal heartbeat yesterday. And now, within the past hour, two of our most respected clinicians inform me that the patient has a widely disseminated, catastrophic disease! Now you tell me, those of you here, just how is this possible—that a healthy young mother-to-be becomes suddenly, mysteriously ill, and for a week in this prestigious institution not a goddamn thing can be found wrong with her until today, when she's found to be nearly moribund! No, don't bother"—he waved his hand disgustedly—"I don't really want to hear it. I'd rather see the patient."

Clements exited somberly, without another word. The entire group rose en masse to follow him, their grumbling held to an inaudible murmur. The day was lovely, but no one bothered glancing through the long window whose panoramic view stretched across downtown Washington as far as the distant Capitol dome. Soon the corridor was filled with white coats. The procession paused outside Mrs. Flanagan's room. A large sign with bold block letters read, "COMPLETE ISOLATION—ALL VISITORS REPORT TO THE NURSING STATION." Led by Clements, everyone donned a surgical mask and cap and put on a sterile gown.

"There are lessons to be learned here," Clements whispered, though his whisper was louder than the average man's conversational tone, "but let me do the teaching. Leave the talking to me." He pushed open the door and the group tiptoed into the room.

Mrs. Flanagan's bed rested inside a humidified isolation chamber, a flexible plastic bubble with germproof access portals. The humidity created a thick fog around the patient. A nurse assisted Dr. Clements into sterile white coveralls. Then she unfastened the plastic entrance vent, and Clements eased himself inside. She zipped up the polyethylene behind him. It was a ghostly scene as Clements walked slowly through the mist, softly calling, "Mrs. Flanagan?"

He paused at the bedside, his movements barely visible. He was bending over the patient. Touching, probing. Suddenly he whirled around. He stormed back to the plastic partition, yanked it open wide, and ripped off his mask and cap. The fog spewed forth and wafted through the room as Clements flung off his outer garments. The nurse started to protest, but Clements cut her short.

"She's dead, you idiot." With that, he abruptly left the room.

No one moved. Warmed by the outer air, the fog cleared. Everyone stared at the cadaver. Annie Flanagan's jaw was slack, the tip of her drying tongue protruding beyond her bared teeth. And then they all inhaled it at the same moment, eyes immediately darting from one person to the next. What was suddenly obvious was not merely the recognition of mortality—the drying, yellow-gray skin growing tighter on the victim's face. Rather, it was the smell. For carried by the mist was the most curious of aromas, an exotic herbal essence portending more of moist green life than of the rancid odor of recent death.

Chapter 2

DEATH WAS A silent visitor that morning, as unwelcome as the guest who arrives unexpectedly for tea. Its dark shadow paused at the bedside of Rachel Garnes, hesitated, and then decided to linger.

Rachel felt its extra presence. In an instant the room's entire atmosphere weighed more, pressing down evenly, a heavy satin quilt that pinned her to the mattress like a down comforter. It was a pleasant sensation. Rachel knew what was inevitable, and she felt almost content to give in to it. She would just as willingly exhale once slowly and let her soul expire, were it not for the smell. Her cubicle was suddenly awash with tropical mustiness, the steamy damp of the jungle trail under a forest canopy of palm. Rachel's eyes twinkled, partly with fever, partly from the sudden aroma. Her tired lungs expanded slowly. She took in the scent of cedar and sapodilla, the earthy aroma of humus and vine, the fragrant bouquet of bromeliad and bougainvillea. The olfactory nerve endings in her brain were stimulated with forgotten sensations. Perhaps this was the start of heaven, she thought, and her weary lids fluttered closed. Greenery was everywhere. Her mind's eye pictured a profusion of leaf and petal, bud and stem, waving stalk and reed. Nearer, my God, to . . .

14

Rachel Garnes joyously let go of life and released her last breath in a susurrant exhalation. She had not been so happy in years.

Rachel's death was undiscovered for a quarter-hour. The young medication nurse, making rounds with her wheelable pharmacy cart, noted the absence of chest-wall movement under the white sheet covering Rachel's thin frame. She felt for the pulse, sighed heavily, and immediately put in a call to the resident on duty.

She dialed reluctantly. It was July fifth—four days after the start of the new medical year. The dubious privilege of proclaiming a person dead went to the junior physician on duty, and she was wondering how the recent medical-school graduate would take the patient's death. It would probably be his first patient to expire since he had received his degree.

Dr. Hassan Mohammed arrived within minutes, stumbling along the corridor. Nervous, surmised the nurse. She tried to size him up as he walked. Certainly not a swashbuckler, she thought. Maybe a lifesaver; or, a cocky-doc?

The nurse bade him to the bedside and pulled down the sheet. He fumbled for Rachel's limp wrist, placing his stethoscope on her rib cage. Then he reached for the lids and shined a light into her pupils. He gazed at the nurse with an expression of wide-eyed dismay.

Oh, Christ, she thought. Not a weeper.

"She's dead," he said softly.

"Yes, Doctor. I kind of gathered that."

"Did you notify Dr. Erikson?"

"No. I have to call the junior resident first to pronounce her."

"Pronounce her?"

"Dead."

"Pronounce her dead?"

"Dead. D-E-D, dead. You have to tell me, 'Nurse, I hereby pronounce this patient dead.'"

"But she *is* dead, isn't she?" he asked.

Gimme shelter, she thought. She glanced at the wall clock, picked up the chart, and made an entry in the Nurse's Notes as she spoke. *"Pronounced dead by Dr. ..."* She glanced at his name tag. *". . . Mohammed at 12:42 A.M."* She flipped the chart closed and handed it to him. "All yours. Make a progress note on the pink sheet. Then you can call Dr. Erikson."

"Do you know the number of his on-call room?"

By heart, she thought. "No, I'm sorry. Dial the operator and she'll connect you. I'll take care of the patient."

Mohammed walked uncertainly toward the nursing station, pausing once to glance back into the room. The sheet was already pulled over Rachel's head. Finally satisfied that there was nothing more he could do, Mohammed proceeded to the nursing station and placed his call.

Dr. Erikson was slow to arrive. He glided sleepily onto the ward, collar open, without a tie. Mohammed leaped to his feet.

"I'm sorry, Dr. Erikson."

"Sorry, Dr. Mohammed?"

"Sorry that . . . I had to disturb you."

"Me too," Erikson yawned. "You'd think Garnes could have waited until six or seven before she cooled it."

Mohammed was confused. "I did right to call?" he asked, in heavily accented English.

Erikson smiled and clapped him on the shoulder. "You did right, good buddy. After you pronounce someone, you call the senior resident. I don't know what they do where you come from. Probably just dump the stiff in the Persian Gulf."

"Oh, no, Dr. Erikson."

"Pollute the oil, huh?"

Mohammed looked flustered.

"Forget it. Did you call the family and the Admitting Office?"

Mohammed's sheepish expression revealed that he had not.

"Christ, Hassan, was I as helpless as you when I first started here?"

16

"I'm sorry, Dr. Erikson."

"Please, let's not dance that 'sorry' waltz again. When you said it before, I thought you were going to tell me you were sorry you couldn't save her life. I'll call the family myself. This is one post we need."

"Post, Dr. Erikson?"

"Postmortem, Hassan. Rack-'em slash-'em."

Erikson reviewed the procedural formalities and paperwork with Mohammed. Then he notified the next of kin. He spoke seriously, sounding contrite and apologetic.

"You seem to have cared deeply for the patient," said Mohammed.

"I care for the post, Hassan. I don't always, but this one's important. Wrap up the chart tonight and meet me in the Administrator's office at seven-thirty. I'll show you how it's done."

Later that morning they assembled in the foyer of Administration. Erikson looked refreshed, while Mohammed appeared positively distraught. Erikson steered him aside.

"Look, Hassan, don't get all misty on me. The family's in there and we're out here. When we go in, look humble and sit in a corner. I talk, you listen. Watch what I do. And for heaven's sake, keep your mouth shut."

Saddled with Mohammed, Erikson thanked God that the Garnes family wasn't Jewish.

While dressing that morning, Erikson had contemplated the overture he would use to get consent for the post. All approaches were variations on a theme, using a handful of common techniques. One was to appeal to the dead patient's liberalism. Another was the plea for science. A third pitch, known as the Brotherhood Ploy, was an offshoot of the second. Suppose, the doctor suggested, that tomorrow another patient with exactly the same condition were admitted to the hospital. If by our doing a postmortem today, that patient could be helped tomorrow—wouldn't the family want that? Certainly the deceased patient would have.

A final variation was something called Assigned Guilt. It

17

had to be carefully milked lest it backfire. The goal was to make the family feel guilty—subtly, but enough so that they felt they had to comply with the doctor's wishes. If only we had gotten to her sooner. Or, perhaps if someone had insisted that Rachel see a doctor when she first appeared ill—who knows what would have happened?

Erikson decided not to take any specific tack. His ability to speak coherently and persuasively was his main weapon. He straightened his tie and, followed by Mohammed, walked in.

There were four of them, three women and a man. Mohammed wordlessly retreated to a corner of the room. The wide office was decorated with Naugahyde furniture encircling a low mahogany coffee table. Plastic potted plants marked the room's corners, and stale prints of modern art embellished the walls. When Erikson entered, the family's faces were downcast. They looked as if they were trying to memorize the wood grain of the table.

They slowly lifted their heads to stare at him. He recognized two of the women from their appearances during visiting hours. The man was a stranger. The other woman was strikingly attractive. Erikson immediately knew that her beauty would prove to be his biggest problem. He wondered about the man. Was he a brother, perhaps?

"I'm Dr. Erikson," he began. "I'm one of the doctors who were taking care of Rachel. I've met some of you before. I'm sorry I didn't have the chance to meet the rest of you."

They regarded him dumbly through red-rimmed eyes, waiting for him to continue.

"I just can't tell you how sorry I am. We all expected this for some time. But now that it's finally here, it's a shock." He paused for effect, looking briefly away. "If there were only something else we could have done, some little last thing . . . I don't know. In a way, I feel we're responsible."

"No," droned the man flatly. "Not your fault."

"I know. I know that logically. But emotionally, it's confusing. I think that's because I became involved with her. I felt as if I knew Rachel. I guess that's because she was so young."

The attractive young woman began to cry. Her blouse bounced when she sobbed.

Don't do that, sugar. I've got a job to do. Of all the times not to wear a bra.

"We made rounds on her two times a day," he continued. "Sometimes three. We were fighting for a ray of hope, a little breathing room. It wasn't there; she just got worse. Still, no matter what her condition was, in the back of my mind I thought we might be missing something. We gave her all the medications we could. But even these wonder drugs didn't bring the miracle we hoped for. They just didn't work. I know, as a physician, that it was because her condition was too desperate. Yet I can't shake the feeling that there might have been something else."

"How do you mean, something else?" asked one of the other women.

"I don't know. I'm not sure. Maybe I'm trying to rationalize our failure. But there must have been a reason why she didn't respond. She should at least have shown some improvement, but she didn't. For all the things that were obvious about her, perhaps the most important was hidden. And we were too blind to see it. There might have been another condition that eluded us."

"What condition?"

"Again, I'm not sure." Erikson shook his head. "I've thought about it a lot, but I can't put my finger on it. Yet I know it's there."

He was really moving now. The family gave him their complete attention. Like any competent actor, he delivered his lines, the words flowing from him with ease and animation. Slowly, he was getting caught up in emotion. He lived the part. Erikson leaned forward, and his eyes captured theirs.

"Please understand me. We did everything possible for Rachel. I don't think she could have received finer care anywhere. But in my heart I know there was something that escaped us. It's something we simply have to find out. And I know that the grief you're feeling now doesn't keep you from wanting to find out too." As he looked slowly from one to the next, his palms inched upward in supplication. "It's because of this, this thing that eludes us, that I ask for your permission to examine her body."

His gaze riveted theirs. He wouldn't allow them to fidget.

"You mean an autopsy?" asked the man.

The word said, Erikson withdrew his gaze. He looked at his hands, surprised that they were trembling. The impact of his words was powerful. His heart raced. His eyes flashed amongst them, a staccato winding of film from one frame to the next. Emotion welled up in his throat.

The young woman uncrossed her legs and sat with knees apart. Her short skirt was ridiculously inappropriate for the occasion. Erikson could see well up the length of her thigh.

"Please don't think of it as an autopsy. That sounds so cold, so cruel. If I had come to you yesterday and said, We can do an operation that may not work, but there's a chance it might save her—you would have given your permission, wouldn't you?"

They nodded.

"Think of it that way, then—as an operation we tried that didn't work. An autopsy is no more, no less. I know it's something Rachel would have wanted. We owe it to her to solve this riddle, this terrible puzzle that destroyed her."

In five minutes they had signed three sets of papers granting permission for an autopsy. Erikson had his post. He walked with Mohammed toward the cafeteria for breakfast, making a mental note to find out the young woman's phone number.

"Dr. Erikson, you were magnificent!" exclaimed a beaming Mohammed. "I don't know where you learned to do such things!"

"Can it, Hassan."

"No, really. Everything you said was true, but it was the way you said it. I'm not sure this is something I will ever master!"

"You'd better, Doctor. If this post turns out to be what I

think, you damn well better. Because there's going to be a whole shit-load of cases just like this one."

THE HOSPITAL'S morgue was similar to those in other university centers. There was ample space for both mundane and exotic, ranging from routine surgical dissection to elaborate teaching cases. Two stainless steel tables gleamed side by side. The room had the smell of formaldehyde and other chemicals, yet the pungent odor of blood was everywhere, saturating even the freshly washed wall tiles.

Each medical resident was expected to pursue a case in its entirety, following the patient from admission to discharge, even if that discharge was to a funeral parlor. Attendance at autopsies was mandatory. Thus, Erikson and Mohammed joined Dr. Hank Cho, the pathologist, later that morning. Dr. Cho was a maverick second-generation Korean-American whose skill at postmortem dissection was second to none.

With the assistance of the residents, Cho began. His scalpel made a neat Rokitansky incision—a Y-shaped slash that began at each clavicle, merged at the sternum, and carried down to the pubis. After retracting the skin, he carved through the sternal cartilage with an electric bone saw. He sliced through the abdomen, baring coiled loops of whitish-yellow bowel. Then they smelled it.

The fruity aroma startled Mohammed, who stepped back. Erikson reached for his arm.

"Steady, Hassan. You okay?"

"Yes, I think so. What is that smell?"

"Good question," interrupted Cho. "We don't know what it comes from. This is the third case we've had in a little more than two weeks. You open the belly, and bingo: take a whiff. Like flowers."

Not exactly, thought Erikson. It was like flowers, and yet it wasn't. It was more like the interior of a plant shop, or a nursery. It was a mixture of smells rather than a single scent.

He could have been pushing a lawn mower, the air filled with the aroma of fresh-cut grass; picking ripe pears and peaches in a sunny orchard; or trimming roses and staking tomatoes in his garden.

"It smells like eucalyptus in the markets at home."

"Where's home, Dr. Mohammed?"

"Don't get him started, Hank," said Erikson. "Once Hassan gets going on the beauty of the Middle East, you can't shut him up. Camel shit turns to caviar."

Cho worked deftly. He made quick incisions in ligaments and connective tissues before extending the incision toward the pubic area. Suddenly he stopped, surprised, as a clearly pregnant uterus came into view, filling the entire pelvis.

"You didn't tell me she was pregnant."

Erikson was dumbfounded; there was no reference in the Garnes chart to pregnancy. "I had no idea. How far along is she?"

"Looks like five months, maybe six. Hard to tell, she's so thin. What the hell. Give me a hand, will you?"

Within minutes he had freed up the patient's innards. Working together, the three of them removed all the cadaver's internal organs, from the rectum to the base of the tongue. The corpse shell was now a hollow. The wet pile of organs glistened in the overhead lamps. The structures were still warm, and the faintest wisp of steam evaporated in the morgue's air-conditioned chill. The scent of a floral bouquet wafted in the air.

"Do other cancer patients have this odor?" asked Mohammed.

"Wish they did," said Hank Cho. "In most cancer posts, it's . . ." He hesitated. "Well, it's something else."

Mohammed flustered, thinking he had made a frightful mistake. "But she did have cancer, yes?"

"Yes, indeed. These nodules," said Cho, pointing to yellowish-gray patches of flesh in the lungs, "are metastases. In another minute, we'll find them in the liver and lymph nodes, too. She's riddled with cancer."

22

"But no primary," said Erikson.

"Not if she's like the others."

"Primary?" asked Mohammed.

"Primary lesion—the first organ affected before the malignancy spreads," said Cho. "In our last two cases, we couldn't find the primary. We wound up signing it out as 'carcinomatosis,' without knowing where the mess started. From the appearance—and from the smell—I'd wager that this one's going to be just like the others."

Cho finished the organ dissection by 11 A.M., taking careful tissue sections from each organ. He had been right: there was no obviously malignant lesion from which the cancer had sprung. The tissue sections would be prepared into slides for microscopic analysis. Ordinarily, the slides were ready for study the following morning. But Cho was in a hurry. He asked his technicians to have the slides ready before the day was over. Perhaps the microscope would reveal what gross inspection did not.

The slides were available by five that afternoon. Cho paged Erikson and Mohammed, both of whom were curious about the diagnosis. Cho's microscope was a twin-headed binocular model, which allowed two people to inspect the slide at once. Erikson looked into the eyepiece across from Cho.

"Obviously malignant cells," commented Cho, sliding the hair-fine pointer across the slide. "Sheets of them. Bizarre mitoses . . . hyperchromasia. But I can't make head or tail out of the organ structure."

He reviewed the slides one by one, first with Erikson, then with Mohammed. In the end he drew a blank. Cancer peppered the patient's body, but examination of the slides gave no clue as to where the malignant cells had originated.

"That's it," admitted Cho. "I'm stumped. I'm going to call Atlanta."

"The C.D.C.?" asked Erikson.

"Right."

Erikson and Mohammed remained within earshot as Cho phoned the nation's Centers for Disease Control. Three nearly identical, unidentifiable malignancies had been discovered in a short period of time. Perhaps it was some sort of epidemic. He hoped the C.D.C. could give him a clue.

After exchanging telephone pleasantries with someone he knew, Cho began describing his findings. He gave a synopsis of the clinical course, physical evaluation, and autopsy results. But while reviewing some further details of the patient's history, he was cut short. His facial expression was curious, puzzled. He listened intently to the party on the other end of the line, offering an occasional interjection.

"Yes, right. . . . But how did you—? . . . Precisely. . . . Okay. I'll send them off to you first thing in the morning. Thanks."

Cho hung up the receiver, obviously perplexed. He seemed deep in thought.

"What is it, Dr. Cho?" asked Mohammed. "What did they say?"

Cho looked away. He rubbed his eyes. "Well. What worries me is that my buddy in Atlanta knew exactly what I was talking about. He knew what I was going to say before I said it. Seems he's been on the phone a lot this week. Two other similar cases have been reported, both in pregnant women. Both rapidly fatal, both unidentifiable. Both identical right down to the smell."

"Well," said Erikson, "that pretty much eliminates an infectious component."

"Not necessarily. Those two cases and our three make five," he said. "But they were all from the Washington area."

Chapter 3

SHE RAN THROUGH the forest, dodging branch and limb. They were there, not far behind, stalking relentlessly, closing the gap. She looked over her shoulder, then tripped and fell. The earth was moist and spongy. Wild-eyed, she scrambled to her feet and darted farther into the woods. A veil of cobwebs splayed across her face. She brushed at the wispy stickiness. The fine strands clung to her eyelids, silky patches across her cheeks. They wouldn't rub free. She shook her head frantically, clawing at the gossamer thread, suddenly horrified by the large, black spider that slowly, slowly inched toward her.

Michelle bolted upright in bed. She was soaked in perspiration. The thin acrylic of her nightgown clung to her skin. Her stomach ached; she placed her hand on her lower abdomen. Now fully awake, recovering from her nightmare, she looked around cautiously. She was in her own bedroom.

A dream. It was just another bad dream, but the worst she'd had so far. She took a deep breath and wiped her damp forehead. Swinging her legs over the side of the mattress, she searched for her slippers with her toes. She wiggled into them and got up. But her legs were so weak that she plopped right down again.

For minutes she sat there in a catatonic fog, the faraway,

thousand-yard stare of a bombing victim pulled from the rubble. Then she blinked her eyes as, by bits, she began to come back to herself. It was hard for her to think, let alone concentrate. She felt drugged. She steadied herself, got up once more, and shuffled to the bathroom.

She looked at her face in the mirror. Tiny dewdrops of sweat beaded her upper lip. There were no bags under her eyes, and her face looked rested. Yet it was only 6 A.M. She felt as though she had been sleeping for a long time.

She was weakened by the nightmare. In spite of her facial appearance, she felt physically and mentally exhausted. She went back to the bathroom and turned on the tub's tap, filling the bath to the rim with hot water. Soon she steeped in its warmth, resting there for hours, until it was finally time to dress for work.

She selected a loose summer knit from her closet. In the bedroom, she held it in front of her, inspecting the fabric. Morning light filled the room. The air conditioner's thermostat sensed the warmth. The condenser kicked in, sending a cool gust through the air. Suddenly, Michelle's eyes darted to her mirror. She saw her bedroom door slowly closing.

She screamed. The dress fell from her fingers as she whirled about. She ran to the door and yanked on the knob. It opened smoothly. She looked quickly into the hall. Seeing that her apartment was undisturbed, Michelle relaxed. She closed her eyes and breathed deeply.

What was wrong with her? She felt spastic, with an edgy tightness she'd never known before. The sudden draft from the air conditioner had pushed the door closed. It had happened dozens of times before. She knew the sound, was familiar with it. Why did she assume that someone . . .

Stop it, she scolded. Forget it and get dressed. Keeping her mind on her task, she fixed her hair and makeup and locked her apartment half an hour later.

Michelle Van Dyne breezed into her office just before nine. Her secretary hadn't arrived yet. She let herself in, contemplating the thousand and one things that awaited her at the start of the new work week. As she put her handbag in a drawer, she was surprised by the tidiness of her desk-top blotter. She distinctly remembered having left a number of items there on Friday, intending to resume work promptly Monday morning. Now the papers were gone.

There was a knock and the office door opened. It was her secretary. Michelle gave her a welcoming smile and returned to her desk drawers.

"Maggie, didn't I leave a pile of stuff on my desk Friday? I can't find a single paper." Locating nothing in the center drawer, she rummaged through the right-hand files. "Maggie?"

Maggie stared at her boss. Speechless, openmouthed, she had the expression of the dumbstruck. She slowly walked in Michelle's direction, staring in astonishment. Michelle looked up and met her gaze.

"Oh, dear. That look means trouble. I misplaced them again, huh? Okay, where'd—"

"Are you all right?" Maggie asked, her tone the barest whisper.

Michelle didn't know what she was talking about. Maggie, suddenly animated, swept around the desk and embraced Michelle, hugging her tight. When she pulled away, there were tears in her eyes.

"We were so worried, Ms. Van Dyne," said Maggie. "Where were you?"

"What?"

"I kept calling and calling. We tried everywhere. We thought something horrible happened to you!"

Michelle smiled uneasily, awkwardly. Was this someone's idea of a joke? "Maggie, why do I have the feeling you're trying to tell me something?"

"You didn't know we were looking for you?"

"When?"

"For the last two days!"

"Over the weekend? What's so important it couldn't wait until Monday?"

"But I'm *talking* about Monday! And Tuesday! We called your landlord, your friends. We considered calling your parents, but we didn't want to alarm them. Mr. Richardson said that if we didn't find you by today, we'd have to call the police!"

Michelle smiled. "You must be kidding!"

Maggie fell silent. Michelle felt confusion and uneasiness beginning to overtake her. She deliberately walked toward the clock-radio that rested atop her file cabinet. Halfway across the room, she stopped abruptly. The clock's digital numbers blinked on and off at 9:04 A.M. Beside the time display was the date.

It said Wednesday, the twenty-seventh.

Michelle's heart began beating faster. "This has gone far enough," she said to Maggie, with an edge to her voice. "I can take a joke as well as the next guy, but it's not funny anymore. Dammit, Maggie, will you please wipe that baffled expression off your face?"

"I'll let Mr. Richardson know you're all right."

"Of course I'm all right! What are you talking about?"

"Just that we were worried, that's all."

Michelle tried to control herself. "Maggie . . ." Then she saw the newspaper folded on top of her desk. She took it and opened it to the front page, searching for the date. When she saw it, she went pale.

It *was* Wednesday. It *was* the twenty-seventh.

The newspaper slipped from her hand. As if in a trance, Michelle shuffled to her desk chair and sat down. She weakly asked Maggie to leave her office; she needed to be alone. Feeling numb, she picked up the phone and pressed an extension for an outside line. She dialed the operator. Her voice was weak.

"Operator, can you please tell me today's date?" There was a pause as Michelle listened. Then the receiver started to fall from her fingers. She tightened her grip and slowly put the phone back in its cradle.

Michelle was stunned. Here she was, arriving for work early, ready to tackle Monday morning head on. Except it wasn't Monday. It was Wednesday.

At least two days of her life were missing.

She had absolutely no memory of the lost hours. She thought back to leaving the office on Friday. She'd gone home and dined out that evening at the new Italian restaurant with the Gilberts. And then . . . what? Michelle suddenly realized she couldn't remember Saturday or Sunday, either.

Between bedtime on Friday and her recent early-morning nightmare, her mind was a blank. There was no hint, no clue. Michelle frowned and toyed with a pencil. Yet there had to be some reasonable explanation! As someone who prided herself on her recall, she now felt impotent, like a mental cripple. The pencil snapped in her fingers. She dropped the pieces and looked at her hands. They were trembling.

Michelle tried to sort out her confusion, but it was no use. She finally got down to work, pushing twice as hard to catch up with her unfinished business. The tedium of the routine was soothing, and the rest of the morning and afternoon passed quickly. Before she left for the day, she called Maggie confidentially aside. Her secretary looked downcast.

"Don't look so glum, Maggie," she encouraged. Then, as if sharing a secret, she smiled and said softly, "I promise to return tomorrow!"

Finally Maggie returned her smile. "All right."

"Just tell anyone who asks . . ." She hesitated, eyebrows arched, searching for the right words. "Just tell them that I was away and forgot to call. Okay?"

Maggie nodded.

Michelle gathered her papers and started for the door. "We women of the world, Maggie . . ." She winked. "Can you cover for me?" Then she gave her cheeriest smile as she opened the door, looking about so that no one overheard their secret. "Someday I'll let you in on it, I promise!"

"Yes, Ms. Van Dyne!"

As she left the building, papers tucked under her arm, Michelle hoped her explanation would suffice. She wondered if her white lie was anywhere near the truth. She smiled to herself. I can't believe it, she mused. I probably had the greatest time in the world, and I can't remember a thing!

Later that evening, her lightheartedness gave way to more serious contemplation. She knew Maggie would do as she was told, and Michelle wanted her explanation to be a simple one. For anything more complex might lead to the truth, a truth Michelle was beginning to find positively frightening: that she had no logical explanation for her absence at all.

SLEEP CAME slowly that night. Michelle curled up under her covers, staring into the dark, trying to summon up the inner warmth of courage. She felt so cold. Could she really have amnesia? It seemed incomprehensible that something so bizarre could ever happen to her. There had to be a logical explanation. Eventually, she thought, she would remember. She hoped she could wait it out.

The next day, Michelle again dived headlong into her work. She took a break at midmorning. She got up from her desk and stretched, then headed for the water cooler just down the hall from her office.

She pressed the button and filled her paper cup. Large bubbles of air floated lazily upward through the glass jug atop the water dispenser. Something about them held her mesmerized. Their globules broke through the surface and rippled the liquid with containerized wavelets.

"May I?" asked the man behind her, waiting his turn.

She heard nothing, her gaze locked on the eddies of water within the glass jug.

"Are you finished, miss?"

Water, sparkling and pure. A fleeting memory locked in her subconscious suddenly evoked images of things past. A dream? She felt a hand on her shoulder. She looked around, saw the man.

"I hate to interrupt your trance, but may I have a drink?"

"Oh . . . I'm sorry."

She stepped aside and sipped from her cup, looking at the water dispenser. Water. Something about water. In her mind the vision was there, vivid and yet hazy, moving into and out of mental focus. A shimmering pool, icy-pure; a gentle waterfall whose cascading sheets of mist glistened with colors of the rainbow. She struggled with the image, wondering why, and where. Her conscious mind was a beachcomber, sifting through the sands of her memory, searching for seashells of remembrance.

She started back to her office. Damn. This thought came out of nowhere, an unexpected tableau with a haunting nuance of familiarity. She had never been a daydreamer before. But now, once again, thoughts began to occur to her. She had a transient image of trickling water and beautiful landscape. The image was lovely, a vision of paradise. What was happening to her? She started back. Reaching her office, she crumpled the cup and tossed it into her secretary's wastebasket.

"Any messages, Maggie?"

The secretary handed her slips of paper. "The Under Secretary called, and said he'll be in his office until noon. And someone from Interior is returning your call."

"Get him for me, would you? And tell the Under Secretary that I'll get back to him."

Michelle entered her office and closed the door. She had a good idea what the man at Interior wanted to discuss. He had a problem, but unfortunately there was nothing she could do about it. The intercom buzzed on her desk.

"Mr. Sykes on four-two, Ms. Van Dyne."

She picked up the phone. "Arthur? Who's on the warpath this time?"

31

"They're staging a sit-in on the Longview slurry line. A sit-in!"

"Who is?"

"Ranchers, some schoolteachers. Local Indians. Isn't there something you can do? Anything?"

"We've been through this before, Arthur. You know I can't stop the pipeline. Anyway, P.R. is your department. I'm afraid it's out of my hands." She listened patiently to his complaints. In the end she promised to speak with the Secretary to see if some sort of conciliatory statement could be worked out.

She hung up and rubbed her eyes. Her job was a never-ending battle that pitted the environmentalists against the energy producers. Dealing with ecological matters was easier than coping with nuclear sit-ins, but it took its toll on her. This particular skirmish concerned strip mining in Wyoming's Powder River Basin. The area was immensely rich in coal, and boomtowns sprang up everywhere, transforming the land.

She sympathized with the ranchers who watched 180-ton-belly dump trucks tear up the land with their massive tires, and for the environmentalists who warned that mining the prairie would leave a permanent, ugly scar. But the country's energy predicament was such that there was no choice. It had to be done.

She finished her calls by noon and left the office, planning to meet a friend for lunch. She strolled down Independence Avenue, savoring the sun's warmth on her shoulders. Pam sat on a bench outside the café and waved Michelle over.

"Want to eat out here?" She pointed to a small table with an awning.

Michelle glanced at the sky. "Yes. It's beautiful today."

The waiter seated them under the Noilly Prat logo and handed each a menu. Pam perused the handwritten fare, speaking casually.

"Where'd you go this weekend? They called from your office Monday."

Michelle gripped her chair, white-knuckled. "I went home."

32

Pam looked up. "Cleveland?"

"Mm-hm."

"Your folks okay now?"

"Yes. I think they're finally over it. Sometimes I wonder if it's tougher on them, as they get older, than it is on me. Well, what shall we eat?" Michelle asked brightly, closing the discussion.

Pam quickly looked back at the menu, sensing her friend's reluctance to dwell on the tragedy that haunted Michelle's family. "God, I'm sick of quiche. And if I drink any more Perrier, I'll float away. What in the world could this be: 'Le Hot Dog Provençale'?"

"A frank on French bread?"

"Outrageous."

Michelle was relieved that her excuse was satisfactory, at least for now. She didn't want to talk about it. They resumed studying the menu, finally deciding on seafood salad and wine. Pam, a journalist who lived in the same Georgetown apartment building as Michelle, was an incurable gossip. She carried the bulk of their conversation. At first she nattered on about the recent cancer deaths in the city, and then moved on to more tantalizing insights into Washington life. Michelle, content to sip her wine, listened halfheartedly without interrupting. She casually looked at the striped tablecloth of bold colors. As she stared, her mind began to drift. Again, sights filled her mind. Visions and images. A circus of color, with light greens and pastels, tones of emerald and bright flashes of pure brilliance. Her vision didn't waver, but her mind spun through the rainbow, around and around and—

"Mike, are you deaf?" Pam was shaking her roughly by the arm, digging her nails in for emphasis. "Mike!"

Michelle snapped out of it. She looked up to see the waiter glaring at her.

"If you please, ma'm'selle."

"What?" She looked blankly at the waiter, then at Pam.

"Your chair, dummy. Move your chair!"

Alert now, Michelle noticed that she was blocking the

waiter's path, as he tried to lead a couple with two small children around her. "I'm sorry."

The waiter moved by brusquely. The children scrutinized Michelle as they sidled past, still peering at her over their shoulders.

"What's wrong with that lady, Mommy?"

"Shhh!"

Michelle looked at Pam, who regarded her with curiosity. Michelle groaned, plunked her elbows onto the table, and put her face in her hands. She felt suddenly weary. Eyes closed, she rubbed her forehead with her fingertips. What *was* wrong with her? She had always been so alert, mentally precise. Should she see a doctor?

"Are you okay, Mike?"

She eased her hands away and smiled. "Just tired."

"Late night?"

"Right."

"Talk about night owls—rumor has it that a mutual acquaintance of ours is a midnight groupie," began Pam, sending another bit of hearsay soaring. Her manner of talking was self-perpetuating, like a lit fuse that either exploded or spluttered out at the end of its wick. She was still speaking when they finished lunch and Michelle suggested they pay the check.

The day passed quickly, as did Friday. Leaving her office, the week's work behind her, Michelle began a long, leisurely walk back to her Georgetown apartment. Her arms were filled with paperwork that would keep her busy most of the weekend. She followed the river route, stopping home in order to drop her briefcase and change into jeans.

After a light supper, she went to a Chaplin movie alone, something she hadn't done in years. It was late when she arrived home. The faint summer sounds of midnight revelry reached her ears when she finally prepared for bed. Wearing an oversized pajama top, she turned off the lights and pulled the cool sheets about her as she slid under the covers. She hoped it wouldn't be hard to fall asleep. For the past few nights she had lain awake for hours, trying to make sense of the nonsensical.

She worried that there might be something physically wrong with her. She had never been inattentive before, or suffered from memory loss. For all she knew, mental lapses might be the first sign of disease—a brain tumor, God knew what. And the fragmented thoughts that shimmered just out of focus were occurring with more frequency: visions of enchanting beauty, bold hallucinations of kaleidoscopic color that lasted seconds before disappearing. Were they memories? If so, of what? If only she understood them. But they meant nothing.

And the faces . . . were they faces? Vague, haunting faces in reeds and tall grass, women indistinct and distant beyond the low howling rustle of leaves bright and glistening . . .

She fell asleep.

HER BED was flooded with moonlight. Its nocturnal whiteness crept slowly across her sheets, whose cool starched linen took on a pale lavender glow. A diaphanous tide of light flowed across her neck like a veil. In the starlight, the arteries in her throat pulsed like small drums that beat out the rhythmic ticking of her heart's clock.

Another building lay across the alley. It was two stories higher than hers, and yet the view from its rooftop barely spilled over Michelle's windowsill onto the bed. From her ledge, the black rectangle of the building's chimney was a crisp silhouette in the moonlight. Its oblong shadow gradually stretched out across her sheets. Another shadow joined it for a moment. It was the flat outline of a man. The gray image paused, peering steadily across the gap. And then it moved on.

THE DINNER plate slipped from her soapy hands and fell to the kitchen floor with a crash. Fragments of shattered china pelted the low cabinets in front of the sink. She stared at her shaking hands, feeling weak. The baby started to cry.

Her husband hurried into the room. He saw what had

happened and shook his head, a worried look on his face. He went to the pantry and returned with a broom. Holding the baby in one arm, he swept up the floor with the other.

"You'd better sit down, Sandy."

"I'm all right."

"You're white as a sheet."

"I'll take the baby."

"Sit down, for God's sake!" he pleaded. "Sit down before you fall down! I'll bring her over in a second."

She shuffled from the room, barely aware of the baby's cries and the muted scuffling of broken crockery being swept across the tile. She sank onto the sofa. Tired. So tired. She closed her eyes. When had she started to feel this way? Two weeks? More? Jenny was barely ten months old. She needed a mother. A strong mother. A warm, protective mother.

But I love her so dearly! she thought. What is happening to me? Dr. Jenkins said all my tests were negative, that there was nothing wrong, that my pregnancy is proceeding normally. I take the extra vitamins like he instructed, drink all my milk. She opened her eyes and looked at her legs. She had lost so much weight that her ankles were bony. The floppy slippers were too big for her feet.

Richard came into the room and sat by the telephone, holding Jenny on his lap.

"Who are you calling?"

"Max."

"I won't see him!"

"Honey, we've been over this a thousand times. Max is a psychologist, not a psychiatrist. He's a good friend. And he can help."

"But there's nothing wrong with me! Dr. Jenkins said so."

"Oh, please," he sighed. "That was ten days ago. And Jenkins could be wrong." He frowned when he heard the busy signal.

"The doctor said depression in pregnancy was normal."

Richard slammed down the phone and leaped to his feet.

Jenny started to cry again. "Enough, already! I'm not going to listen to any more medical crap from him! The guy's a quack—you know that? Depression, my ass! Look at you! You're thin as a rail! You can't keep your head up, and you're getting weaker every day! Not to mention the afternoon you disappeared altogether. Who knows if you'll pass out again, disappear again."

Sandy began to cry. It was hard, for she barely had the strength to weep. Something was wrong. She knew it. Maybe she *should* go to see Max. Richard came toward her, trying to soothe Jenny as he walked. He cooed to her, kissed her. He cradled the baby and sat next to his wife, taking her hand, stroking her fingers. She looked at him apologetically.

"I'm sorry, Richard," she sobbed. "I've tried so hard. . . . I can't remember. . . . I—"

"I'm sorry too, San. I didn't mean to yell at you. I just can't stand it anymore. I can't stand to see what's happening to you. You're due in only two months, and here you're withering away before my very eyes! Maybe it is depression—I don't know. But I love you. You and Jenny. I need you both. Let me take you to see Max. Please!"

She sniffled and wiped her nose. "All right."

"Will you go with me tomorrow?"

She nodded.

"Good girl. This is the right thing—you'll see. Let me try his line again."

"I have to nurse Jenny."

He handed her the baby. Sandy took Jenny in both arms and held her close. She adored her daughter. Slowly, unsteadily, she walked to the bedroom as Richard dialed. Jenny's crying lessened. Sandy pressed her damp cheek to her daughter's. She hadn't thought any mother could love her child as much as she loved Jenny. Would she have enough love for the new baby too?

She propped the pillows against the wall as a backrest. When Jenny was a newborn, she had nursed her in a rocking chair. But now she didn't have the strength. It was all she could do to lean against the pillows. She opened her robe and unfastened the snaps of her maternity bra. Her nipples were already leaking, stimulated by the baby's cry. Funny, she thought, how nursing was supposed to prevent pregnancy. It certainly hadn't in her case. No matter. She put Jenny to her breast and closed her eyes again.

The baby suckled contentedly. Nursing was such a private thing. So warm, so wonderful. How close she felt to her child! A smile curled her tired lips. She breathed deeply, savoring the emotional bond. Strange, the scent in the room. Herbal. Almost floral. Delightful.

In the other room Richard was finishing his conversation with Max. It had taken him fifteen minutes to bring the psychologist up to date. Now it would be up to Max, and Sandy. The sudden sound of crying came from the bedroom. It was Jenny. The noise grew louder, continuous—a plaintive bleating. He covered the mouthpiece with his hand.

"Sandy!" He waited for a reply. The only response was Jenny's wailing. "San . . . ?" It bothered him that she let the baby cry so long. He spoke into the phone. "Hold on a second, Max."

He put down the receiver and strode into the bedroom. What was going on, for Christ's sake? "Daddy's coming, Jen."

He halted inside the bedroom door, trying to comprehend what he saw. His wife slouched against the pillows, face away from him. But his eyes were drawn to Jenny. The baby lay on the rug beside the bed. Flat on her back, tiny fists held tight about her red face, she screeched incessantly. He hurried toward her and scooped her up, soothing her. What in the name of . . . ? He sat on the bed, kissing Jenny, hugging her. He reached for his wife's shoulder. "For God's sake, Sandy, you . . . "

Sandy's body slid slowly off the pillows and fell heavily onto the mattress. A stain of wet saliva moistened the linen where her cheek had been. Her skin was as cold as her eyes, which stared sightlessly across the room.

SHE HAD to get away for a while. A four-day weekend would be ideal. She would leave the city for three days, and then spend a leisurely Monday amidst the sights and sounds of Washington. She owned a quarter-share in a summer rental near Ocean City; it was there she headed Thursday night. The white sand and brilliant sun would be a warm anodyne, easing away her tensions.

By Sunday afternoon, her once-pale skin had a radiant tan. As a child, she had sunburned quickly. Her complexion was very fair, in spite of her dark hair, a sharp contrast to her glowing blue eyes. Her father had called her Snow White. Yet she loved the seaside. As she grew older, Michelle had learned to tan without burning, using proper timing with adequate emollients and sunscreens.

Her friends were now back at the house, yet Michelle remained on a chaise longue in a far corner of the beach, savoring the sun and the solitude. She just needed to be alone. In minutes, her skin was baking again. The vivid memories of her recent confusion drained from her in the sun's warmth. Lying limp in the recliner, she tried to concentrate. Maybe what was happening to her was a delayed reaction. Psychological backlash. The time sequence wasn't right, but perhaps she could piece it together. Could it all be related to what had happened to Trish? No, of course not. She was over all that. She had long since stopped thinking about the publicity, filing the newspaper clippings in a far corner of her memory. The Van Dyne sisters, they were called. Olympic-caliber track stars destined to wrest the title from the Russians and the East Germans. They were lovely, they were feminine. And they were winners. For eighteen months, both Michelle and her older sister had emerged victorious at nearly every amateur track event in the country. Competing singly or in relays, they combined skill

39

and speed with a grace and beauty never before seen in athletics. The public adored them. Posing together, they adorned the pages of *People* and *Newsweek*, looking spectacular in their brief running outfits. And then it ended, with suddenness and finality. Trish was dead.

It had happened in February, six months before. They had been living in Washington two years, working by day, training morning and night. They had both had good jobs in government, and they were as respected for their growing bureaucratic skills as for their athletic prowess. The police had called one morning with the news about Trish just as Michelle arrived for work.

The whole thing had happened so quickly that Michelle couldn't deal with it. Her parents, shocked and emotionally frail, had completely fallen apart. At the Ohio funeral she had shuffled among the mourners, shunning reporters, dazed and numb. The flight to her former Cleveland home, her parents' hysteria, the burial, and the return trip to Washington occurred in a fog.

Over the next six months, Michelle somehow managed to pull herself together. She threw herself into her work with a frenzy. At twenty-six, she was Senior Executive Assistant to the Secretary of the Department of Energy. She was the youngest executive of her rank in the D.O.E., and perhaps in any Cabinet department. She disciplined herself toward newer, longer working hours. After all, there was nothing else to do. She hadn't used her track shoes since the day her sister died.

Could that be it? she now wondered. Were her strange thoughts and recent amnesia a manifestation of suppressed feelings, now surfacing months later? Determined to succeed in her self-analysis, Michelle took a lazy walk down the beach before returning to Washington Sunday night.

The following morning, feeling rested and refreshed, she willed herself to concentrate. She got out of bed and opened the shades. She stretched. It was a bright, sunny day. She took a shower and dressed in a light, summery frock, a belt-waisted white cotton dress hemmed at the knee. Her long tanned legs were a lovely contrast to the pale fabric. She accented her lids with blue eye shadow and inspected herself in the mirror. She liked what she saw. Filled with confidence and determination, Michelle locked her door and strolled toward the river.

She bought a newspaper and folded it under her arm. As she slowly plodded along the pavement, she mentally wrestled with what was happening to her. It seemed peculiar that events from months ago should now have such a sudden and dramatic effect on her. And even if Trish's death was at the root of it all, why would it manifest itself in amnesia and the bizarre content of her visions? They just didn't seem related. Deep in thought, she looked philosophically somber as she gazed in front of her. By the time she reached Memorial Bridge, she was no nearer a solution than when she had started out. She sat on a bench and looked across the river toward the National Cemetery at Arlington.

Swirls and eddies danced through the river current, water bugs skittering across a pond. The Potomac had an unusually rapid stream that morning. Its turbulent flow at high tide sucked at passing flotsam, briefly submerging a floating bottle before launching it from wavelet to wavelet.

From the bench by the river's walkway, she watched the bobbing bottle. How different her life had been from the precarious existence of floating glass, destined to sink or be shattered! Until six months ago Michelle had been secure, safely moored in the sheltered harbor of her career and her sport. Trish's death had changed all that. And now, with what was happening in her mind, her future seemed as uncertain as that of the bottle.

Did anything make sense anymore? Maybe she should stop trying to unravel these enigmas on her own. Even if it meant going to a doctor—a shrink—she'd do it. She was not about to lose her mind.

She riffled through the *Post* halfheartedly and sighed. She really wasn't interested in the news. A tall man seated at the other end of the bench seemed to be watching her, yet when she glanced up he was looking the other way. Something about him chilled her. Then he got up and walked away.

Michelle watched him depart. He had an unusual appearance. Dark hair; chiseled features, with a slightly Mongoloid shape to his eyes and high cheekbones. Not Hispanic, she thought; an Eskimo? When he was gone, she felt relieved and she resumed looking through the paper, trying to take note of late-summer sales. She needed a new fall wardrobe as well. Suddenly, an item caught her eye.

She stared at the small item in the corner of the page. It was an obituary. The victim's photo rested atop three small paragraphs of print. It was a handsome picture of a young woman, probably taken from a college yearbook. Michelle narrowed her eyes. There was something vaguely familiar about that photo. She *knew* that woman. But from where?

The terse copy didn't help. It simply stated that Sandra Fischer, a twenty-five-year-old pregnant woman, had died suddenly after a short illness at her home in Alexandria, Virginia. She was survived by her husband, Richard, and a ten-month-old daughter, Jennifer.

Fischer? Michelle didn't know any Fischers. Not around here, anyway. Maybe when she was in Cleveland . . . or back in school? No, she decided, there was nothing in the name. But that photo . . . the haunting eyes, the smile. Yet she couldn't make a connection.

Enough! Michelle threw down the paper and rubbed her eyes. She got to her feet and strolled briskly back to her apartment, concentrating on nothing but the steady drumming of her even strides. By the time she returned to Georgetown, she had forgotten the news item entirely.

Chapter 4

Dr. Wolfe's receptionist buzzed the intercom. "Dr. Clements for you, Dr. Wolfe."

"Thank you."

Samuel Wolfe finished his instructions to the patient before him and escorted her from his office. He knew what Ridley Clements wanted: advice. Wolfe and Clements had been classmates decades before. Clements was a loner then, as now; only Sam Wolfe could penetrate his austere veneer, and bring friendship to a man whose sole devotion was to medicine. There was no one else Clements trusted.

"Reporters are breaking down the doors," Clements began. "They want a statement from me at eleven. I cannot put them off forever."

"What happened to remaining noncommittal? Two days ago you swore that was the only way to go."

"Two days ago there were five dead. Today there are seven. Today they want answers. They want facts. You've seen the newspapers. The public is beginning to be scared. These Woodward types will just fan the flames unless I give them something to go on."

"Like what?"

"If I knew that, I wouldn't have called!"

Clements was right. The mystery surrounding the cancer deaths was creating unprecedented hysteria, similar to the hue and cry over Toxic Shock Syndrome or the panic surrounding Legionnaire's Disease. The cancer fatalities were becoming a media event. There was even speculation about sealing off the metropolitan area. Fortunately for Wolfe, he was an internist. The impact on his own practice was nowhere near the price his obstetric colleagues had to pay. And Clements, so close to becoming the new Surgeon General. But he had no idea if his bland assurances to Clements had any basis in fact.

"What does the C.D.C. say?"

"They're just as much in the dark as we are. They're going to present what little they have at Grand Rounds here soon, but I can't wait that long. I have to say something now."

"Tell you what. Give them a hook, enough of a hint to get them off your back."

"Such as?"

"Make them believe there's a strong likelihood this is something infectious. In fact, pretend you have some preliminary organisms under study which may be involved, and that you should have results within a week. That should give you breathing room."

"And when the week is up?"

"You can dump it in the C.D.C.'s lap by then, right?"

There was a pause as Clements weighed the advice. "Good. Very good. I like it." He rang off with neither thanks nor goodbye.

Wolfe smiled and put the phone back in its cradle. Clements was so easy to deal with if you understood him. The problem was, nobody did. Except Wolfe.

If only the disease were as simple as the man. What confronted them was a horrifying riddle, a catastrophe that struck at the very foundations of the family itself, that destroyed the unborn child in its mother's womb.

Unborn child. Pregnant women. A fragmentary thought intrigued Samuel Wolfe, and he unconsciously toyed with the plant on his desk as he became lost in concentration. He fingered the bloom spike of the miniature pink orchid with dainty gemlike blossoms. There was something to it, he knew—something about pregnancy that was killing those women.

"Here it is, honey. It's on now."

"Coming."

While he adjusted the volume and fine tuning on the color TV, his wife put away her toothbrush and tied the sash to her robe. The belt was hiked up atop her protuberant abdomen, swollen by her pregnancy. She pulled down the covers and crept into bed beside him. Her hand found his. She squeezed his fingers hard when the newscaster delivered the first few lines of the story.

"This brings to ten the number of fatalities reported in the Washington metropolitan area," the reporter continued. "Of the nine previous victims, six lived in the District itself, two in suburban Virginia, and one in nearby Maryland. Today's fatality occurred in a twenty-eight-year-old Rockville woman. She leaves behind her husband and three young children."

"Turn it off. I don't want to hear any more."

"Just a second."

"—of the Medical Examiner's office announced that preliminary examination of the victim suggests findings identical to those of the nine cases reported thus far. What puzzles authorities is why this peculiar form of rapidly fatal cancer seems to strike only young women about to give birth. In an exclusive interview to be broadcast later, *Action News* has learned that no similar cases have been reported from anywhere outside the Washington, D.C., metropolitan area. Speculation persists as to the disease's cause and clinical course. So far, medical authorities have been unable to come up with any satisfactory answers. Pregnant women everywhere—"

She pressed the button, changing the channel.

45

"Why'd you turn it off?"

"I want to see something else."

"I thought you wanted to listen to the news."

"Not anymore." She rolled on her side, turning her back to him.

"You want to watch anything? Johnny Carson?"

Her soft crying began, shaking the mattress.

"Aw, Jesus, Gloria, not again?"

"I'm scared, Vinnie."

He touched her shoulder, pressed himself next to her. "Will you stop it, hon? This is such a crock. I told you a thousand times that you've got nothing to worry about. And what'd your doctor say? Huh?"

"I don't care what he said," she sobbed. "All I know is that I'm due any day. Didn't you hear the announcer? All of those women were just like me! There was nothing wrong with them either. How do you expect me to feel? Doesn't it worry you at all?"

"No, it doesn't. TV news is a business. These guys will do anything to help their ratings."

"Oh, Vinnie!"

"You're getting yourself worked up over nothing."

"You don't believe there are women out there dying?"

"What if there are? They take a coincidence and blow it all out of proportion. There is nothing wrong with you. I mean, you are so damn healthy—have been for nine months—you put a flabby guy like me to shame!"

"I wouldn't care so much if it was here and there. You know—a case in California, or maybe Rhode Island. But why here? Why is it only happening in Washington?"

"Maybe it's politics. They're trying to scare people, or something."

"*Politics?*"

"Look, all I'm saying is, you're making too much out of this."

"I'm not just worried about me. I keep thinking that in a week from now, if something happens to me, how will you—"

"Gloria, Gloria, stop thinking about that stuff," he soothed. He put his arms around her and nuzzled her neck, wondering how long he could continue the charade, wearing a mask of nonchalance in spite of the growing horror he felt within.

"DID HE say that? Did he come right out and promise you full partnership after one year?"

"Sure did. I'm telling you—the guy's been after me for two years. You know that."

"Sounds too good to be true."

"So what do you think?"

"I think you'd be crazy not to take it," said Taylor. "But I still have trouble picturing your names on the same shingle: Samuel Wolfe and Craig Erikson III."

Erikson laughed. "I hope the patients won't be too surprised. But sooner or later, some old lady's going to screw up her appointment and wander into the office to have a checkup and a few laughs with old Sam. Only guess who she'll find at the other end of the EKG machine."

"She could do worse."

"My feelings precisely."

Erikson and Taylor continued their banter throughout lunch, as they had done for three years. They had met when they were both starting specialty training—Erikson in internal medicine and Taylor in obstetrics and gynecology. Soon they were fast friends. Each enjoyed the other's easygoing manner and quick wit. Both were single and socialized often, playing racquetball together twice a week. At thirty-two, Erikson was three years older than Taylor but regarded him as more of an intimate peer than younger brother.

It was early in their friendship that Taylor had discovered a lighter side to Erikson's personality. Erikson was an incurable practical-jokester. Where the somber hospital atmosphere was concerned, his wit was sardonic. He was intent upon eliminating grief and brightening up the place. As a result, though he might toil endlessly to save a patient's life, his respect for the newly deceased was nonexistent. He was far too professional to poke fun at the dear departed; but his dark humor helped many a medical student cope with the difficult transition from life to death. Evenings would find him frequenting the anatomy lab, but it was the morgue that became his sanctuary and inspiration, the scene of his most outrageous pranks. Erikson cajoled Taylor into accompanying him; and he soon found that Taylor shared his grisly sense of humor, even encouraging it.

Time after time, unsuspecting interns or medical students fell victim to their conspiracy. Hassan Mohammed in particular never seemed to catch on. He was the one who discovered the fortune cookie in the Chinese woman's vagina while Erikson and Taylor convulsed with laughter.

They would finish their residency training in June of the following year. With no geographical or family commitments, they could pursue their respective careers wherever and however they chose. They had long talked of working in the same locale. Private practice held the greatest lure. As a result, they spent long hours considering the various pros and cons of different parts of the country. It was time for a change. After ruling out the East, they investigated Colorado and the Southwest. Finally, they settled on San Diego. It was a tough area to break into. But with minimal financial needs, they could endure a few lean years before they developed successful practices. And then came the offer from Sam Wolfe.

Wolfe had one of the finest practices in internal medicine in Washington. A widower in his early sixties, Wolfe was recognized as an astute clinician, compassionate healer, and excellent teacher. He was also a first-rate businessman. His ever-burgeoning practice, well run and efficient, grossed over $400,000 per year. After his former associate died several years earlier, he had considered retiring. But his patients wouldn't permit it. They were as devoted to him as he was to them. The problem then became one of finding a new partner.

Wolfe and Erikson hit it off well together. The older man

soon hinted that a job with him was in the offing. He knew about Erikson's friendship with Taylor and learned of their California fever. If he wanted Erikson to stay, his job offer had to be a good one. And it was. If Craig Erikson entered practice with Samuel Wolfe, he was assured of professional and financial success.

Taylor took the news in stride. He recognized his friend's quandary. Friendship was one thing; career was another. He couldn't expect Erikson to refuse such a fantastic offer. So the ball was now in Taylor's court. Would he consider staying in Washington?

"I don't know, Craig. The capital ain't what it used to be."

"There's almost a year left. Suppose a guy like Durosier asked you to go in with him?"

"Not likely."

"But suppose he did? Or Marshall, or Levine. Those solo guys are killing themselves working alone. And you know you have a damn good reputation. If one of them made you an offer, would you stay?"

"Hard to say," replied Taylor, finishing his lunch. "Those characters have a way of stringing you along for a year or two—you know, cheap labor—and then finding some excuse to kick you out. Anyway, the city's rotten with gynecologists. What we need is a good plague."

"Then you just might be staying yet," said Erikson. "There was another cancer death last night, just like that Garnes I had a few weeks ago. I'm presenting it at today's conference. At this rate, there'll be more than enough business for everyone. A good plague you want? You got!"

THE CPC, or clinicopathologic conference, was the medical highlight of the week. It attracted medical students, attending physicians, and residents from all services. The conference was devoted to a formal, thorough discussion

49

of an unusual or interesting case, usually a fatality. The resident would present the history and physical examination; a radiologist would review the X-rays; a professor or guest speaker would try to put the pieces of the puzzle into diagnostic perspective; and then the pathologist would reveal the autopsy findings—occasionally to the surprise of everyone. But today would be no surprise. All assembled knew that the conference would be a discussion of the most baffling malignancy anyone had ever encountered.

Taylor sat in the rear of the amphitheater, listening to his friend's presentation. He watched the young nurses watch Erikson. Erikson's boyish good looks reflected his Scandinavian heritage. His sandy-blond hair fell in a slight wave across his forehead, and his greenish-blue eyes sparkled.

A good speaker, Erikson made his mundane presentation dynamic and exciting. There was little in the patient's history those in attendance did not already know. The victim, a twenty-five-year-old mother of two, had been due to give birth to her third child in a month. She had arrived at the Emergency Room in a coma and been admitted to the combined Obstetrical and Internal Medicine services for evaluation. She never regained consciousness. After a rapid and inexorably downhill course, she died a quiet death. Erikson eloquently painted her death a tragedy and turned the podium over to Dr. Clements, who started his presentation with some slides.

The films from Radiology were typical of metastatic cancer. White, golf-ball-like circles filled the dark shadows of the patient's lungs. Similar densities were scattered throughout the abdomen. The CAT scan revealed metastatic lesions everywhere.

The professors of medicine and gynecology, the main discussants, tried to make some sense out of the case. Until recently, Clements commented, neither had seen anything like it. Now, in little more than a month, they had accumulated six nearly identical cases in the same hospital. Another seven were scattered across the city. Clements' voice boomed at the audience.

"Not long ago, we hypothesized an infectious etiology for this disease. I'm the first to admit that we were mistaken. We don't know what's behind these cancers. If anyone can help us out, it will be today's guest speaker."

The guest pathologist was a scholarly man. He was Chief of Cancer Epidemiology at the Centers for Disease Control. If anyone could shed some light on the illness, it would be he. He began his talk with an epidemiologic review of known malignancies. Why was it, he said, that cancer of the breast was almost unknown in Japan, while cancer of the stomach was so prevalent? And why did second-generation Japanese-Americans suddenly develop an incidence of breast malignancy which equaled that of other Americans? He spoke of dietary and environmental factors. Then, his overview complete, he moved on to the topic at hand.

The victims had a single characteristic in common. All were pregnant women, and most had due dates within three to seven weeks of their deaths. Aside from that, they seemed quite different. They had various racial, ethnic, and religious backgrounds. The deaths were randomly distributed around metropolitan Washington, with no prominent locale or specific hospital. Some victims came from semirural areas, others from the concentrated inner city. There was no common denominator regarding their pregnancies or anticipated deliveries. Some were to have their first babies, others had one or more previous children. While most of the women had appeared likely to deliver vaginally, a handful had been scheduled for cesarean section. Although an infectious etiology seemed likely, no organism had yet been isolated. Most puzzling of all, not one case had been reported from anywhere else in the United States.

The audience listened with fascination. It was still hard to believe that thirteen deaths had now been attributed to the new disease—a figure that had long since caught the eye of the press. Newsmen were barred from the conference, but filled the halls outside with their bright lights and minicams, waiting for the right word or key phrase with which to begin their next report.

What sort of malignancy was this, he continued, that ravaged the victim's body so rapidly, and against which no known remedies would work? He flashed a slide on the screen which compiled the therapies for the first ten cases. The list was lengthy. Antibiotics had been used, along with radiotherapy, chemotherapy, interferon, and hyperimmune serum. Nothing worked. The disease was relentless, fatal from a week to ten days after appearance of the initial symptoms. The unborn child succumbed shortly after the patient became ill, before it could be saved.

At autopsy, the findings were virtual carbon copies of one another. The stillborn fetus was never affected by the nodules. These soft, rubbery, yellowish-gray masses were deposited throughout the victim's body. The odor upon entrance into the body cavity was universally described as floral. He extracted an empty pint-sized glass jar from his briefcase.

"In this container we've managed to bottle the essence of that smell," he said. "Those of you in the back row may want to come closer as I open it."

Coughs and confusion arose from the audience. Several people started toward the exits. The pathologist smiled, satisfied at the success of his attempt at levity. Anyone sleeping in the amphitheater was now surely awake.

"I thought that might shake you up," he continued. "No, I won't open it, unless some of you are interested at the conclusion of my presentation. But it's harmless enough. Analyzing this scent with gas spectrophotometry, we've found it to be composed of various aromatic hydrocarbons, and of other organic compounds similar to ambergris and musk oil. The mixture of components is never the same, but always has a decidedly fruity aroma. It's completely nontoxic, so far as we know. If it weren't, those of you sitting here who have already smelled it would be either dead or quite ill."

The pathologist concluded his presentation with color projections of the microscopic slides. To Hank Cho, sitting in the darkened audience, they were identical to the slides he had shown Erikson and Mohammed. The last few slides were of photos taken through the electron microscope. The cellular ultrastructure was similar to that of malignancies in general, but specific for none.

"So we know a great deal, and yet we know nothing," said the pathologist. "We know the symptoms, characteristics, and outcome of this disease. But we know nothing about its cause or epidemiology. We don't know where, when, or how a victim will contract it. The present number of cases is probably underreported. Most disturbing to us in Atlanta is that the number of case reports is increasing geometrically. Assuming no change in the incidence rate, by the end of this year there will be hundreds of deaths. Ladies and gentlemen, this is truly a public-health problem of major proportions."

Murmurs rippled through the assemblage, hushed chats here and there. The question period was a round of verbal speculation as each participant voiced his opinion. Some were hopeful, in the spirit of progressive medical science; others, dismally fearful. The only truly scientific question came from Samuel Wolfe, who asked that the last electron micrograph be shown again. The room lights were dimmed, and Dr. Wolfe was handed a flashlight pointer. He shined it at a corner of the slide.

"My question may sound silly, but I'm an amateur botanist at heart. Not long ago, in the *Journal of Investigative Biology*, there was an article on unusual fungal infestations in a rare tropical variety of *Oncidium* orchid. This array of microtubules," he said, pointing to the slide, "looks just like the pattern in a magnified cross section of the fungus."

The pathologist regarded him curiously. "An interesting point, and very astute of you to notice it. At the C.D.C., some of my botanical colleagues mentioned the same thing: namely, that the microtubular pattern—and particularly the tubulin-dimer subunits—resembled patterns in certain plant species, and of some plant pests as well. We concluded that it was a coincidental observation. For as you are aware, there are no known plants, or plant diseases, that can affect humans to this degree."

"You say *known* plants."

"Are you suggesting that some sort of toxic plant product or fungus could be responsible for this kind of human malignancy?"

"Well, no. I'm—"

"Because if you are, we'd simply feed our patients fertilizer and douse them with bug spray. And that would be the end of that."

The audience laughed, and Samuel Wolfe laughed with them. The conference ended and the crowd dispersed. Erikson joined Dr. Wolfe, walking with him toward the door.

"Dr. Wolfe, you old codger, when do you have time to read all that plant stuff? You actually sounded like you knew what you were talking about."

Wolfe smiled. "But I do, Doctor. Biology was my love before medicine. I have a green thumb—and two greenhouses, in fact. Orchids are my specialty. You'll have to see them sometime." They were joined by Taylor, and the trio disappeared down the corridor, trying to dodge reporters on their way.

The last person to leave the amphitheater was a dark man with slick black hair. He was wearing a white lab coat, as were all the hospital employees, but one that did not fit properly. He walked quietly to the doorway, pausing to look down the hall, his piercing gaze fixed intently on the departing figure of Dr. Samuel Wolfe.

Chapter 5

IN HER OFFICE the next morning, it was just after nine when her secretary buzzed.

"Mr. Richardson would like to see you, Ms. Van Dyne."

"When?"

"Right away, in his office."

Michelle straightened her blouse and walked down the corridor to the office of Daniel Richardson, her immediate superior. They, along with several others, conferred every Monday at ten. No doubt he wanted to review some topics before the meeting began. Richardson greeted her politely and showed her into his office. Once they were inside, his smile vanished. It was replaced by a look of concern.

"You look tired, Michelle."

"I am, a little."

"Is it the job, the hours? I know damn well how hard you work."

"It's not the work. I've just been under a little strain, that's all."

Richardson walked around his desk and sat down. "I won't beat around the bush, Michelle. We're worried about you. You *are* under a strain, for whatever reason. I know it, you know it. Around here everyone knows it."

"It's that obvious?"

"Plain as day. We all have problems, and some of us bring them to work with us. But in your case, it's gone beyond that. You're not yourself. I simply won't allow one of our best executives to suffer like this."

She looked at her hands. "I'm sorry. It's something I'm trying to work out."

"Maybe you shouldn't try by yourself. I won't pry into your private life, Michelle. It's none of my business. But I think you should talk to someone about it. Your friends, or relatives, or a doctor."

"A doctor?"

"Perhaps. We need you, Michelle. You're far too valuable to this department for us to let you go to pieces before our eyes. You have a magnificent future ahead of you. Don't ruin it now. So I'm asking you, as a friend. And as your boss. Please get some help."

She left the office tearful, with mixed emotions. They had been so good to her at work, so supportive. They had understood, when she was shaky after Trish died. And they had stuck behind her, helping her over the hurdles of pain and grief. Now it was happening again. She knew she was letting them down.

She'd always been independent enough to solve her own puzzles, but now it was different. She wasn't on a cinder track, running against the sweep of a second hand. What was happening was far more complicated.

That night, Pam and Andrea had invited Michelle to share pizza with them. She arrived at seven, bringing a six-pack of beer.

"How do you get away with drinking that stuff?" asked Andrea.

"I thought you liked beer."

"I do. That's the problem. It goes right to my hips. Are you running again?"

"No."

"Amazing. I guess once you're in shape, you always stay

firm, you know? All I have to do is look at a bottle of beer and my cellulite starts to bulge."

"What's new at work?" Pam asked offhandedly.

Michelle had to smile. Pam's casual queries bore the mark of the skilled journalist she was, forever fishing for that small item of political gossip to which she could attach her by-line. "Not much. But even if there were, everything in this town is an afterthought to those awful cancer deaths."

"You're right," Pam lamented. "Can you imagine how horrible it would be to be pregnant now?"

"It was always horrible," quipped Andrea, the confirmed single.

They talked a little about their work, but they always returned to the epidemic that was terrifying them all. Throughout the conversation, Michelle slowly tore the labels off the bottles of beer. She had a habit of playing with something while others talked—picking pieces off empty Styrofoam coffee cups, or twisting paper clips into circles. Now she listened carefully, realizing she had been so wrapped up in her own problems that she hadn't taken in the true terror of the cancer deaths. She looked down at the shredded beer labels, wanting to change the topic to what was foremost on her mind. She hesitated about confiding in them, but she wanted her friends' opinions, needed their advice. She didn't know how to bring it up; it seemed such a delicate issue. Realizing that no moment would ever be right, she finally blurted it out.

"I'm planning to see a psychiatrist."

Pam and Andrea exchanged stares. "Why? When?" asked Pam.

"Why? I'll explain. When? As soon as I find someone. I don't really know who to call. You were both in therapy. Were your doctors any good?"

"I saw four different shrinks," said Pam. "There was only one I really liked, but he doesn't take private patients anymore."

"You know, Mike, I knew something was bothering you," Andrea chimed in. "Making paper dolls is one thing," she said, nodding toward the torn labels. "But you've been starting to act really weird."

Michelle was about to explain her situation when she suddenly realized that it was unnecessary. It seemed that her friends were already aware of her bizarre behavior. With no need for further prompting, they both began to relate anecdotes that revealed the extent of Michelle's absentmindedness. They were little things—small incidents like the episode in the outdoor restaurant the day she and Pam had had lunch. Michelle was shocked for the second time that day. First it was Daniel Richardson, and now her friends. Had it really gone that far?

Dozens of their friends had been in therapy at one time or another. For the next hour, they debated the pros and cons of various analysts' reputations. Finally they agreed that Dr. David Bender would be the best.

THE WASHINGTON Psychoanalytic Institute was a nondescript walk-up in northwest Washington. There was little to set it apart from the other buildings in the block except for a small black shingle with gold lettering. Michelle paid the driver and walked up the front steps. She pressed the doorbell and heard chimes ring inside. A harsh buzzing signaled that the door had unlocked.

The inner foyer was dark. A wide staircase led upstairs, and a narrow corridor ran the length of the first floor. At the end of the hall was an antique desk with a china lamp, whose dim illumination bathed the plaster walls nearby.

Having just traveled in bright sunshine, Michelle's eyes were unaccustomed to the poor light. She closed the door behind her and squinted toward the desk. She started down the corridor, her vision improving. There seemed to be no one else there. She was alone.

There were several doors, but no names or directions. Beside the desk was a long couch with a magazine rack. Michelle sat down to wait, thumbing nervously through the periodicals.

A few moments later, one of the doors opened. A well-dressed middle-aged woman walked into the waiting area. She found her sweater in a closet, slung it over her arm, and left. Michelle was watching her depart when someone addressed her.

"Miss Van Dyne?"

Michelle looked up. Standing in the open doorway was a man who appeared to be in his late fifties. He had a short-cropped gray beard and warm eyes. His white shirt and striped tie had the slightly rumpled look acquired from long hours of sitting.

"Dr. Bender?"

He nodded in a fatherly manner. "Come in, please."

He held out his hand, and she took it. The palm was cool, the handshake firm. He escorted Michelle into his book-lined office, which contained an analyst's couch, a wide desk, and two chairs. He motioned toward one of the chairs as he sat in the other. Michelle smoothed her skirt and sat down, wondering what Dr. Bender would say. Instead he watched her face, saying nothing.

"I wasn't sure I was in the right place," said Michelle. "I spoke with a secretary this morning."

"I arrange my sessions through an answering service."

"I heard it was hard to get an appointment with you."

There was a hint of a smile. "There are always cancellations in the summer."

His expression was both interested and polite, but still he said nothing. Michelle realized he was leaving the opening to her. As he watched her face, she grew more and more self-conscious, until she nervously blurted out what was uppermost on her mind. "I think I might be going crazy."

He leaned back in his chair and raised his eyebrows in a most reassuring manner. "I feel that way myself half the time."

His attitude put her at ease. He was still waiting for her to continue, but casually, the way a friend might wait to hear her share an intimate secret. Still, she held back. "Don't you take notes, or something?"

Bender leaned forward and looked her directly in the eye.

59

He had an expression of concern. "Look, Michelle. We should get something straight, up front. I'm not a stenographer, and I don't have any hidden tape recorders. All I do is talk. No hype, no bull. I'd like you to forget all the books on the walls and just let your hair down. Tell me what you're thinking. I'm not going to laugh at you. I'm here to listen." With that, he leaned back again, still gazing at her with his warm eyes.

She took a deep breath. "Where should I begin?"

"At whatever you think is the beginning."

Well, he certainly was direct. She didn't have to think too long about the beginning, either. Everything had been going along smoothly at work, she explained, and she thought she had been doing reasonably well. Damn well, in fact. And then, recently, she had been having these . . . thoughts.

"What sorts of thoughts?"

She hesitated, trying to find the words. "I'm having trouble remembering something. There's a blank space in my memory, like a chunk of time that was cut out with a cookie cutter. Four whole days. I seem to have a lot of nightmares, too, like the kind you have when you're little."

"Tell me more about the thoughts."

"The thoughts are . . . different. They're images—almost visions."

"Visions of what?"

Suddenly, "Do you think I'm going crazy?"

"You're hung up on terminology, Michelle. Why not just talk to me? Tell me about the visions."

Beautiful visions, she said. Exotic images. Pictures of greenery and waterfalls. It was a paradise, somewhere, in her mind. A lovely place. A place of liquid whiteness, and purity. And there were faces. Perhaps faces of women. Sad women. But on this she was less clear.

Michelle finished the session and began the next, the following day, with a continued narration. When she finished, she felt drained. She had had no idea she could talk about it at such length. Throughout, Bender looked at her with concern. He hardly fitted her preconceived notion of the stereotypical psychiatrist. He talked a lot, drawing her out on this point or that, smoking cigarettes occasionally.

"So?" she asked. "What do you think?"

"About what?"

"Am I losing my mind?"

"We all are in one way or another. Do you realize that all the time we've been talking, you haven't said one word about your family?"

"They have nothing to do with this!"

"Oh—touched a raw nerve, have I?"

"No, they're just not involved!"

He looked away and seemed thoughtful for a moment. "They may not be involved, but don't you think they're worth mentioning?"

"But that's not the point. You have no right to assume I'm avoiding my family. They're just not part of this!" she said, suddenly feeling near tears.

Bender stopped pacing and stood in front of her. "You're not angry at something, are you?"

"No, I'm not angry!"

"You wouldn't say you were shouting, would you?"

"Goddammit, I am not shouting!"

Bender sat in his chair and leaned slowly forward until he was only a foot away. Infuriated, she looked away. "Michelle," he said softly. She ground her teeth and looked at the wall. Again, "Michelle," and this time he turned her face back with his fingertips. "Look at the way you're sitting."

She looked down at her fists held tightly against the wooden knobs at the end of the armrests. She was sitting on the very end of her cushion, leaning forward in an attitude of fury. Surprised, she relaxed her grip. She was unnerved by her own vehemence. She breathed deeply, and slumped back into the chair.

"You did that on purpose, didn't you? Want to *make* me angry?"

"No, Michelle. You did that to yourself."

"I'm sorry."

"To hell with being sorry! Now I'm the one who's going to get angry if you pull that 'sorry' stuff on me. Has it occurred to you that you might have a very good reason to get pissed off, to yell and scream and shout? One thing is for certain. You're a woman who is capable of a great deal of anger, and for some reason, you're afraid to let it out."

She looked into his concerned eyes, wanting so much for him to explain it to her. "Is that what's wrong, then? Is this some sort of hostility thing?"

"There's no need to put labels on everything, Michelle. It's how you feel that counts. And when I talk about your family, you get very protective. Why is that?"

"I . . . I don't know."

A pale haze of blue cigarette smoke ringed his head like a halo. "I do find one thing very curious."

"What?"

"That one of the country's most promising athletes has been in my office for two visits, and in that time hasn't mentioned a word about her sport. Or her sister."

Michelle knew this was what he had been leading up to, the reason he had provoked her. But she didn't want to talk about it. Not now. It still hurt too much. She bit her lip and turned away. "Don't. Please don't."

Bender leaned closer and touched her wrist. He soothed her with his words. "You can't escape life, Michelle. Fame will follow you wherever you go. You might not want to remember it. But if I'm going to help you, I have to know more about the Van Dyne sisters than what I used to read in the papers."

Michelle grew tearful. Her eyes were watery, and she shook her head, tight-lipped.

"I have to know what's in *here*," Bender continued, pointing to his chest. "I want you to let your heart out. It will be painful for you; that kind of memory always is. But I'm here to listen. It's the only thing that will help. So tell me, Michelle. I want you to tell me with all your heart and all your soul. Tell me what happened to Trish."

Chapter 6

THE BALL HIT low on the baseboard and quickly fell to the floor, an unreturnable winner. Taylor raised his racquet in futility. It had been going like that all night.

"I don't believe it. No contest. This is a slaughter."

"Was that the greatest shot you've ever seen? Huh?"

"Bloodsucker."

The buzzer signaled the end of their court time. Erikson tossed a towel to Taylor, and they returned to the locker room with the terry draped around their necks.

"Face it," said Erikson. "I'm unbeatable."

"In a pig's eye. Last week you couldn't return one shot."

"Raw talent, that's all. Indoor court or outdoor. Borg, I'm ready when you are."

"You're nuts, you know that? Come on, get dressed. I'll buy you a beer."

They showered and dressed lightly for the warm summer evening. Leaving the racquetball court, they walked to a quiet lounge two blocks away. It was a sedate pub they frequented after each week's play, free of the one-upmanship and singles competition of noisier night spots. The tavern had a black vinyl bar top with a brass rail for edging. They drank draft beer in frosted mugs, making halfhearted small talk in the manner of people accustomed to each other's presence.

They were close. There was never jealousy or rivalry between them. When one spoke, the other might casually touch his arm or shoulder—an offhand gesture as natural as spring showers, easily misinterpreted by those nearby. Taylor wrestled with the thought of remaining in Washington. He would have to make his choice soon.

"Did you see that the N.I.H. is offering a one-year fellowship in high-risk obstetrics?"

"How much?"

"Thirty-five, plus perks. What do you think?"

"What's in it for you?"

"Prestige, I guess. You learn a lot over there. They've got a bench full of heavy hitters."

"Is it something you really want? I think you'd just be marking time."

"I won't know unless I try."

They left the tavern and, still deep in conversation, passed the Watergate complex on their way home. They were close to Dr. Wolfe's apartment. On impulse, Erikson suggested they stop in and see Sam. He'd looked under-the-weather lately. They walked into the wide lobby and announced themselves to the doorman. After a quick phone call upstairs, he announced that Wolfe would be happy to see them.

Wolfe had moved to his new residence a year before. He had sold his house in Montgomery County and moved into a penthouse apartment near Watergate. A man who had once lived frugally, he decided to splurge when he relocated. The last of his children was in college; the time had come to spend his accumulated wealth. As a lover of plants, he gave the real estate broker only one requirement: that the apartment had to have a rooftop terrace, facing west.

Wolfe was delighted they had come. He showed them around the apartment. His new quarters were ideal. The interior was decorated simply, except for the kitchen, which boasted a growing collection of woks, pasta machines, and crêpe pans. But he lavished most of his time and money on the terrace. He had enclosed it in solar glass, creating a perfect greenhouse. Evenings would find him puttering about among the flowers as the sun set low across the Potomac.

It was to the greenhouse that he led Taylor and Erikson when they arrived. He showed them in with a flourish. Taylor was delighted, and even the cynic in Erikson was quieted by the beauty of Wolfe's collection. Most of it was composed of orchids. The plants were arrayed in three tiers that ran the length of both sides of the greenhouse. As they walked, Wolfe explained the characteristics of each orchid in a manner so buoyant that both young doctors were excited by the older physician's enthusiasm. He showed them the velvety, butterfly-shaped lavender blossoms of a *Doritaenopsis* still in bloom, and pointed out the green streaks in a *Paphiopedilum* just beginning to flower.

"I've never seen green petals," Taylor remarked.

"Orchids come in colors that defy description," replied Wolfe. "Here, look at this one," he said, holding up a slatted clay pot. The plant had broad green leaves, with a bloom spike that bore a single brilliant magenta flower the size of a small plate. "This came in the mail the other day. It was bare root. I potted and watered it and went back to work on my other plants. The next thing I knew—not half an hour—it had bloomed. Never saw anything like it."

"Where did you get it?"

"Good question. I buy a lot of my stock through the mail, but this came in an unmarked box. Could be a mail-order bonus. Or a gift, but there was no card."

"A woman, Sam," said Erikson. "C'mon, you old charmer. What are you doing in that office when the doors are locked?"

"Hah! I should be so lucky."

"Does it smell as nice as it looks?" asked Taylor, bending over.

Wolfe fended him off. "Don't do that, my boy. It smells, all right. Stinko. I got a noseful the other night, and it's not at all pleasant. Funny how something so lovely can have such a foul odor." He put the pot in a corner and led them away to drinks. "Strange plant, that one."

In the living room, they sipped brandy from oversized snifters. As Wolfe chatted about his plants, Erikson watched him. Wolfe's skin was shiny, thin and moist and vaguely yellow. He was perspiring; the pale hue of his flesh hinted at poor health.

"What do you think, Craig? Want to try your hand at orchids?"

"Not on your life. My idea of gardening is hosing down the pavement."

"That's too bad. Horticulture is most rewarding when it's a joint venture, something shared."

"Then share this with me: what's wrong with you? You don't look so good."

Wolfe looked surprised. "I'm fine, really. But the work is hard and the hours are long. I'm not as young as I wish. That's why I need you with me." They both looked at Taylor, sensing the pressure he must feel.

"Leave me out of this. What you guys decide is none of my business."

"You sure you're okay?" Erikson repeated. "I don't want to start practicing with some senile character who needs every night and weekend off. And stays home to care for his plants. Why don't you just get a poodle, like everyone else? You make like those plants are human."

"They're much more than human. The plants around us are the essence of life itself. We're surrounded by death in our line of work. Plants remind me of what we have to live for." He looked suddenly philosophical. "Did I ever tell you I grew up on a farm?"

"You mean pigs and chickens and all that?"

Wolfe nodded. "Born and raised in Nebraska."

"A cornhusker," said Taylor.

"No, wheat was our stock-in-trade. Oh, we had corn, and

66

a few barnyard animals. But just for our own use, you see. Back then, we didn't have the combines and threshers they use now. Everything was horse-drawn, or done by hand. It was a marvelous thing, raising a wheat field."

"You sound like the original Old MacDonald."

"Don't kid yourself. Farming was damn hard. But it had its rewards. You would plow your fields, sow the grain, and water it well. And then let the sun do its work. Before long, there'd be row after row of tiny seedlings pushing skyward. It was a transformation. That brown earth would turn into a sea of golden wheat. I used to lie there at night, looking at the stars. And I swear, I could almost hear it grow."

"Sam, you're a poet."

"I have a feeling for the land, that's all. But that's all changed now. The feeling's still there, but the chemistry's gone." He got up slowly and walked to the wide living-room window. The lush panorama of Virginia beckoned in the distance. He gestured toward it, his hand wandering across the horizon as faint orange touches of the setting sun lingered in the west. "A pity," said Wolfe. "Such a pity."

"What is?"

Wolfe was deep in reflection. He looked wistful, his tone melancholy. "The way we're destroying the land. In my day, we used manure for fertilizer. Now everything's chemicals. And poisons. We use pesticides by the ton, and pollute our air and water. Acid rain denudes the forests, killing fish and wildlife. It won't happen while I'm alive; but there'll come a time, in your generation, when everything ceases to grow."

"You sound like one of those environmentalist fanatics. A regular Jane Fonda!"

"If she's leading the protest march, I'll join it every time."

They all laughed heartily, and Dr. Wolfe poured one last nightcap. While the younger doctors talked, Wolfe again scanned the horizon, feeling a strange uneasiness.

．．．

THE LONE woman guard sat atop the bluff, perched on a chair of stiff reeds woven like polished wicker, listening to the sounds from the area below. She guarded her prisoners casually now, indifferently, at times leaving them unattended for hours. There seemed little time left for preparation; and yet their leader said it would be enough.

Her thoughts strayed to stories told her in her childhood, of the thousand years that had passed since the longboats sailed north across the Great Water, leaving their priestly bastions forever behind. In their new land, they had lived in splendid isolation for centuries, existing in harmony with the vast ocean that pounded the nearby shore of the continent's eastern coast. On a seabound plain, near a stormy cape called Hatteras, their plants had thrived; with proper care, even their most tropical species had mutated, adapting to the new environment. And so their small civilization had prospered for ages, until the arrival of the fair-haired strangers in their tall ships, cannon booming. Yet remaining apart was paramount. The past had borne witness to the mistakes that came from mingling.

Again they had moved, journeying slowly, taking years, using their plants to sustain them. They had first gone up the Pamlico, following the River Roanoke to its headwaters. Higher and higher they had traveled, westward into the mountains of Appalachia. And then, by accident, they had found it. The entrance to the crater was hidden, the long-extinct volcano silent. High above the valleys, the air was fresh, the water pure. They had sealed off the entrance, once and forever. Only rarely did they venture forth, and then only when necessary. This was to be their home.

In the past, they had been content to wait decades, generations, to achieve their goals. In this foreign sanctuary, the grandeur of the passing ages had witnessed abundant growth of the thick, verdant foliage so necessary to them, and had even seen maturation of the mighty ceiba and magnificent cedar as they tapped the water that poured through underground aquifers and formed cisterns and caverns in the porous limestone. The immutability of the ages had been their ally. Now it was their enemy.

It was imperative that the priesthood survive. The peculiar loss of their fertility had never been expected. They were months behind schedule. Yet once they had the final tool they needed, their problem would be corrected.

The dark-skinned woman rose to stretch, ignoring the sounds from below. She turned her back and tried to block them out. Then it came again: what seemed to be a moan. The guard frowned, turned back again, and moved slowly forward along the trail to where it ended in a wide forest glade. She stood on a mossy green plateau that bounded the top of a sharp cliff. The ominous noises came from beyond its edge.

Another moan.

Tight-lipped, the guard stood on the cool moss of the rocky precipice. Below, in the glen on the forest floor, the two pregnant women were unaware of the guard's face gazing into the valley. Nor did they see the expression of contempt that overcame her. For they saw nothing. Strapped to their chairs, they stared blankly ahead, unseeing, in numbness and catatonia. They were unconscious of the belts that cradled their protuberant abdomens, and of the thin needles that pierced their skin to suck forth a substance from within their uteri. Yet every once in a while, one would stir and moan—a low, guttural sound.

TALKING ABOUT Trish was no problem at all, once she allowed herself to do it. The months of agony she had repressed now gushed forth in endless run-on sentences. Michelle had no shortage of memories. The dizzy montage of reminiscence welled up in her mind like a giant balloon, ready to burst while she wrestled to verbalize her thoughts. She talked for days about every aspect of their life together.

She told Bender about the track meets in which they had

run. They were good, very good. The weaknesses of one were compensated by the strengths of the other. She had adored Trish. It was partly the love of a younger sister, partly the respect of a close competitor. Bender brought her out on this: her feelings of dependence, and trust. But her strongest reaction came when they discussed Trish's death. To Michelle, it was still an exposed nerve.

"You don't believe she could take her own life?"

"Maybe someone else, but not Trish. She had everything to live for."

"How can you be sure?"

"I just know, that's all. And why wasn't there a suicide note?"

"There wasn't something on her mind, something that might make her consider suicide? Perhaps she was ill—something she didn't tell you."

"Dr. Bender, Trish and I were like this!" She held up her crossed fingers. "We saw each other every day, and spoke on the phone three or four more times. If something was bothering her, I would have known it."

"There are, unfortunately, many suicides that go unexplained. How did she appear the day it happened?"

"I told you, she was fine! We'd just done five miles that morning in the park, in the snow, shivering all the way. And she kept cheering me up, saying stuff like 'C'mon, icy-buns, I'll freeze to death waiting for you.' I'm telling you, Dr. Bender: Trish did not jump out that window."

"Meaning?"

"Meaning she did not take her own life."

Bender was pensive, fondling his gray beard. "Sometimes, Michelle, being a younger sister can cloud objectivity."

"How?"

"By idolizing her the way you did. You may have blinded yourself to the truth. There are many cases where emotions can obscure judgment."

"I'm sure that *can* happen."

70

"But not with you?"

"Not when it comes to my sister," Michelle said adamantly. "Trish Van Dyne did not commit suicide."

The sessions with Bender were helpful, in a general way. Michelle felt better about herself. Her friends remarked that she seemed better. But the time spent in therapy did not eradicate her strange thoughts. The visions persisted, compounded by the nightmares. And throughout, though she saw the point, Michelle would not admit to the truth of Bender's implication: that what was happening to her was based in the deep well of guilt and denial she felt over Trish.

The summer was fast drawing to a close. Only a few weeks remained of her beach-house rental. Though the weather forecast was gloomy, she decided to escape the city. It rained or threatened rain for three straight days; it was maddening. On Sunday morning, a light drizzle and foggy mist obscured the ocean. Nonetheless, she put on a swimsuit and a raincoat. She knew the combination was ludicrous, but did it matter?

Michelle dragged her beach chair to the water's edge, a trail of damp tracks behind her. The beach was deserted except for scores of gulls and sandpipers. Huddled in her chair, arms wrapped around her, she watched the birds circle leisurely overhead, occasionally diving to the waves below. The surf pounded the shore, and the wind carried the spray toward her, crystal fragments of icelike mist that stung her cheeks.

She closed her eyes and allowed her mind to roam. The mist on her skin stirred her memory, bringing to the surface thoughts of a similar day a year before. It was at the A.A.U. Outdoor Championships in Philadelphia. The fog that swept off the Schuylkill River had socked in Franklin Field, making the air dank and heavy. The track was slow, the heats uninspired. Just when it seemed that the meet would be a disaster, Trish infected Michelle with enthusiasm. They decided to set a record that day.

Trish ran the first leg of their 880 relay. Michelle waited

in her lane, eyes on Trish, who seemed to laugh as she ran, leading the field by ten yards. As her sister neared, Michelle exploded down the track. "Do it!" Trish's eyes urged, as she slapped the baton into her sister's palm. Michelle's legs pumped like fluid springs. She raced through the fog and mist, her lightning strides spewing cinders behind her. As she rounded into the home stretch, she saw Trish jumping up and down like a schoolgirl. Michelle burst through the tape, exhausted but beaming. She slumped into her sister's arms. Breathless, they shared a light-headed, giggly embrace when their time was posted. They had knocked four seconds off the record. She smiled at the memory.

Michelle returned to Georgetown after dark in a downpour. The cab pulled up in front of her building, and she opened the car door in the pounding rain. She leaped onto the pavement, clutching her satchel, and ran toward the protective overhang. A bolt of lightning illuminated the sky.

In her rush to get inside, she thought she saw something—someone?—at the building's corner pillar. Was it her imagination? The rain soaked her hair, washed down her face. Her heart was pounding. A booming clap of thunder rumbled overhead. Standing motionless, washed by sheets of rain, she looked like a child's forgotten doll left out in the storm.

"Come on, Miss Van Dyne! You'll get soaked!"

She turned toward the sound. The building's doorman held the door open, beckoning with his free hand. She looked back at the vacant pillar, then slowly walked into the lobby.

"Look at you, wet as a mop! You'll catch some cold in a storm like this, Miss Van Dyne."

Water dripped from her chin. Michelle pointed through the lobby's plate glass. She tried to keep her voice calm. "Frank, did you see someone standing over there, outside, at the corner?"

The doorman squinted and shook his head. "I haven't seen anyone in rain like this. Some traffic, a few stray dogs. You'd have to be crazy to be out there now."

"I thought I saw a man when I got out of the cab."

The doorman peered again, and shrugged. "Could be, Miss Van Dyne. Lots of crazies on the street. But I didn't see anyone."

"Must be my imagination," she said finally, taking the stairs. She now felt the wetness, and was chilled to the bone. She started to shiver. Inside her apartment, she donned a warm terry robe and wrapped a towel turbanlike around her hair. There was some brandy in the kitchen, and she poured two fingers into a snifter. She returned to her darkened bedroom, and looked out the window to the lighted, rain-washed street below. She had to hold the snifter in both hands. Her whole body was shaking.

There was no one on the street. She studied the sidewalk for blocks and saw only empty pavement. My imagination, she thought again. Soon I'll be seeing flying saucers.

Chapter 7

    "YOU'D BETTER LIE down, Sam."

    "I'll be all right."

    "Come on. We'll help you."

    Erikson and Taylor assisted Samuel Wolfe to his feet. He walked unsteadily. They each held an elbow and led him to a couch in a den just off the kitchen. He lay down, breathing heavily.

    "This is ridiculous," he wheezed.

    "Stay put," said Erikson. "Doctor's orders. Don't get up until we come back for you."

    Wolfe was exhausted. He closed his eyes without further comment. The younger men retreated from the room, leaving the door ajar. They returned to the kitchen table, where the three of them had just begun dinner when Dr. Wolfe was stricken.

    Wolfe was an excellent cook. Ever since his wife's death several years before, his culinary horizons had expanded. His current interest was pasta. But as he carried a platter to the table, his body had shuddered, and his eyes had rolled backward. When he fell to the floor, the tray of fettuccine splattered across the tabletop. Now Erikson and Taylor carefully tidied up the mess.

    "You're the internist," said Taylor. "Was that a stroke?"

"I don't know what it was. The guy needs a thorough workup. EEG, cardiogram, the works."

"Should we take him to the hospital?"

"Not yet. He's a fighter. Better not push him. We'll work on his ego tonight, and maybe we can talk him into being admitted tomorrow."

The table cleaned, they sat down and nursed their drinks. Dr. Wolfe had invited the two of them to dinner when he learned that Taylor had decided to take the postgraduate fellowship. It was to be a celebration, of sorts: Wolfe had the associate he wanted, and Taylor and Erikson could remain together.

Now, as Taylor and Erikson finished their wine, Wolfe had gotten up and reappeared in the kitchen.

"Sam . . ." Erikson rose from the table.

Wolfe waved reassuringly. "Sit down, sit down. I'm all right. Just needed a few minutes' rest." He looked at the stains on the table. "Just as well. I thought it might be a little too *al dente.*"

"How many attacks have you had, Sam?"

"Do you like linguine? It'll only take a minute or two."

"How many, Sam?"

Wolfe walked unsteadily toward the pantry. "This is the third in three days."

"What are your symptoms?" asked Taylor.

"Just weakness. Then I feel dizzy, and the next thing I know I'm waking up on the floor." He found a box of noodles on the pantry shelf.

"No pain, or numbness?"

"Nothing. It's high blood pressure, that's all. Let it alone and it'll pass."

"Let it alone and we could be pallbearers," said Erikson. "Don't be silly, Sam. You know you have to go to the hospital."

"Let's talk about it after supper, all right? You two must be starved."

Erikson shook his head. "Doctors. The worst patients."

As the water boiled on the stove, Wolfe went to his study and returned with a manila envelope. He sat at the table as he opened the package. "As much as I enjoy having you to dinner, I do have an ulterior motive," Wolfe confessed. "I want to pick your brains."

"Slim pickins."

"Oh, I don't think so. I respect your judgment. Here," he said, emptying the envelope. "Do you notice any differences in these?" He handed them two glossy eight-by-ten photos. Each was an electron micrograph.

Taylor and Erikson studied the pictures, passing them back and forth across the table.

"Look the same to me," said Taylor. "What do you think, Craig?"

"I guess so. I'm no expert, but I can't tell the difference." He handed the photos back to Wolfe. "What about them?"

Wolfe made a steeple with his fingers, composing his thoughts. "See if you can remember your academic sciences. Bacteriology, epidemiology, and so forth. Unless things have changed drastically since I was in school, human and other mammalian diseases are essentially nontransmissible, except for some rare exceptions. Rabies, for example. And some kinds of worms. But for the most part, animals don't get the Asian flu, and feline leukemia can't affect people. Right?"

They both nodded.

"The same is true of plant diseases. Oh, you can get a rash from poison ivy, or a bellyache from eating castor beans. But those are toxic effects, not plant diseases. Growing things—grass, trees, cotton—have a whole spectrum of their own maladies, and none of these afflicts humans. At least, not until now."

Taylor and Erikson exchanged stares.

"You remember my comment at the CPC not long ago, about how the slides that guy from Atlanta showed looked similar to something in my botany journal?"

"Go on."

76

"It was just an afterthought, but I was curious. You see, it involved a plant disease—orchids, to be specific—so I was all the more interested. I called the author of that article. We spoke for a while, and he sent me a few pictures. This photo on the left," said Wolfe, "is one of several he mailed."

"And the one on the right?" asked Taylor.

"An enlargement that Hank Cho made for me. It came from his latest cancer autopsy."

For a moment, no one spoke. Taylor stared at Erikson, and then looked back at Wolfe. He took a deep breath and whistled softly.

"I haven't mentioned it to anyone but you. I think they'd laugh me right out of my own department."

"You're suggesting that this plant disease causes human malignancy?" said Erikson.

"I'm raising it as a possibility. What do you think?"

"That Atlanta pathologist was pretty sharp, and he said there was no common denominator. Maybe he missed something. Were all the victims orchid fanciers?"

Wolfe got up to stir the pot on the stove. "That would make it simple, wouldn't it? But they weren't. I pulled the charts on all the cases to date at the hospital. My nurse called some of their families. None of them raised orchids. Some had other indoor plants; a few raised vegetables. And there were a couple who couldn't stand plants."

"Maybe they were near orchids outside the house. At a wedding, or a funeral. Or at work."

"I thought of that too, but I'm afraid it doesn't check out."

"So it might have nothing to do with orchids."

"Now you're getting somewhere," said Wolfe, as he finished stirring. "It does, and it doesn't. You see, this particular plant malady doesn't affect orchids alone. It's found in several other rare tropical species."

"You're still left with the plant-exposure angle."

"Not necessarily. Intimate contact may not be that important. I think I know how it's happening. I'll give you a clue: you don't have to grow ragweed to get hay fever, do you?"

They both looked at him blankly.

"You lost me, Sam," said Erikson.

A buzzer went off in the other room. "Think about it for a second," said Wolfe. "I'll be right back. I just have to get something in the pantry." He left the kitchen.

"Think he's on to something?"

"I don't know," said Taylor. "Those pictures are impressive. So far, everyone else has drawn a blank. At least he's headed somewhere."

There was a loud crash from the other room. Taylor and Erikson leaped from their chairs. In the living room, Samuel Wolfe staggered toward them, blue-faced, one hand extended toward them. They caught him just as he fell. Taylor rolled him onto his back, feeling for his pulse. Wolfe was struggling to speak.

"Don't talk, Sam. It's going to be okay. Lie still."

Wolfe's trembling hand fluttered up, and Erikson took it. Their eyes locked together. With the greatest effort, Wolfe pursed his lips. He could barely breathe. His voice was a faint, gurgling rattle.

"Hold on, Sam. Hold on!" Erikson pleaded.

Wolfe's head slumped back. His sightless eyes stared beyond them, as his last breath escaped in a moist wheeze.

Erikson immediately ripped open Wolfe's shirt and began giving closed-chest cardiac massage. Taylor frantically began mouth-to-mouth respiration. They worked furiously for fifteen minutes, until the pulseless body with the fixed, dilated pupils bespoke the futility of their efforts. Kindly Samuel Wolfe had departed from the living a stone's throw from the plants he had tended so gently.

THE NEXT day seemed interminably slow to Erikson. He and Taylor asked Hank Cho to call them as soon as the autopsy results were available. They had summoned an ambulance to take Dr. Wolfe's body to the hospital the night before; if they hadn't, Wolfe's remains would have become the property of the District of Columbia Medical Examiner. Cho himself had come right over, before midnight. But because of the lateness of the hour, and the need for the requisite consent and notification, the autopsy wasn't begun until the following morning.

Erikson had spoken with Dr. Wolfe's daughter. Dr. Wolfe had been in excellent health. Because of the unexplained suddenness of his death, Erikson recommended a postmortem. Wolfe's daughter, too upset to make a decision, gave the phone to her husband. The son-in-law knew of her father's fondness for the younger internist, and he said he would trust Erikson's judgment in the matter.

Erikson delegated his morning rounds to a junior resident and made only a perfunctory appearance in the clinic. The remainder of the time he paced the hall outside the morgue. Finally, at four, Cho called him in. Erikson paged Taylor from the morgue's telephone.

"You said his symptoms looked like a stroke?"

"Not exactly," said Taylor. "I thought he might have a neurological problem, but it didn't appear to have any pattern."

"It wasn't a stroke," said Cho. "His brain was clean—at least, the cortex. And his heart was in great shape. He had the coronaries of a thirty-year-old."

"Then what?"

"Look at the slide under the 'scope."

They both inspected it; it took no time at all. Taylor muttered a faint "Jesus" before shaking his head in bafflement. Under the microscope was the characteristic appearance of the devastating cancer they had come to know so well.

"How the hell is this possible?" said Erikson. "This disease doesn't affect men."

"I can't figure it," admitted Cho. "We're back to square one. Maybe it is infectious after all."

"Then we're all in real trouble just standing here," Taylor

said nervously. "The whole hospital staff should get antibiotics, or at least gamma globulin."

The telephone rang, and Cho frowned. "I bet that's Clements," he said. "His timing is uncanny. He's been after me all day to rush this through." He walked across the room and stepped on a pedal under the phone. The device activated a wall-mounted intercom, installed to enable a gloved pathologist to speak without having to pick up the receiver.

"Are you finished, Dr. Cho?" Clements' voice boomed.

"Yes, sir. Just now."

"Well, then? Do I have to come down there myself to get an answer?"

Cho shook his head and shrugged toward Erikson. "No, Dr. Clements. Dr. Wolfe died of the same cancer that's killing our pregnant women."

There was a pause. "Are you absolutely positive?"

"No doubt about it, Dr. Clements. I think we're going to have to notify Infection Control."

"You'll do nothing of the sort," Clements said in even tones, his voice ringing with authority. "Who knows about this besides you?"

"Dr. Taylor and Dr. Erikson are here now. Besides the four of us, no one."

"Was Dr. Wolfe's pattern the same as that of the women?"

"Not exactly. It wasn't widespread, like all the others. It started in his lung. What killed him was a single metastasis, no bigger than a dime. Right in the middle of his brain stem."

"I want your written report on my desk in an hour, Dr. Cho. Dispose of Dr. Wolfe's organs in a sterile manner. Drain all of his blood and fill his blood vessels with antibiotics before you release the cadaver to the mortician. As for the three of you, not one word of this is to leave the morgue."

"But we can't withhold this information!" interrupted Erikson. "There could be an epidemic!"

Clements' voice exploded over the loudspseaker. "I don't

recall asking for your opinion, Dr. Erikson! Dr. Cho, did I understand you to say that Dr. Wolfe's disease was unlike that of all the others?"

"Yes, sir, but—"

"Then let me handle it. The three of you take the usual sterile precautions. One hour, Dr. Cho. I want that report in one hour." There was a click, and Clements was gone.

"He's mad!" said Taylor.

"Maybe not," said Hank Cho. "You know as well as I that you never underestimate Dr. Clements. Maybe he knows something we don't. And he's right, in a way. If we start shouting infection without having any proof, the whole District will be in a panic."

"How long could Dr. Wolfe have had it?" asked Erikson.

"Good question. This is the most rapidly lethal cancer we've seen. I spoke with his internist. Apparently Sam had a completely normal checkup a month ago."

"He died of cancer in less than a month?"

"The pattern fits, right? A quick illness, just like all the women. But you two keep your mouths shut, like the man says. Not a word about this until I investigate it further and until we hear from Clements. Funny, though. I didn't even have to prepare the microscopic slides. I knew what was wrong as soon as I opened the chest cavity."

"How?"

"I could smell it."

BREAKFASTING IN the hospital cafeteria the next morning, Taylor cracked open two soft-boiled eggs while Erikson drummed his fingers impatiently on the tabletop.

"What do you make of what Sam said the other night? The photos and all that?"

"Impressive. Dr. Wolfe did his homework."

"Do you think he was leading up to something?"

"No question. But I don't know what. It would be nice if

he'd stumbled onto some new epidemiological perspective. Did you hear the news this morning?"

"No, why?"

"The *New England Journal of Medicine* ran the first good article on the cancer in this week's issue. Straightforward—just facts. And a bunch of question marks. Apparently, one of those sensationalist weeklies got hold of the *Journal* article in advance and hyped it all to hell. 'Killer Cancer Stalks Capital,' or something like that. Today both articles hit the regular media. And they're having a field day. All the facts are distorted." He finished his eggs and looked at his watch. "Got to go. Keep me posted if you find anything, okay?"

"Sure."

Erikson had difficulty accepting Wolfe's death. It was their own hospital's seventh similar fatality, yet the only one involving a man. But to Erikson, it wasn't a statistic, a faceless stranger. He was genuinely fond of Dr. Wolfe and had looked forward to working with him.

Wolfe's daughter was an exceptionally levelheaded individual. After the funeral, she phoned Erikson and discussed the disposition of her father's practice. She would try to have the other attendings cover the practice over the next nine months until Erikson finished his training. She knew that her father had intended to share it with Erikson, she said. If Erikson would make himself available for emergencies and assist in administrative matters, she would see to it that the practice was his.

She asked a favor in return. The lease on her father's apartment came due at the end of the year. She couldn't bear the thought of packaging his belongings and rummaging through the memorabilia. Could Erikson possibly see to those matters? And, oh, there was one more thing: the orchids. She knew her father had loved them dearly; she hoped Erikson could place them somewhere suitable. The doorman was instructed to give Erikson the apartment key anytime he requested it.

It wasn't easy to visit Dr. Wolfe's apartment again, but

Erikson thought it best to do so as soon as possible. The dead man's memory was still fresh, troubling him. But he knew it was what Wolfe would have wanted. Wolfe had seemed to be on the verge of a discovery; maybe Erikson could fit the loose pieces together. He got into his car and drove crosstown to Wolfe's home.

A different doorman was on duty from when he had been there last. The man eyed him suspiciously. Erikson still wore his hospital whites. In the lobby, he saw the wall-mounted video surveillance cameras he hadn't noted two nights before.

"What can I do for you, Mac?"

"I'm Dr. Erikson. Dr. Wolfe's daughter said you would have a key for me."

The doorman rummaged through some papers. "Erikson . . . right. You got some kind of I.D.? Driver's license?"

Erikson took out his wallet and extracted various cards. The doorman waded through them slowly.

"We got to crack down on security. Okay, Doc. Here's the key." He returned Erikson's cards and handed him an envelope. "Too bad about Dr. Wolfe. Helluva guy." Erikson began to walk away. "And a great tipper."

Erikson sighed, reached into his pocket, and gave the man a dollar.

"Thank *you*, sir. Take all the time you want."

Wolfe's apartment was untouched. Erikson cleaned the dining area and put the kitchen utensils in the dishwasher. Then he made a tour of the rooms. The apartment was spacious. There were a small den and kitchen, living and dining rooms, two baths, and two bedrooms, one of which had served as a study. He opened the door to the greenhouse. The air conditioner and humidifiers were on separate timers, controlled automatically. The plants would probably be fine for several days. But since he knew nothing about their watering requirements, disposing of the orchids would be his first priority. He hoped Dr. Wolfe had made an inventory of his collection.

There was no such list in the greenhouse. He searched the

living room, found nothing, and then entered the study. The wall was lined with bookshelves. The books were about two subjects: botany and medicine. There were innumerable texts on gardening, internal medicine, orchid culture, and cardiology. None of them, though, contained the inventory he sought. He turned to the desk.

The desk blotter was spotless and uncluttered. In the top right-hand drawer, though, Erikson found the list he was looking for. It was in a blue vinyl three-ring binder. Inside were several hundred pages devoted to Wolfe's collection. Each orchid was listed by name and number. There were also columns for parentage, date acquired, source, price, description, and culture. Wolfe had made detailed notes on each plant, underlining some items, placing exclamation points after others. It was a labor of love.

Erikson decided to take the binder with him and make his calls the next day.

But the next day was hectic. There had been just enough time to squeeze in a call to the local chapter of the American Orchid Society. The person Erikson spoke with had known Dr. Wolfe, and was shocked by the news of his death. He assured Erikson that there would be no trouble disposing of Wolfe's orchids. It was one of the finer private collections in the city, and could command a tidy sum. But Erikson insisted that it be a donation. He knew Wolfe would not have been interested in capitalizing financially. All he would have wanted was to dispose of the plants with simplicity. His contact instructed Erikson that a pickup could be arranged the following morning, if the plants could be gotten ready. He told Erikson how to package them. A truck would be sent over at nine.

Filled with a sense of duty, Erikson returned to Wolfe's apartment. The superintendent had located cartons for him. After filling scores of them with books, he set to work on the orchids. Although he was tired, he placed the plants in the boxes with great care, mindful not to knock off a bud or fracture a leaf. It was tedious work. He didn't finish until mid-

84

night. Then he took the cartons individually down to the lobby.

By 1 A.M., the boxes were assembled. Erikson paused to survey his work. Aligned in row after row, the cartons were a floral phalanx that paid tribute to the man who had cared for them so dearly. They were beautiful, thought Erikson. Alive with color, they reflected the years of painstaking work devoted to them. He looked at them one last time. It was such a pity. Then he turned and left, not noticing the absence of one particular flower.

The large magenta orchid was gone.

Chapter 8

MICHELLE AWAKENED IN the middle of the night, dry-mouthed, with a sudden pain in her abdomen. She had been nauseated before she went to bed, thinking it was from the enormous lunch she and her girlfriend Cheryl had consumed at O'Callahan's. Was it the cheeseburger, or the sausage? She had gone to bed expecting to be fine in the morning.

Now she felt worse than ever. As she stumbled from the bed to the bathroom, Michelle found herself incredibly weak and horribly dizzy. She sank to her knees and crawled across the rug. She hadn't gone two feet when she couldn't continue. Her mouth and throat were parched. Yet her mind was lucid. She knew she needed help.

The cord to the bedside phone reached the rug beside her. She would call Pam. She tugged on the cord. The phone fell with a crash. The receiver had a lighted Touch-Tone dial. She struggled against the lassitude that overcame her as her shaky finger pressed the buttons.

Pam answered sleepily after five rings. Michelle had trouble speaking; even her neck muscles were weak.

"Pam . . . it's Michelle. Pam?"

"Hello? Who is this?"

Michelle's voice was terribly faint. "Michelle," she repeated. "It's Michelle. Pam, help me. I'm sick."

"Mike, is that you? I can hardly hear you."

Even her breathing was becoming labored. She struggled desperately to make herself heard. "Pam . . . sick . . ." She couldn't continue.

"I'm coming right over."

Michelle heard the click, then the high-pitched whine that follows the dial tone. The shrill noise pierced her eardrum. She couldn't move. Her vision was blurry. She could barely talk, and it was hard to breathe. It was going to be all right, she told herself. Pam was coming.

Lying there aware that she was unable to move, Michelle thought she was going to die. Strangely, the pain receded. In its place was total fear. And tears of bitterness filled her eyes. Something horrible had been happening to her, was happening to her. Something over which she had no control. And now it seemed she might never find out.

Sounds at the front door: Pam? The doorbell rang, but she couldn't get up. There was no way she could open the door. There was banging, and Pam's muffled shouting. Then it stopped, and Michelle's panic intensified. Pam had gone away. A minute passed, then two. Michelle tried to calm herself. Again there were noises, and this time her lock unbolted. She heard the door swing open. Lights were switched on.

"Mike?"

She tried to answer, but couldn't.

"The bedroom," directed Pam.

There were footsteps. The room lights went on.

"Jesus God," said Pam, as she knelt beside Michelle. "Mike, can you talk?"

In her dim vision, Michelle could make out the superintendent, holding his passkey. She struggled to turn her face toward Pam. Her mind was surprisingly clear; only her body wouldn't work.

Pam looked at her frantically. "Are you in pain?"

"I'd better call an ambulance, Miss Magnuson," the super said, and quickly found the phone.

Pam gently rolled Michelle onto her back. "Mike, honey,

it's going to be okay," she soothed. "Just tell me: it wasn't drugs, was it—something you took?"

Somehow Michelle managed to inch her head slowly from side to side, indicating no. She hoped Pam wouldn't get hysterical. But Pam was growing frantic. "Oh, Christ, why can't you talk? Dammit, Mike!" She jumped up in frustration. "Is it in the kitchen? Something you ate?" Infuriated by her own helplessness, she yelled, "Shit!" and stormed off toward the refrigerator.

The super returned and felt Michelle's pulse. "Just take it easy, Miss Van Dyne. The ambulance'll be here soon." For lack of something else to do, he put a cold compress on her forehead. Pam returned to the bedroom.

"There's almost nothing in the refrigerator, and the trash is empty. Do you think it was something she ate?"

"I don't know, Miss Magnuson."

"I can't believe this! Isn't there something we can do?"

"I don't know, Miss Magnuson."

The distant siren wailed on cue. "Thank God!" said Pam as she went to the window, watching the flashing lights below.

Michelle was aware of everything. The ambulance attendants wheeled a stretcher into the room. One of them wore the insignia of an emergency medical technician. They spoke calmly to Pam and the super as they examined Michelle. On the count of three, they put her on the stretcher, and as soon as they were loaded, the ambulance sped off, siren wailing.

The medical technician checked Michelle's vital signs. He flashed a light into her eyes, tested her reflexes, and listened to her heart and lungs. He then spoke into the microphone of a two-way radio. "Central, this is Forty-two. We have a twenty-six-year-old white female who seems to have a neurological problem. A friend found her lying on the bedroom floor. The patient can no longer talk.

"On physical examination, blood pressure is one hundred over sixty. Pulse is eighty. Respirations twenty-two and shallow. The patient seems alert but is unable to speak. There are no signs of trauma. The pupils are slightly dilated. Reflexes are normal. No apparent drugs or alcohol. Our E.T.A. is four minutes. Over."

Soon they arrived at the Emergency Room. Michelle was wheeled inside. Pam, wearing her bathrobe, spoke with the Emergency Room admitting clerk. She had found a health-insurance card in Michelle's wallet and gave it to the clerk. The clerk fed the card into the computer.

Inside the Emergency Room, the doctor on duty knew the case was grave. The young patient before him was seriously ill, but he had absolutely no idea what was wrong with her. He hoped she wasn't one of those cancer cases. It was at this point that Dr. Mohammed decided to call in Dr. Erikson.

"Hassan, Hassan," said Erikson wearily. "You're going to be the death of me." Erikson pulled open the curtain in the Emergency Room cubicle and fixed his gaze on an attractive woman in obvious distress. He was instantly alert. The patient before him was lovely, but she was also critically ill. She was struggling for air, but each breath was faint. Her face had a cyanotic hue of dusky pallor. Erikson's stethoscope was in his hand at once.

He examined her thoroughly, quickly. From her appearance, there was little time left before she would stop breathing. History was all-important, yet his evaluation was hindered by her inability to speak. After a few minutes he was finished. He stared at Michelle. Mohammed was just behind him.

"Is it a seizure, Dr. Erikson?"

"No. Anybody with her?"

"A friend is in the waiting room."

"Did you draw bloods when you started the IV?"

"Yes, Dr. Erikson."

"Call the lab and tell them it's stat. Did you order an EKG and chest film?"

"No, sir. I called you first."

"Listen carefully, Hassan. Tell the nurse to call Anesthesia and Neurology immediately. Sit on the lab people yourself.

I'm going to talk to the friend. Bring a stomach tube when you come back. Anything on the computer?"

"I don't know, Dr. Erikson."

"Then find out. Get back here as soon as possible."

A nurse stayed at the bedside when both of them left the room. As Erikson walked toward the waiting room, his mind sorted through diagnoses. The clinical picture was almost clear in his mind. He halted at the clerk's desk.

"Do you have a printout on the patient in Three?"

"Coming through now, Doctor."

She tore off the sheet of paper and handed it to him. It was nearly blank. According to the summary the computer had gleaned from the I.D. number on the health insurance card, Michelle Van Dyne was single, twenty-six, and in excellent health. She had no known diseases, did not take medications, and had never been hospitalized.

Worthless, he thought. He pushed open the waiting-room door. "Who's here with Van Dyne?"

A nervous young woman in a bathrobe snuffed out a cigarette and hurried toward him. She was carrying two handbags. "How's Michelle?"

"Not good. What happened to her?"

"I'm not sure. She called me—we live in the same building—and sounded terrible. When she wouldn't answer the doorbell, I had the super open up. We found her lying on the floor, and she could barely talk. It's not that cancer, is it? Please, not Michelle!"

He ignored the question and glanced at the handbags. "Is one of those hers?"

"Yes, this one."

"Did you look through it?"

"No. I didn't think—"

"She have a boyfriend?" he asked, as he rummaged through the contents.

"Michelle? Not anymore. Her sister died a little while ago. She hasn't dated much since then."

"Oh, is she *that* Van Dyne?"

"Yes."

"Has she been sick lately? Fever, abdominal pain?"

"I don't think so. But I haven't seen her in a week."

"Well, look what we have here,"exclaimed Erikson, as he located a credit-card receipt in Michelle's purse. "P. J. O'Callahan's, and it's stamped today."

"What is it? Does that mean something?"

"Why don't you have a seat, okay? Someone will talk with you in a little while." With that, he went back into the ER, leaving Pam worried and confused. The woman didn't know much, he thought, but she had been of some help. He knew O'Callahan's; it was open until dawn. He beckoned to a nurse.

"Cindy, call this place and see if they keep their guest checks. Find out what the patient had to eat."

Inside the cubicle, the anesthesia resident looked worried. "If she doesn't come around soon, I'm going to tube her."

"I think you'll have to."

"Get me a cart," said the anesthesiologist to the nurse. "And call Inhalation Therapy. Have them bring a respirator."

The small cubicle was alive with activity. The X-ray technician had no sooner completed a portable chest film than the EKG nurse pasted leads on Michelle's chest. As the anesthesiologist set up his equipment, the neurologist arrived.

"Problem?" he asked Erikson.

Erikson nodded. "Here's all you need to know: progressive respiratory paralysis in an afebrile, previously well patient. She's got postural hypotension and dilated, unreactive pupils. And check her mouth—dry, crusted mucous membranes. Get the picture?"

"Poisoning?"

"Sort of. Just tell me she doesn't have meningitis or something weird like myasthenia, okay?"

The neurologist began his examination as the nurse handed Erikson the cardiogram. He scanned the strip, then took the still-wet X-ray from the technician and stuck it onto the fluorescent view box. Mohammed returned, breathless, and handed Erikson the lab slips. He looked at one after another, then announced the results.

"Normal EKG. Her chest is clean. Electrolytes, blood work, and urinalysis are normal." The nurse who had called O'Callahan's handed Erikson a list of what Michelle had eaten for lunch. "Christ, what an appetite."

The neurologist finished. "It's not a neuro problem. Last time I saw a case like this, it was mushroom poisoning."

"She didn't have mushrooms." Erikson circled an item on the lunch list and showed it to the neurologist.

"Sausages?"

"Homemade, and probably bottled. Cindy, call that dump back and tell them they better find out if anyone else ordered the sausage today."

"What is it, Dr. Erikson?" asked Mohammed.

"Something camels don't get, Hassan. This patient has botulism."

THE SNOOZE alarm went off just as the phone rang. The Medical Examiner was jolted into wakefulness by the clamor. After fumbling for the snooze control on his telephone, Dr. Marvin Greenberg realized his mistake and lifted the receiver with one hand while he located the clock-radio with the other.

"Hello?"

"Marv, it's Ron Stillwell. I hate to wake you, but I need your help."

"That's all right. I was just getting up." He eyed the clock: six-fifteen.

"Didn't want to bother you at home, but it's important."

Greenberg didn't doubt that it was. As a respected family practitioner in the area, Dr. Stillwell had the reputation of a man of few words but abundant common sense.

"No problem. What've you got?"

"An emotionally wiped-out family, a diagnostic puzzle, and a very tired old doc."

"Meaning you?" Marv smiled.

"Meaning me. I can't pull these all-nighters anymore."

"That'll be the day. You're a workaholic."

"Wish I was. Anyway, here's the story. I've been providing newborn care for a very nice young couple. She delivered about three weeks ago—normal delivery; no problems in the nursery. She's developed some complications now. I'm not sure from what. But anyway, a few days ago, they brought in the baby for a checkup. He was very listless, lethargic. I couldn't find anything specifically wrong, but there was definitely something going on. I ordered some tests and sent the kid to Jerry Finkle, the pediatric neurologist. They were on their way to see him yesterday afternoon when they were in a car crash."

"What happened?"

"A freak accident. It was a hit-and-run collision, and should have been just a minor fender bender. Except the poor little kid went right through the windshield."

"Oh, God. How'd that happen?"

"That's another story. The baby was really smashed up. They rushed him right to the hospital, and he was in the Neonatal Intensive Care unit most of the night."

"And then?"

"He died a few moments ago."

"Jesus." Greenberg swallowed. "You really know how to start a guy's day off."

"The baby's in the morgue now, Marv. The family wants a post because of the child's symptoms before the crash. Which is why I'm calling you."

An autopsy? Greenberg knew that Stillwell was head physician on the Workers' Compensation panel, and active on medical-malpractice committees. Surely he realized that a postmortem on a routine motor-vehicle accident could open a legal can of worms.

"You know we don't do posts on M.V.A.s. Especially the

93

fishy ones. This isn't a Comp case, but a good lawyer would have a field day. Why don't you have the hospital pathologist do it?"

"I just spoke with him, and he won't take it."

"I don't blame 'im. Why don't you just tell the family there's nothing to be gained from an autopsy in this situation?"

"Because I can't convince myself of that. I honestly feel there's some underlying pathology here."

"What if there is? Even if I find something, it's a little late for therapy."

"It's a very, very complicated situation. The family, the emotional element ... I can't sell it too scientifically, but could you possibly do this one for me as a favor, and put it on my tab? I'll owe you one."

Greenberg hesitated. It just wasn't done. The Medical Examiner's office ran by rules, protocols. Yet he knew that Stillwell was not the kind of man who would ask a favor if he did not have a terribly urgent reason. "Okay, Ron. I'll get on it this morning."

In his office two hours later, Greenberg quickly dispensed with his morning chores and went directly to the morgue. He wanted to be finished with the case and have it off his mind before it disrupted his daily activities. The mortuary technician had unwrapped the baby's body and prepared it for his arrival.

The naked infant looked utterly frail as it lay atop the steel dissection table. Its body had nearly cooled to room temperature, but still held enough warmth to imprint a dull, foggy silhouette on the much colder stainless slab supporting its flesh. Greenberg stood at the baby's side and gazed at the small, still cadaver. He hated doing autopsies on children. There was something so absolutely pointless about their deaths. He put his finger in the baby's tiny palm, felt the limpness, and inwardly mourned the warm, clutching grasp that had once been there.

His gaze wandered across the baby's chest where purple

blotches started at the breastbone and continued upward, a harlequin bruise that enveloped the shoulders. His face was relatively unscathed. The small nose was flattened, obviously broken, clotted blood filling the nostrils; and there was a raised discoloration just above it where the forehead must have met the windshield. But what had killed him was an ugly, ragged discoloration below the chin, extending from ear to ear, where the window glass had ripped into his neck. He hadn't had a chance.

He was still a beautiful little boy. A good mortician, with a little skill . . .

"Hell of a way to get crackin', huh, Doc?" said the technician.

"Yeah. Poor kid. What's he weigh?"

"Five thousand grams on the nose. Eleven pounds."

"You'd think his parents would have had him in one of those car seats."

Greenberg sat on a stool at the end of the table and positioned himself behind the child's head. He'd dispense with the brain first. It should be relatively intact. He found a craniotome and plugged in the electric bone saw. Using a scalpel, he circumcised the scalp at ear level. Then he peeled back the thin skin, glovelike, and deftly incised the underlying muscles. When the skull was clean, he turned on the saw and put it to the bone. The blade whined, then tugged and bit. A fine powder of pulverized bone wafted into the air. Shortly, he had worked the bone all around. He lifted off the calvarium intact.

He pared away at the dura mater and set to work on the supporting ligaments. As he had suspected, the brain appeared uninjured. Soon he had freed up the sides and back of the brain before beginning work on the frontal lobes. Finally he severed the brain at its base, and gently scooped it out of the skull.

Greenberg handed the cerebrum to the technician. A few more seconds in the head, and he would be ready for the thorax. He peeled away the membranous diaphragm overlying the

95

pituitary gland. Suddenly, he stopped, and peered intently. What . . . ? He got off the stool and walked to the side of the table. He inspected the baby's mouth and throat. Then he lifted back the upper lip, drawing it over the broken nose. In spite of the dried blood in the mouth, he could see it clearly.

A fine, healing incision stretched across the gum line, where the gum met the lip.

Perplexed, he let the lip fall and began work on the chest, storing the observation in the back of his mind. With the help of the technician, he completed the gross dissection in half an hour. He took some organ samples for preparation into slides. Then Marv Greenberg pulled off his gloves, washed his hands, and picked up the telephone. He located Stillwell in a matter of minutes.

"I've drawn a blank so far," said Greenberg. "I think the hemorrhage and shock from the accident killed him. I'll have the cultures back and preliminary slide reports in forty-eight hours, but I don't think they'll help."

"No pneumonia, sepsis—nothing?"

"I doubt it. But you should have told me about the hypophysectomy."

"The what?"

"Hypophysectomy. When was it, about a week ago?"

There was a pause. Then, "What are you saying?"

"Come on!"

"I repeat—"

"I'm saying that this infant had major surgery when it was two weeks old."

"Impossible! I've seen the baby regularly since its birth. It's never been hospitalized."

"Then tell me: why does it have an incision in its mouth, and an empty sella?"

"Marv, this child hasn't left its mother's sight for a minute. Except . . ."

"Except what?"

"I mentioned this morning that the family situation was

96

complicated. Emotional problems, I think. You see, the mother claims that the baby was missing for a ten-to-twelve-hour period one night about a week ago, while her husband was away."

"And then it just turned up again?"

"Like I said, I think there's a strong psychological component here."

"Psychology's one thing; physical findings are another. I'd hate to be stuck with the explanation you're suggesting."

"Why?"

Greenberg pictured the scar, saw the empty pouch at the base of the skull. "Because I, for one, find it hard to believe that this child was abducted overnight, during which time someone stole its pituitary gland."

THROUGHOUT, ALTHOUGH she knew she was gravely ill, Michelle was struck by her mental clarity. Her body wouldn't function, but she was totally lucid. She was completely paralyzed, and could neither breathe unaided nor speak. What little she knew she gleaned from snatches of conversation between the scores of people who attended her. Early on, she understood she had botulism, and the knowledge terrified her. At one point, listening to the muted "ffft" of the respirator, she realized how tenuously she clung to life. If the machine were accidentally turned off, or if someone tripped over its cord, she would die. It was this sense of impotence that horrified her most.

She was utterly unable to communicate. Tubes protruded from every orifice. In addition to the breathing apparatus in her lungs, she had a stomach tube, which continually sucked out what little was left in her stomach. There was an intravenous dripping into each arm. A urinary catheter was draining her bladder. And throughout the night, and well into the morning, she was receiving enemas. "Cleansing enemas," one of the nurses called them.

97

The irony was that she had never felt so unclean in her life. In spite of her paralysis, her sensory ability was untouched. She felt everything. The enemas left her with a rancid fecal residue that clung to her inner thighs. It dried in place, sticky and foul-smelling. Caught up in the medical ministrations, no one bothered to clean her up.

After she had been wheeled into Intensive Care, the neurologist returned to do a spinal tap. The catheter was tugging on her bladder—a steady ache. One of the IVs had slipped out of place, and her arm began to swell painfully. As they rolled her onto her side for the spinal, she braced herself for the inevitable stabbing pain. But then, not far away, a man's voice reminded the nurse, "Don't forget the local." She silently blessed him, forgetting the discomfort. At least someone remembered. It was the first consideration anyone had shown her.

The voice belonged to a Dr. Erikson. She gathered that he was in charge, as he did most of the talking and gave the bulk of the orders. Toward noon, fewer people descended upon her, with their tests and tubes and pinpricks. She hoped that she was holding her own, or at least not getting worse. She was exhausted. Because she hadn't been able to blink, her lids had been taped shut to keep her eyes from drying out. But she was unable to sleep. She sensed someone hovering over her. The tapes were lifted away gently. Her eyelids were eased open, and a light shined into her pupils. The handsome face of a young doctor slid into view. He peered into her eyes. With his fingertips, he brushed back the hair on her forehead. He had a kind, gentle touch. "Sleep now," he told her. Then he helped her close her eyes with the tape, and he drew the curtains about her cubicle, giving her some privacy. It was a small gesture, but it was wonderful. She wanted to cry.

Hours later, she awakened. The curtains had been opened. She heard the pouring of water, and the wringing of a washcloth. They had come to bathe her. Her gown was removed. The water was barely lukewarm. She wanted to shiver, but couldn't. Her skin prickled with gooseflesh.

"Christ, this is cold!" It was Dr. Erikson. "Can you make it a little warmer?" he asked someone. One of the nurses walked away. Michelle lay there naked. For the first time, she felt embarrassed. Her nipples hardened from the chill. But then he covered her with a warm blanket. Again she wanted to cry. God bless you, she thought. Her lids eased open against the tape; a tear trickled from one of her eyes.

"Well, I'll be damned," said Erikson. He came into her view, looked at her, and smiled. With his finger, he wiped away the tear and removed the protective tape. "You're crying—you know that? That's a good sign." He found her hand, squeezed it with his. "I think you're going to make it, kid," he said.

That night, he slept on a cot by her bedside. His mere presence soothed her. It was the closest she had felt to someone since Trish had died. Dr. Erikson was the only one who seemed to consider her something more than a fascinating disease. She wanted to talk to him. Even if he was only doing his job, she wanted to thank him.

"Some women are a little more responsive when you lie next to them," one of the nurses said to Erikson. There was a playful slap, and giggling. Whispers were exchanged, and then the nurse left. Erikson lay down again. Surprisingly, Michelle felt a sudden pang of jealousy. This annoyed her. She had no right to feel that way. But comforted by his nearness, she slept.

It was morning again. Erikson took the tape off her eyelids and told her to blink. Michelle found that she could. She felt incredibly weak, but at least her body was starting to function again. "Very good," he said encouragingly. "Now see if you can squeeze my fingers." He slipped his hand into hers. "C'mon," he urged. "Aren't you supposed to be some kind of athlete?" She surprised herself when she was able to close her hand slightly. He seemed pleased. "Great," he said. "You're doing great. Keep that up and we'll take those tubes out in no time."

An hour later, with Michelle propped up in bed, Erikson examined her thoroughly. He had a firm but gentle touch. He described his findings to another doctor, who scribbled in the chart while the examination proceeded. Then he was finished.

"We start rounds here in fifteen minutes, Hassan," he said to the other man. "Make sure you have all her X-rays and lab results." Then Erikson sat on the edge of the bed and spoke softly. "How're you feeling—all right?" She was able to nod. "You're making an incredible recovery—you know that? It must have been the fantastic shape you were in. What a stroke of luck to have a famous athlete for a patient. I know you have a lot of questions. I'll go over everything with you soon. But first you have to make *me* famous."

Moments later, what seemed like dozens of physicians and medical students surrounded her bed. From their hushed murmuring, she gathered they thought she was a pregnant cancer victim. But then Erikson stepped to the front of the assemblage, slipped open the chart, and began his presentation. Michelle noticed the students' eyes widen as their interest grew. Botulism? Most of them had only read about it. They were even more fascinated when they learned who Michelle was. Was this really one of the Van Dyne sisters? The most pointed questions came from the Chief of Internal Medicine.

"Are you sure it's type B?"

"Yes, sir. Verified by mouse testing in the lab just a little while ago. And I just received word of two more suspicious cases at D.C. General—courtesy of O'Callahan's."

"How has she managed to improve so quickly?"

"We were fortunate enough to make the diagnosis fairly early. The Public Health Service had the trivalent antitoxin we needed, and we got it on board within an hour of her admission."

Excited discussion continued for the next few minutes. Satisfied that the diagnosis was correct, the conversation focused on treatment. All agreed Michelle was ready for extubation. The anesthesiologist loosened the attachments to the tube in her throat, then slid it out of her trachea. Michelle gagged and spluttered. Erikson patted her on the back. In a moment, she was able to breathe more easily.

"Young woman," said the Chief of Internal Medicine, "you can thank God you're alive. And Dr. Erikson here. We all admire you very much, and would hate to lose you to something like food poisoning. Now that you can talk, do you have any questions?"

Michelle didn't have to think long. "When can I take a bath?"

Everyone laughed. After a few more questions, the entourage moved on to the next case. Erikson lingered. He leaned over and whispered to her. "I'm golden," he beamed. "I won't thank you for getting sick. But I will thank you for getting better. You have no idea what you've done for my reputation. I'll be back after rounds, and we'll talk." He turned to leave.

Michelle watched him depart, thankful. She had started to relax when he suddenly walked back into her room. "Oh," he said. "You can have the bath tonight." And he was gone.

ERIKSON DOWNED the last of his beer and laughed heartily. Sitting in the lounge with Taylor, he filled in the details of his diagnostic coup. They hadn't seen each other in days. Taylor was unusually occupied in Obstetrics, and Erikson was busy with the Van Dyne case. She was doing exceptionally well, and it now looked as if she might be going home shortly. Erikson suppressed a snicker. He was a little giddy from the beer, but Taylor knew he was holding back.

"Out with it, man. What's the big joke?"

"You want to know what really happened?"

"Sure."

"If you ever tell anyone, I'll break your goddamn neck"—knowing, as he said it, that Taylor never would. He recited with gusto the tale of how he had been reading one of the many "throwaway" journals in the Doctors' Lounge. The article on botulism had fascinated him, from a forensic point of view; it had struck him as an interesting way to kill someone, if you had a quantity of purified toxin. But then he had forgotten

101

about it, until—presto: there she was, in the Emergency Room. A disease made to order.

Taylor laughed, relishing his friend's secret. A quick diagnosis for a rare disease was a doctor's dream. No wonder they were lauding Erikson with kudos.

"You are so damn lucky. Always were."

"To top it off, she's not bad-looking."

"Gorgeous, I heard."

"Yes, she is," said Erikson. "In fact, she really is," he said again.

MICHELLE WAS discharged after a week in the hospital. She had recovered fully. She was rested and mentally refreshed. She sensed she had come to a turning point in her life. The strange thoughts that plagued her seemed less frequent. She wondered if it took this sort of physical jolt to put one on an emotionally even keel. Most of all, her spirits were buoyed whenever Erikson came to her hospital room. She was flattered that he seemed to lavish so much attention on her. She left the hospital wondering if their paths would ever cross again.

It was clear she had to find some way to thank him. But she wanted it to be more than a simple handshake or expression of gratitude. It wasn't just that he had saved her life. He had also sent her soul soaring, helping lift the depression that was smothering her. That called for something special. Perhaps a gift, if she could discover his interests. At any rate, she would have to think it over carefully. It had to be just right.

Being back in her apartment was wonderful. She called her close friends and assured them of her full recovery and made arrangements to be back at work in a few days.

She was stiff from her week of inactivity. For the first time in months, Michelle made her way to the rear of her clothes closet. There was a shoe rack hidden there, behind her dresses. Two dozen pairs of track shoes were on its rungs. She selected a pair and laced them tight. Digging into a footlocker, she found a stopwatch. When she finished dressing, she locked her apartment and headed for the track. On her way downstairs, she felt a sudden pang of guilt. She had never run without her sister.

Outside, Michelle jogged to the track. God, she was slow! There was no spring in her step. She felt like a novice. It took forever to get to the university. Her feet ached, and her knees were sore. Reaching the track, she was dismayed by her physical condition. It was as if she had never run before.

She paused to limber up, doing her own form of yoga and stretching exercises. After a few minutes, she was ready. She walked slowly to the starting line. Few other people were there, and that was fine with her. She didn't want anyone to witness this dismal performance.

She hit the stopwatch and started off, deciding to warm up completely before beginning her sprints. A slow but comfortable seven minutes per mile should suffice.

After the first half-mile, she felt more comfortable. She closed her eyes, tuning in to the rhythmic pace of her steps. It felt good. She was at home again. It seemed like so long . . . Suddenly, she heard footsteps on the cinder track behind her. Her eyes jerked open. She looked straight ahead, keeping calm. The vision of the man in the rain flashed in her mind.

Don't be silly, she told herself. It's just another runner.

The steps grew nearer. The gap closed between them. Michelle was determined not to become alarmed. She continued her pace. The other person would pass her soon enough. But gradually, the steps behind her slowed. The runner behind her was moving at precisely her own speed. Following her. She was about to turn around when she heard his voice.

"You look great with your clothes on."

She stopped running, smiling and excited. Erikson, dressed in street clothes, ran past her.

She quickly caught up to him. "You scared me."

"I couldn't resist. You've got a World Class tush."

All at once, her aches evaporated. She felt on top of the world. "Where did you come from? How did you find me?"

"Easy. I drove by your apartment for one of those popular house calls you used to hear about and you practically ran in front of my car. I followed you here."

"I didn't see you come onto the track."

"I'm a sneaky little devil."

She felt awkward, at a loss for words. She wanted desperately to make conversation. Something witty, clever. But somehow it seemed enough that he was there, beside her, again, comforting her with his presence. Every so often he would lag behind her, then quickly catch up.

"What are you doing?"

"Admiring your legs. Sleek. Very sexy."

Michelle laughed. "Do you always sleep on a cot next to your patients?"

"Sometimes, in Intensive Care. Or when they're very beautiful."

"Is it true what they say about doctors?"

"Sure. We're all perverts."

"No, I mean about seeing a woman naked, and it having no effect on them."

"Not with me. I nearly dived into your bed while you were on the respirator."

"What stopped you?"

"Fear of getting caught."

"That's too bad," she ventured. "I may have been paralyzed, but I could feel everything."

He laughed. "I read you were fast, Van Dyne. But even I'm not that kinky."

Minutes later, he stopped, out of breath. He was worn out.

"I can go slower," she said.

"No, keep on going. I'll just sit on the bench awhile."

"I didn't mean to push you."

"You weren't. But there's no way I can compete with an Olympic sprinter."

"I'm sorry."

"Van Dyne, get your lovely ass back on the track. At least give an old man like me the pleasure of watching you."

"Are you sure?"

"Doctor's orders!"

She practiced for another half-hour. He took her stop-watch and called out her times. She was happy. He seemed pleased by her effort. When she stopped, sensing the first tightness of fatigue, he waved her over to sit beside him.

"Feel good?"

"Yeah." She nodded, gulping air.

"How long has it been? Six months?"

"About that. How did you know?"

"I read more than medical books. It was in all the papers, about how you dropped out of sight when your sister died. Trish, wasn't it?"

"You remember her name."

"Yes, reading is a required skill for doctors. We have to know how to count, too."

"Why are you teasing me?"

"Because you look beautiful when you get angry. And because I don't want you to think you've cornered the market on tragedy."

"I guess a lot more people than I thought remember Trish."

"*I* sure did. It's hard to forget a figure like hers." He got up. "Let's go. I'll buy you a Coke."

They drove slowly back to Georgetown. She felt good in his presence. He amused her with humorous anecdotes about hospital life. They found a small coffee shop not far from her apartment. Inside, they sat by the window and ordered drinks.

"Feel better?" he asked.

"From the run?"

He nodded.

"Yes. I never should have stopped."

"Obviously botulism agrees with you."

She laughed, looking casually through the glass. Outside,

the narrow street was lined with city elms. A gentle breeze gusted along the thoroughfare. The boughs of trees dipped in the wind. The leaves rippled with the air current, reflecting the overhead sun like sparkling coins of green and gold. The colors attracted her, capturing her gaze. She became lost in their twinkling. There, amidst the branches, the haunting faces reappeared. The faces . . .

"Michelle?"

She snapped out of her daze and turned toward the sound. It was Erikson. He held tightly to her wrist, shaking it to capture her attention.

"What?"

"Where were you? I lost you for a while."

Embarrassed, she pulled her hand away. Her face was red. She would be mortified if he knew. "Just a daydream. I'm sorry."

"About what?"

"Nothing."

Erikson made a wincing expression and looked at her out of the corner of his eye. "Oh, man, I picked a real winner here."

"I'm sorry," Michelle said firmly. "I just don't think you'd understand."

"Understand what?"

"Nothing." By now she was beet-red, and he was staring at her with a half-smile on his face.

"Don't stop now."

"Stop what?"

"Blushing. I get completely turned on when a beautiful woman blushes." He reached under the table and squeezed her knee.

"You're impossible!"

"Try me."

"But I don't even know you!"

"That's *my* fault? *You* were the one who was paralyzed. It was all I could do to keep from panting at your bedside."

"I didn't hear any panting."

"Comes from lots of practice. Breath control. I'm a very subdued heavy breather."

She adored talking with him. If only he were a little more serious, she might . . . No. He wouldn't understand. She wanted to change the subject. "I never had a chance to thank you."

He looked at her incredulously. "Cut!" He looked over his shoulder, toward the soda fountain. "Cecil, have the crew take five. We'll rewrite Miss Van Dyne's lines and then do another take." He turned around again. "Where the hell did you dig up that dialogue? First, I ask about your daydream, and you pull a Garbo. 'I vant to be alone'—you know? And now this thank-you business—what is that, *Dallas?* Who writes your script?"

"But I'm serious!" she laughed.

"Yeah, and this is the Pepsi Challenge," he said, rearranging their colas with new straws. "Viewers, today Mrs. Crave-your Body from Parsippany, New Jersey, will try to determine. . . ."

He stopped then, smiling at her warmly, watching her wipe a tear of laughter from one of her eyes. She looked back at him with responsive warmth.

"You're never serious, are you?"

"Doesn't pay to be. I was in therapy once, and—"

"You? *You* were in therapy?"

"Sure; isn't everybody at one time or another? I wasn't always this handsome, witty, and virile."

"What in the world for?"

"It's a long story. I nearly freaked out once, early in my internship. One of those identity-crisis things. Anyway, I had this really great shrink. He taught me to laugh at myself. And I haven't stopped since."

That settled it for Michelle. "Well," she said, "I'm in therapy now. I think I'm freaking out a bit myself."

"You?"

"Yes."

"Why not tell me about it? I almost went into psychiatry."

"Why didn't you?"

He slammed his fist on the table, rattling their glasses. "Dey all sleep mit deir patients, und dat is *verboten!*"

Michelle cracked up. She longed to talk with him, to tell him everything. In fact, she decided she would.

An hour later, they were still in the coffee shop. Michelle talked for a long time. It was a catharsis, infinitely more relieving than her sessions with Dr. Bender. She purged herself of the confusion that recently had filled her life. She told him everything. Beginning with what had happened to Trish, she moved on to the four days she had lost and the first bout with her strange thoughts. She talked about her therapy, and about the mixed feelings she had about it. She considered telling him she had sensed someone following her, but thought that might turn him off completely. She hadn't even tried it on Dr. Bender.

She found him a good listener. And she felt comfortable with him—a feeling that had begun in the hospital and continued even now. He had an interesting way of keeping the conversation going, of speaking without speaking. If he had a question, he would raise an interrogatory eyebrow: one eyebrow, just like that. Or if something wasn't clear, he would silently purse his lips and narrow his eyes, coaxing the words from her.

In an hour, Michelle didn't think he had said more than a few words. She was grateful; she needed to talk. His personality had a dual quality. In the hospital, he had been voluble, often sarcastic. Now he was the most patient of listeners. She looked at him candidly, content. A lock of his sandy hair fell in front of one eyelid. She pushed it back and looked into his blue eyes.

"My hour's up. You're a better psychiatrist than Dr. Bender."

"Should I send you a bill?"

"Are you expensive?"

"I'll take it out in trade."

"One of *those* doctors, huh?"

"Only when it comes to track stars." He was suddenly pensive, and toyed with the ice in his glass. "All in all, I'd say you've had one helluva few months."

"I know it sounds like a fairy tale, but it's not. It's like a nightmare. Just do me one favor: don't tell me if you don't believe me. Now that I finally got up the courage to talk, I don't think I could take it if I thought you were laughing at me."

"I don't know what to believe. Fairy tale or nightmare, it boils down to the same thing: you're the one going through it. You could be some kind of wacko. But with legs like yours, I'm willing to listen to anything."

She touched his fingers. "Thank you."

"Michelle—"

"Call me Mike."

"You're on." He looked at his watch, then out the window.

"Do you have to go?"

"There are some patients I promised to check on at the hospital."

"Is it very busy, with all those cancer deaths?"

"Very. You see, I'm also working on the vaccine."

"Really?"

"Yes. We can cure them of cancer, but they turn into raving nymphomaniacs."

She laughed too, and soon their laughter was uncontrollable, bringing tears to their eyes as they held their sides. Then slowly their laughter subsided, and they gazed at each other with fondness. Michelle put her hand on his.

"Thanks, Craig. I haven't laughed so much in . . . God, I can't remember. You know what? It doesn't bother me that you think I might be a flake. You're very kind."

"Do you have any plans for tonight?"

"Just some stuff I have to get ready for work. Why?"

109

"There's so much more I'd like to talk with you about. Would you like to get together later?"

"I'd love to."

"Mike?"

"Hmmm?"

"Don't worry, I'll help you."

Michelle lifted her face and softly kissed him on the cheek.

Chapter 9

"AND NOW WITH an update on the latest developments in the cancer epidemic, here's *Action News'* Public Affairs Correspondent, Meredith Bernard."

"Thanks, Jim. Joining us today is Dr. Ridley Clements, one of the leading forces in obstetrics and gynecology here in Washington, and one of the names most often mentioned for the soon-to-be-vacated post of Surgeon General. Dr. Clements, you've been at the forefront of much of the controversy surrounding these continued cancer deaths. Do you think that the criticism of your role has been justified?"

"That depends on what you consider my role to be. I've been a little more available to the press than some others. Perhaps that makes me more vulnerable to criticism."

"Then just who is the spokesman for the medical community?"

"There is no one spokesman. We're all working in concert—"

"But it seems that this is precisely what the public is saying, Dr. Clements. No one seems to be in charge."

"That's not quite true. Every department chief oversees the cases in his hospital."

"But aren't those efforts coordinated? Shouldn't they be? In something as serious as this, why isn't there a master strategy, a sort of game plan?"

"There is. We're working together with local and federal authorities toward a solution."

"Have you found one so far?"

"Unfortunately not. But this is the kind of situation where there can be surprising developments anytime."

"What is the status of the cancer epidemic, to date?"

"I don't like to use the word 'epidemic.' 'Epidemic' implies some sort of infection, and we have no evidence for that."

"Yet not long ago you said yourself that you thought it was an infectious process. In fact, some of your critics have said that your comments were typical of the stalling by the medical community."

"No one is stalling, Miss Bernard. At the time of my statement, I thought we had evidence to that effect. Unfortunately, we didn't."

"What about the actual number of cases, epidemic or not?"

"The most recent figures we have are several days old. As of last Friday, there were fourteen confirmed cancer deaths."

"And how many more women are being hospitalized?"

"I can't be sure, but I imagine around half a dozen."

"So you're talking about twenty cases?"

"That is correct."

"It's been reported that one of the victims was male. Could you confirm that for us?"

Clements hedged. "To my knowledge, all cases have been confined to pregnant women."

"What is it about these women that makes them so susceptible to this rapidly fatal form of cancer?"

"I wish I knew. It would certainly help in our research."

"You don't have any clue, then?"

"As I said before, we're actively working in a number of different areas."

"There has been speculation about placing the District and adjacent counties in quarantine, or imposing some form of martial law to prevent spread of the disease."

112

"That's nonsense. Those are the types of rumors that have been the most irresponsible. In fact, just the opposite is true. The local birthrate has dropped by fifty percent. Pregnant women are leaving the Washington area in record numbers to have their babies elsewhere."

"We're almost out of time, Dr. Clements. Just one last question. In the past few days, there have been unconfirmed reports about the disappearance or death of a handful of babies in our viewing area. Do you have any comment on that?"

There was a sudden twitch in Clements' cheek, a nervous tic unnoticed by most. The first droplets of perspiration moistened his hairline.

"I'm afraid I haven't heard anything about it."

"Thank you, Dr. Clements. Back to you, Jim."

The spotlights went off as the broadcast returned to the anchorman. Dr. Clements' hand trembled as he fumbled with the tiny microphone clipped to his tie.

NADINE FUSSED with her son's hair as she watched TV. Within a week of his birth, his unusually plentiful hair had turned a luxuriant red. She ran her hand through the fine strands as he slept, making ringlets with her finger. The news item worried her.

"Did you hear that, Joe?"

"Hmmm," Joe grunted as he read the sports page.

"Joe?"

"Don't pay no attention to that crap, Nadine."

"But now they said babies were dying."

"There ain't nothin' wrong with our kid," he insisted, still studying the paper. "The only people dyin' are the Redskins."

HANK CHO sat alone in front of his TV. He admired Clements' performance. The man was a diplomatic orator. He skillfully sidestepped the reporter's questions and adroitly elucidated what they knew about the epidemic: nothing. If the public discovered how frightfully little they'd learned so far, there would be panic.

The last question about something happening to children intrigued him, though. He was sure it was just media hype, their peculiar brand of sensationalism. With that thought in mind, he turned off the TV and headed for the bedroom. The phone rang.

"Dr. Cho," the voice boomed, "did you happen to watch the evening news just now?"

"Yes, Dr. Clements. I thought you fielded those questions pretty well."

"I would have fielded them better if I had been prepared. Why haven't I been informed about these infant deaths?"

"Because there haven't been any. At least, not in our hospital."

"Then find out where, and when. If it's rumor, so be it. But I want to know for sure. I won't be embarrassed like that again."

Cho sighed. "When do you need the information, Dr. Clements?"

"I needed it ten minutes ago." He hung up with finality, leaving Cho to stare in irritation at the silent receiver.

TAYLOR WAS unusually busy in Obstetrics. The cancer deaths had risen to sixteen. Clements' ranting was heard throughout the hospital. There were instances when Taylor had to remain on duty days at a time. His weekly racquetball session with Erikson had to be postponed, and they had little opportunity to see each other except in the hospital cafeteria. Now, early in the morning, they were having breakfast there together. After a few light conversational moments, Taylor broached a more serious topic.

"Do you still have those photos Dr. Wolfe showed us in his apartment?"

"Yes, somewhere. Why?"

"I've been thinking about it ever since he brought it up. I keep remembering his suggestion that a plant disease might cause a human malignancy."

"He merely raised it as a possibility."

"But it's such a nice little theory. Covers all bets."

"Much too farfetched," said Erikson, spearing a piece of bacon.

"I'm not so sure," said Taylor. "There are all kinds of carcinogens, so why not something botanical?"

"I can't swallow the contagion angle. He mentioned that too, remember?"

"That's because you figure the same thing we were taught in medical school, that communicability indicates a role played by some sort of virus or bacterium. But maybe Dr. Wolfe had something else in mind."

"Like what?"

Taylor shrugged. "Who knows? What I find hardest to accept is the implication of intent."

"What intent? Sam said nothing like that. That's really reading between the lines."

"Maybe. But when you talk about something contagious that strikes only pregnant women, it sounds like a form of germ warfare."

"You're out of your gourd."

"You don't see that as a possibility?"

"Nah. Even if the Russians did discover a great new way to poison our water, *everyone* would get sick, not just those women—right?"

"Come on, I wasn't thinking about the Russians."

Taylor's name was paged over the loudspeaker, and he rose to go.

"Then who were you thinking about?"

Taylor took one last bite of his toast. "Beats the hell out of me." He gave a noncommittal shrug and walked out, leaving a perplexed Erikson to stare after him, wondering if the long hours were finally affecting their sanity.

115

• • •

THE INTEROFFICE memo reached Clements' desk by midday. It was a tersely worded statement from Hank Cho, a follow-up to their conversation the night before. Clements read it twice and frowned. Cho had written that according to the District of Columbia Medical Examiner, only one death had occurred in an area infant. The child had died of trauma, though the Medical Examiner parenthetically added that its pituitary gland had been removed for reasons unknown. Interestingly, the M.E.'s office had several other reports of bizarre pituitary dysfunction—infants with unexplained nausea and vomiting, persistent drooling, changes in the texture of their skin—though none had resulted in death. Cho concluded that it was coincidence, yet he could not rule out the possibility of stress or a new viral syndrome.

Clements opened his lower left desk drawer. He found the folder with Cho's report on Dr. Wolfe's death and autopsy. He shuffled through to the last page, inserting Cho's latest memo behind it. Then he put it back into his desk and locked the drawer.

Chapter 10

THE MORE HE saw her, the more he wanted to see her. Her effect on him was magical. The grim hospital atmosphere seemed more tolerable whenever he thought of her. The quickness with which she lifted his spirits surprised him. He had had girlfriends before, and dated dozens of the hospital nurses. But those relationships had always been loose and casual. If he had to choose between staying with a patient and going out to dinner, he usually chose the patient. His work was more important. But now, he couldn't wait for the workday to end.

He thought the feeling was reciprocal. At least, he hoped it was. He managed to see Michelle at least every other day. She was gay and carefree in his presence. She seemed much more relaxed than when they had first met at the track. Her fears and apprehensions were largely gone. She was back at work, fully engrossed in her job. The strange thoughts and visions that had plagued her before seemed to have disappeared. It was because of this that she had temporarily postponed her sessions with Dr. Bender.

It was hard to maintain professional objectivity, to remain uninvolved. Being close to her didn't help. Michelle had the most endearing habit of unexpectedly touching him. While he was talking, she would cock her head and listen; and then, for no apparent reason, she would reach out, and her fingertips would graze his cheek. He would stop talking, overcome by the intimacy of the gesture, a little embarrassed by it. But when he continued, what she had done seemed the most natural thing in the world.

They didn't talk much about Michelle's first conversation at the coffee shop. Her confessional episode over, and her strange thoughts and dreams too infrequent to consider a problem, there seemed to be no reason to bring the subject up again. Michelle was happy with her work, Erikson content with his. They spent more and more time together. Michelle resumed running, and even talked of returning to competition. Erikson joined her at the track, running occasionally, but more often just watching. He could watch her for hours and never tire of being a spectator. She was a joy to behold, a superb athlete who was utterly feminine at the same time. She ran with fluid grace, seeming more like an ice skater than a sprinter. He enjoyed watching her liquid figure most of all. From a distance, she was all curves and softness, like flowing chiffon. Up close, she was firm and tight, but with no trace of the bulging calves or muscular arms that distorted the bodies of other female athletes. Erikson would just lean back, fix his gaze on her sleek legs, and smile.

He was confused by his feelings. He truly liked this woman—loved her, he thought—and yet he was acting out of character. With anyone else, he would try to leap into the sack the first chance he got. But for some reason, not with her. It wasn't that he didn't want to; it was more as if his feelings were sabotaging his libido. Yet their emotional intimacy seemed to grow even without any corresponding contact or a physical relationship, save for an affectionate touch, a kiss on the cheek, or a warm arm around the shoulder. They had been together constantly for almost two weeks, yet they hadn't spent one night together. Lying in bed alone, he would imagine her beside him. She filled his mind with fantasy. But he didn't want to push things; he wanted it to just happen naturally.

That night they had a light dinner out and attended a concert at the Kennedy Center. The six Bach Brandenburg Concertos; classical music was his love. They returned to her apartment for a nightcap, and to look through Erikson's prized picture albums. When he had picked her up earlier, Erikson had brought along his memorabilia. They had discovered they had something in common: they had both been history majors in college. In fact, Erikson had taken his Master's in history, specializing in North American studies.

"I was a Civil War buff," he'd told her. "I couldn't get enough of it. I used to collect stuff—muskets, uniforms, old posters. In the end I gave it all away, except for my photos."

"Civil War pictures?"

"Albums and albums. Some tell me it's one of the finest private collections in the city."

Now he stacked the albums on her low coffee table. Michelle held them on her lap one at a time, turning the pages slowly. Each photo was captioned. Erikson had typewritten several lines under each picture, placing the scene in historical perspective. Michelle was impressed by the care he had taken. The frayed edges of the fading brown-and-white photos had been meticulously mended.

They sat side by side, discussing the photos and sipping beer. He enjoyed watching her turn the pages. Her facial expressions had fascinating range and depth, the visage of a mime. In the middle of the last album, she turned a page and became motionless. "My God," she said, staring at one of the photos. Erikson recognized the picture of a squad of Union cavalrymen and their scout. Sitting on horseback, they struck rigid, unsmiling poses as they gazed at the camera.

"What is it?" he asked.

She didn't answer at first. Her pose evoked the frozen grace of a startled fawn alert to the hunter's footfall.

"Mike?"

"Where was this picture taken?"

He glanced at the caption. "Probably somewhere in western Virginia, in the Blue Ridge Mountains. Why?"

Michelle's finger seemed to tremble. Her nail circled the face of the scout.

"I know him," she intoned.

"You couldn't."

"It's uncanny how familiar he looks," she said. She wasn't sure why, but the image in the photo sent a sudden chill through her body as it summoned up the vague recollection of something frightening and evil in her past. "I could swear I've seen him in person before."

Erikson looked back at her reassuringly. "That's impossible, Mike," he said, in carefully measured beats. "That picture is over a hundred and thirty years old."

HUNDREDS OF miles from Washington, the dark-skinned man perched high atop the mountain in a carved-out granite niche, surveying the countryside below. Beside him, a rectangular box glowed with a peculiar phosphorescence as it monitored the signal that came from the nation's capital. To watch the monitor was his sole function; yet all-important though his task was, every so often the man was overcome with worry, and his attention wandered. His gaze would shift to the lush valleys whose crops awaited the fall harvest.

They were twelve, and twelve they would remain. When one of their lot was claimed by the passing centuries, they would restore that which had been lost, male for male, female for female. The shocking loss of their fertility was contrary to all the laws of nature, the cumulative experience of millennia. It was only in their desperation that they dared violate the very principles they held sacrosanct.

The man brushed the hair from his squinting eyes. When had their symbiosis begun? he wondered. It had been thousands of years in the past, distant and forgotten, when their ancestors first began to appreciate flowers as something more than lovely trinkets, when their forebears discovered that the leaves above did more than offer shade from the fiercest sun. But secrets learned demanded something equal in return: and thus the nurturing had begun. As the priests prospered, so did they protect, lavishly caring for their plants, according them respect.

They were as much at home outside the crater as within, though there was seldom reason to leave. Centuries before, they had transplanted beaver away from their new abode, and lured foxes and deer to points distant, thus banishing the trappers and hunters.

He prayed they had enough time left. There would be no more chances after this one. In their desperation, they had at last pried forth the remedies that, when applied, would restore their fertility. He was suddenly buffeted by a windy gust, and he was chilled. He wrapped his arms around his back and returned his gaze to the steady signal.

IT WAS getting to be a habit. They spent the next evening at his apartment. Michelle openly admired the diversity of his eclectic tastes. One entire paneled wall housed his elaborate stereo system—complete with electronic apparatus and the latest in C.B. equipment. He had photographs everywhere—landscapes, cityscapes, portraits ("My Steichen phase," he said). His books covered a wide range of subjects; his leather furnishings were masculine but warm; and Michelle grew to feel as comfortable with the home as she did with the man.

She searched in her tote bag and took out a long, thin box, gift-wrapped.

"What's this for?"

"For saving my life. And for being so wonderful to me."

"You didn't have to do this. Your insurance covered everything."

"Go on," she laughed. "Open it."

Erikson removed the ribbon and gift wrapping. Inside the

box was a gold-plated stethoscope. He smiled. "Is this the real thing?"

"Eighteen-karat. And it works. I didn't know what to get you. Do you like it?"

He frowned. "Let's see, now . . . which end do I put in my ears?" Then suddenly he looked up, grinning widely. "I love it, you adorable sentimentalist! But this must have cost a fortune!"

"You're worth every penny."

"Christ, I might be the first person to be mugged for a stethoscope." He took the small gift card from its envelope. It was signed simply, *"Love, Mike."* He looked at her with a feeling of deep affection. Then he leaned over and kissed her on the cheek. "Thanks, kid."

The air about them seemed charged. Erikson felt suddenly awkward—the self-consciousness of a first date.

"I guess it's getting late," he said awkwardly, rising to get her sweater.

"Do I have to go?" She stared at him and he looked back without talking. They searched each other's eyes, feeling the longing, but not knowing what to do about it. His hands hung loosely at his sides. She reached over and took hold of his fingertips. Her touch was electric. She took a step closer, letting her fingers slide up to his elbows.

"Craig . . ."

Neither dared look away. Their nearness was heavy and magnetic. He lifted his hands and cupped her face in his palms. They kept their eyes open as he drew her face to his. Their lips came together gently, without kissing. Finally their eyelids closed. Her mouth was warm and silky-dry. He moved his lips softly against hers—a feathery grazing, deeply sensual. Then he pulled away to look at her again. They breathed heavily.

His arms went around her, and he pulled her against him. She gave the slightest whimper and nestled her chin against his neck. Her nails pressed into his back, drawing him nearer still.

When their hips touched, her warmth seeped into him. She pushed her chest against his. There was no holding back.

His hands were under her blouse, their lips together. Her mouth opened, soft and pliant and searching. His hand slid under her bra. He pressed her breast against the flat of his palm, rubbing the nipple in small circles. Michelle moaned softly. He led her to the bedroom.

Half-clothed, still embracing, they sank onto his bed. Again he held her, and they kissed tenderly. She hugged him tight. Cheek pressed to cheek, they caressed each other. Then she returned her mouth to his, lips parted. She lay back on the pillow.

"I've dreamed about how it would be."

"I have too."

"Please make love to me."

She rolled her body next to his, pressing urgently. Her hand slid between his legs. She held him there. Then her palm rose to his waist. She undid his belt buckle and eased down his zipper. Her fingertips glided along his velvety length. Firmly, she encircled him.

He unbuttoned her blouse. She shrugged out of her bra straps, freeing her breasts. She had the whitest skin, almost opalescent. He kissed her nipples while she softly stroked him. Michelle closed her eyes. Her fingers roamed through his hair. She wished he wouldn't be so gentle. She urged him onto her.

Her hand quickened its pace, and his resistance was gone. She lifted her skirt and thumbed down her underpants, flicking them aside with one foot. She drew him toward her. Now very much aroused, he lowered his trousers to his knees. But before he could remove them, her legs locked tightly around his calves. She arched her hips. He slid smoothly into her. She sucked in her breath, pressing his face into her breasts. Both of them, half-clothed, her skirt hiked up about her waist, made wild, frenzied love with an intensity only the first time can bring.

Their damp faces rested together on the pillow. He was

still inside her. He raised himself to his elbows, taking his weight off her, and softly kissed her eyelids. He looked at her face, her eyes still closed. She was lovely.

While he watched, he thought he saw a subtle frown crease her forehead. Then she winced. He pulled away from her, rolling onto his side.

"What is it?"

"I don't know. . . . Maybe because it's been such a long time for me."

"Was I hurting you?"

"Oh, no, it felt wonderful."

"Then what?"

"Pain." She grimaced. She touched her lower right abdomen.

"Christ," he muttered. "I *was* hurting you. Let me see."

He placed his hand horizontally along her abdomen. He pressed in gently, watching her expression. She knitted her brow. Then he let go suddenly. The pain seemed more intense.

"Which hurts more—when I press, or when I let go?"

"When you let go."

"Damn."

Michelle touched his lips. "Don't quit on me now. I plan a very long evening for us."

But she was growing shockingly pale. Michelle sat up and swallowed deeply. Then her hand went to her mouth.

"I feel sick."

"Come on." He helped her out of bed and started for the bathroom. Halfway there, she gagged. Her stomach heaved, and she almost vomited. Erikson steadied her shoulders. "Almost there, Mike." They made it to the bathroom just as she began to retch. She emptied herself into the sink. Her breath came in shuddering spasms.

He wet a towel and wiped her face and lips with cold water. Slowly, she began to breathe more easily.

"Any better?"

She nodded.

124

"I want you to lie down."

"I will. Let me just stay in here for a while."

"Do you need help?"

"I'm okay."

He stepped outside, allowing her privacy. Finally she came out of the bathroom looking pale and shaken.

"I'm bleeding." Her voice quavered.

"Is it your period?"

"I'm not due yet."

"That's it," he decided. "Let's go. I'll help you dress."

"Where?"

"To the hospital. Hell, I was going anyway."

"Oh, no," she said, shakily.

"Don't worry. It's nothing serious."

"Are you sure?"

"If I'm not worried, I don't want you to worry either."

But he *was* worried. Very much worried. He had no idea what had happened; there were all sorts of possible diagnoses. The abdominal pain disturbed him most. She seemed to be in quite a bit of discomfort. "Just so happens that my best friend, Taylor, is a gynecologist in the hospital. I want him to take a look at you."

He helped her get into her clothes. As he dressed, she sat on the bed, arms crossed, bent forward. He dialed Taylor's home number. There was no answer; he had to be at the hospital. Michelle got up unsteadily as he hung up. His arms circled her waist for support, and they walked, sometimes lurching, down to the front door.

"WE HAVE about a dozen patients in labor," Taylor told his friend a half-hour later. "Is it something I can do between contractions?"

But Erikson was serious. "Remember that botulism patient?"

"Who doesn't?"

"Yeah. Anyway, we sort of got involved, and—"

"You dirty old man!"

"It's not what you think. She's really special, Taylor. I brought her in because she's bleeding vaginally and in a lot of pain. I'd like you to take a look at her."

"Pain like cramps?"

"No, more like an acute abdomen."

Just then the nurse motioned for them from the examining room. "I'll just introduce you," said Erikson. "Then I'll wait outside."

Twenty minutes later Taylor and a nurse came out of the examining room.

"I want a flat plate of the abdomen," he said to the nurse. She nodded and left to order the X-ray. Overhearing him, Erikson went over to his friend just as the loudspeaker blared, "Dr. Taylor, to the Delivery Room stat."

"Oh, shit," he muttered.

"What gives?"

"I have to run. Look, your girlfriend has one hell of a vaginal laceration. I put in some packing, but I still might have to throw in a few stitches under anesthesia. Give me a hand, okay? Check her blood count, look at her X-ray, and get started on her surgery consents, IVs, and all that. I should be free in about an hour." With that, he turned and ran up the stairwell.

Confused, Erikson walked slowly into the examining room. Michelle reached for his hand.

"Something's wrong, isn't there?"

"Don't be ridiculous. Taylor was in a big hurry, but he didn't seem all that worried."

"Does he know why I'm bleeding?"

"Just a little vaginal laceration, that's all."

"A what?"

He leaned over and whispered secretly in her ear. "Baby, I promise not to let the word get out, but just between you and me, why didn't you tell me you were a virgin?"

126

She laughed in spite of the pain. "He did *not* say that!"

"Eh, what does he know, anyway?"

"Please tell me!"

"All right. What it boils down to is this: I don't care what Xaviera Hollander says. Size *is* important. They're not banging down my door for nothing, you know."

Michelle was growing impatient. "Craig—"

"A tear. Satisfied? A vaginal laceration is a tear. No big deal. Happens to my women all the time."

"If it's no big deal, what am I doing in a hospital?"

"Well, maybe yours is an eensy bit bigger. Nothing to brag about. And even if he does have to take you to the Operating Room, don't let it go to your head."

"Oh, no!"

He saw the look of fear in her eyes. Erikson leaned over and kissed her reassuringly on the cheek. "Hey, you're not going to get all misty over a few stitches, are you?"

"Is that all he has to do?"

Erikson nodded. "And that's only if the vaginal packing doesn't hold. We're going to take an X-ray, and do a blood count. That'll give him more to go on."

"How soon will you know if he has to operate?"

"Soon. Don't worry."

She pulled him toward her. He leaned over and kissed her cheek, hugging her as best he could. Her skin was cold and pale. After a moment, he straightened up.

"Let's get that X-ray now, okay?" He pecked her on the forehead and walked out.

Dizzy and confused, Michelle stared at the bare bulb in the ceiling which seemed to go around, and round, and round.

Across the hall moments later, he studied the X-ray. There was a dull haziness in the right lower quadrant of Michelle's abdomen, which he thought indicated an accumulation of some sort of fluid. All the other structures looked normal. The nurse came over and handed him the blood count. Michelle's hemoglobin was low: seven point nine grams.

127

"Type and cross-match her for four units of blood," he said. "And get a consent for surgery. Call Anesthesia and tell them Dr. Taylor might have to do surgery."

"She wants to see you."

"I know. I'll be right there."

He spent the next forty-five minutes by her side, holding her hand and wiping away her mascara-stained tears. She wouldn't take anything for the pain. Then he repeated her blood count and went outside to await the results. The clerk was on the phone with the lab when Taylor called.

"Craig, this place is so busy, we even got Clements out of bed. And he is busting chops. I presented Michelle's case to him. He says it all depends on her repeat hemoglobin. Did you have a chance to get one?"

He paused while the clerk finished writing the numbers down. "Just coming through now." She tore off the slip and gave it to him. "It's down, Taylor. Six point eight."

"That settles that. Clements says he'll cover the cases from the Delivery Room if you can get her upstairs now. Anesthesia's running ragged too, but they can give us half an hour. Can you manage it?"

"Sure. And thanks."

Fifteen minutes later, Taylor was lathering his hands in the scrub sink outside the Operating Room. Through the glass door, he could see the anesthesiologist inserting a tube into Michelle's throat. He thought about her dropping hemoglobin level. She probably had a small "pumper" spurting from one of her vaginal blood vessels. Unless it was tied off soon, she could go into shock.

He wished he had more time to talk with Erikson. No matter. If he could see the outline of the laceration clearly, a few stitches should be sufficient. As he rinsed his hands in the sink, Taylor made a conscious effort not to try to figure things out before he had more facts. He'd know soon enough.

Inside the Operating Room, he gowned and gloved while a circulating nurse positioned Michelle. She put Michelle's feet into stirrups, knees bent, so that her legs flopped wide apart. She gave Taylor a stool after he applied sterile drapes. He sat down and removed the packing. There was seven yards of it, compressed into a tight wad. But even that amount wasn't a sufficient tamponade. When he pulled it free, it was soaked with blood, and liver-sized gobs of gelatinous clot expelled themselves behind it. He put a heavy weighted speculum into her vagina while the nurse adjusted the overhead lamp. He dabbed away the remaining blood and peered closely at the edges of the laceration.

"Will you need sutures, Doctor?"

"Give me some zero chromic on a taper."

A half-dozen figure-8 sutures should be enough, he thought. While waiting for the nurse to open the packets, he plucked away a strand of material at the vaginal apex. It looked like a piece of grass. He held it in his palm and placed it under the light.

It was some kind of suture material, yet it was the most unusual he'd ever seen. It wasn't catgut, or one of the newer dissolvable types. Nor was it nylon, silk, or a synthetic. He rolled it between his fingers, baffled. It seemed utterly foreign.

Taylor took a long, slender forceps and probed the upper edges of the tear. There were a few more of the strange sutures present. He gently eased them free. But as he did, the margins of the laceration widened, and both of Michelle's ovaries came into view.

Taylor didn't like it. He wasn't prepared for complications that might lead to a lengthy pelvic procedure. Not that seeing an ovary was unusual; in fact, the laceration was situated in the precise spot where one might intentionally incise the upper vagina, as in a tubal ligation. Was that it? he wondered. She had given no indication of it when he talked with her, no mention of any vaginal tubal.

He probed deeper into the laceration and located the fallopian tubes. They were intact, with no sign of surgery. Following the prescribed format, he carefully examined her internal pelvic region in detail. It would be folly to overlook something, sew up her tear, and then have to go in once more. He flipped over the tubes and inspected their entire length. They were in perfect shape; he doubted that Michelle would ever have trouble conceiving children. By carefully manipulating the ovaries, he could see both front and back surfaces. But then he narrowed his vision on the anterior surface of the right ovary as something else came into view. On the outermost pole of the ovary, not easily seen, was a greenish mass. It was somewhat rounded, not quite the size of a dime. A cyst—a small endometrioma? he wondered. The ovary was the right spot for it, and certainly the benign condition was common enough. He took a long Allis clamp and gently tugged on the edge of the mass, not wanting to cause bleeding. It came free instantly.

Seen better in the light, it was more perfectly round than he had first thought, and it had the dark green color of kelp. He felt the blob with his gloved hand. It was slightly compressible, but firm, unlike any endometriosis he was familiar with. He didn't know what to make of it. He gave it to the nurse and asked her to send it to Pathology for examination.

Minutes later, he finished the vaginal suturing. He placed a cotton sponge firmly against the incision line, then looked again: it was dry. He peeled off his gloves just as another nurse poked her head into the operating room.

"Dr. Clements wants you in the Delivery Room right away, Dr. Taylor."

"Who does he think I am, Houdini?"

"What's your post-op?" asked the circulating nurse, as Taylor took off his mask.

He gazed at the green sphere in the specimen basin. His thoughts were far away.

"Dr. Taylor? You did a repair of vaginal laceration, and what?"

"Oh. A repair and removal of small ovarian . . . cyst: probable endometriosis."

"Thank you." She penned something on the Nurse's Notes.

130

"Save the chart for me, will you? I'll get to it soon."

"Sure." She finished writing as he left the room, and then she located a plastic specimen jar. She filled it with saline, inasmuch as the OR porter had broken the bottle of formaldehyde swabbing up after the last case. It didn't matter. Saltwater would do. She picked up the small green mass and dropped it into the fluid. It bobbed up and down, floating. It was the most curious thing she had ever seen.

Erikson was waiting on a bench at the end of the corridor outside the Operating Room. He rose to meet Taylor.

"How is she?"

"No sweat. She'll be fine."

"Was it a vaginal laceration?"

Taylor swung his arm around Erikson's shoulder in brotherly fashion. "Craig, I know you like pretty things in skirts, but what you did was a no-no. You've got to give them time to heal, old man."

"Give who time?"

"Look: it's the old story—when the husband asks how soon they can have sex after the delivery, the answer is 'Gentlemen wait until after the placenta has been delivered.' I know you're hot to trot, and she *is* very attractive, but what you did was naughty, naughty, naughty!"

Erikson pulled himself away. "What are you saying?"

"I'm saying that there are times to play and times not to play. And as your friend, I'm saying you should know better. I don't care if you're crazy about the girl or not: you don't screw someone while she's still convalescing from vaginal surgery. Period."

"Now, wait right there," said Erikson, holding up his palms in front of his chest. "I can't believe I'm hearing this. Are you trying to tell me that she had major vaginal surgery recently, and I disrupted a suture line?"

"By Jove, I think you've got it!"

"Taylor—level with me. There's no doubt about what you're saying?"

Now it was Taylor's turn to be surprised. He'd been so

131

sure that Erikson knew about the previous operation that he had been content to admonish his friend. But he saw that Erikson's confusion was real, not one of his pranks. "There's no doubt," said Taylor.

"But what for? Did she tell you?"

"No—in fact, she said she'd never had surgery. Look, old man, I know she's good-looking, but are you sure she's all there?"

Just then the tall figure of Ridley Clements burst into the hall. His white hair was unruly, and his voice was tired and irritable.

"Dr. Taylor, I am waiting for you!"

"Yes, sir." Quickly, to Erikson: "You'd damn well better ask her for your own sake, Craig. I'll meet you at breakfast, okay?"

Erikson stood there in the corridor, annoyed and confused, like an abandoned Little Leaguer whom the big kids won't play with anymore. He waited outside the Operating Room as they placed Michelle on a stretcher. When they passed him in the hall, he took hold of one of the rails and helped wheel her toward the Recovery Room. He looked at her face. Michelle's eyes were closed, and she was still slightly pale. She was extubated, breathing on her own, but not quite awake. A blood transfusion dripped into her vein.

The nurses in Recovery busied themselves with the new arrival. They gave Michelle oxygen and adjusted the intravenous solutions. Erikson sat at a nearby desk. His lips were pressed into a thin line. Soon, Michelle was substantially more alert, and the nurses were occupied with other patients. He quietly approached the bedside.

Her eyes were closed. He reached for her hand, found it, and squeezed. Her lids opened, and she squeezed back.

"Hi. Are you awake?"

She nodded.

"How're you feeling?"

"All right." Her voice was hoarse, for her throat was dry

and still felt irritated from the endotracheal tube. He gently brushed back the loose strands of hair about her eyes. Her lids were heavy from the anesthetic, and her eyes began to close again.

"Pssst."

"Hmmm?" Her gaze fixed on him, and she struggled to focus.

"I'll come back later. Get some sleep."

She held tightly to his hand. "Don't go. I'm up."

"Good. Run out and get me a paper, and I'll have coffee with my bagel."

She smiled, more alert now, but also more serious. "Am I okay?"

"Good as new."

"Was it what you thought?"

He wouldn't press her about it, not now; but she had a right to know. "Yep. Just a little laceration, right where your vaginal scar was."

Michelle blinked. "What?"

"Your scar. The incision from the other operation wasn't quite healed, and it tore a little. But don't ask me to apologize. I loved every minute of it."

There was a ringing in her ears, and she wasn't sure she'd heard him right. She was still groggy, and the annoying ache between her legs was getting painful, and he was saying something . . . "Scar?" she managed, as her vision began to drift.

"The scar."

Her eyes were leaden, and she seemed to be trying to comprehend what he had said. But then she drifted away. Far away. And he feared that she was gone again, temporarily lost in the imaginings that he had thought no longer occurred. Yet maybe it was the anesthesia. A nurse came to the bedside carrying a syringe.

"I have some sedation for her."

"Yeah. I'm going."

Erikson released Michelle's hand and left the Recovery

Room. He was tired. He'd let her rest and try to get a few hours of sleep himself. Her reaction was strange. It had truly seemed as if she didn't know what he was talking about. He reached his on-call room exhausted and went to sleep. When he awoke, it was nearly seven. He quickly showered and put on his whites. He called the Recovery Room and learned that Michelle had been transferred to her own room. He would see her after breakfast.

In the cafeteria, Taylor looked haggard. He ate his cereal mechanically. The dark bags under his eyes sagged, and his clothing was wrinkled. Erikson pulled up a chair beside him.

"You look like Van Gogh did before he cut off his ear."

"Don't hassle me this morning. I'll bite."

"One of those nights, huh?" said Erikson, as he watched Taylor's face sink lower and lower. "If your chin gets any closer to the table, you can throw away the spoon and drink right out of the bowl."

Without further prompting, Taylor did just that. Then he put down the bowl, wiped his lips on his sleeve, and belched loudly.

"Class," said Erikson. "That's what I always liked about you."

"Thank Clements for that. He brings out the best in the breed. In fact, he insisted I honor him with my presence in the OR in precisely ten minutes."

"Sounds like a swell fellow."

"A real sweetheart. Speaking of class, did you talk with Little Miss Muffet yet?"

"Not exactly. She wasn't awake enough in the Recovery Room."

"If I were you, I'd watch my derriere. I don't know what she's trying to pull, but that wasn't a very clever stunt."

"When do you estimate she had that operation?"

"Three, maybe four weeks ago."

Erikson frowned. "Impossible."

"Why?"

"That's precisely when she was hospitalized here for botulism."

Taylor shrugged. "So maybe it was a little before that. But there's no doubt she had surgery. There were still sutures in place."

"What kind of surgery was it?"

"A colpotomy."

"Don't confuse me with that mumbo jumbo. What's a colpotomy?"

"An incision in the upper vagina to expose the pelvic organs. Usually for something like a tubal ligation."

Erikson was astonished. "Are you trying to tell me she had a tubal ligation?"

"No, her tubes were normal. I'm not sure what she had done." Taylor looked at the clock and started to rise. Erikson tugged on his coat sleeve.

"Hold on a minute. Run that by me once more."

"Clements will nail me to the wall if I'm late, Craig."

"Just answer this for me: what are the legitimate indications for having a colpotomy?"

"Christ, there are dozens."

"Just name a couple, so I can get a feel for it."

"Well, it might be for fertility studies. Was she trying to get pregnant?"

"*Pregnant?* I certainly hope not. What else?"

"Well, maybe the surgeon thought she had a pelvic infection."

"Did you find any suggestion of that?"

"Not a trace."

"What else?"

"Or maybe just to get at her ovaries."

"What for?"

"Could be *in vitro*–fertilization studies. There's a lot of that going on."

"You mean test-tube babies?"

"Among other things. Look, I've got to—"

135

"One second, one second. How come the surgery wasn't on the interhospital health-insurance record?"

"How should I know? Maybe it wasn't done in Washington. Or she could have had it as an outpatient, if she wanted."

"And if she didn't want it?"

"What?"

"I mean, could she have had the operation against her will, the way research labs do surgery on stray dogs?"

"Are you *nuts?*"

"I know it's farfetched, but is it possible?"

"Anything's possible. But one thing's for sure: that girl has you so strung out that you're grasping at straws. Why not make sure *she's* not hiding something from you? That's more logical, isn't it?" Taylor gave his friend an encouraging clap on the shoulder. "Think about it," he said, and left.

Erikson finished his breakfast in sullen silence.

HANK CHO was rushing into the Pathology lab. He was supposed to give a lecture at Johns Hopkins Hospital in Baltimore at ten o'clock, and he had forgotten his notes. Finally he located his briefcase, and was on his way out the door when he saw the specimen that had been sent down from Surgery during the night.

"What is that thing?" he asked the technician in the lab. He handed him the plastic jar.

"There's nothing in here, Dr. Cho."

"Look again, Joe. The little green thing floating on top. Is this in formalin?"

"No, the OR ran out. It's in saline."

"Where'd it come from?"

"From an ovary, according to the Pathology slip."

"Did they culture it?"

"I don't think so."

Cho was already late, but his curiosity was aroused. He could spare a few minutes. He assembled several petri dishes of various jelled media and streaked the green sphere across their surfaces. In twenty-four hours he would have a preliminary indication of the presence or absence of microbial growth. Wearing gloves, he picked up the specimen with sterile forceps and looked at it closely. "You sure this isn't a contaminant? It looks like it fell off somebody's shoe."

"The slip says it might be endometriosis."

"No, too green. Almost polished, you know? But soft. I wonder if this is some kind of fungus, like actinomyces. Weird."

"You want to use my microscope?"

"I'll use the one in my office, Joe."

He unlocked the door and went to his desk. He switched on the lamp to his microscope and placed the object on a glass slide. He eased the object under the low-power lens and looked through the binocular eyepiece. Then his vision froze. "Incredible," he softly uttered.

Through the lenses, he saw a complex network of interconnecting wires. They looked like electrical connections, reminiscent of microcircuits in a solid-state computer chip. He narrowed his eyes, peering intently. Something bothered him, and creases lined his forehead. He moved the slide back and forth, observing it from all angles. His jaw muscles tensed. For several minutes, he scanned with the microscope. When he finally looked up, the color had drained from his face. He couldn't believe it.

"This object is alive."

Chapter 11

NADINE HEARD THE baby cough. She sat upright in bed, her mother's ear now trained, listening to the sound. Joe continued sleeping undisturbed, snoring loudly. There it was again—a croupy, deep rasping of phlegm. She put on her robe and hurried to the baby's room.

The night light cast a pale glow across the crib. Her son was beginning to wake up. Although he was no more than a month old, his features had changed completely. His face was filling out, and his head was covered with the reddish curls he'd inherited from Nadine's father. The baby's hair was damp now. She put her palm on his forehead, and thought she felt fever. The baby started to cry.

She picked him up, cuddling him, fretting about his worsening condition. It *had* to be more than the simple virus the doctor had claimed last week. She sat in the rocking chair and unsnapped her nursing bra. She put her son to her breast.

She was terribly worried. He had been feeding poorly for days, and his cry had become hoarse as he grew more and more somnolent. Then the vomiting had started. And now, fine wrinkles had developed about his eyes and mouth, delicate creases in skin that had become dry and waxy. Nadine stroked his hair, listening to the slight wheeze of his inhalation.

138

He found the nipple, and his crying ceased. But he wouldn't nurse; his small tongue seemed too thick for his mouth. His tiny lips opened and closed lethargically, and a small stream of saliva ran down Nadine's breast as her son began to drool incessantly.

ERIKSON WENT to Michelle's room. Her blood transfusion was completed. She was awake and alert, and she smiled as he neared the bedside. Her complexion was glowing, almost rubicund. The blood seemed to agree with her. He looked around self-consciously and kissed her on the forehead.

"Afraid the nurses might see?"

"We're not supposed to fraternize with the patients."

"I hope that doesn't include making love."

"No, but holding hands is definitely out. How're you feeling?"

"Better."

"Any pain?"

"Sore, but not really painful anymore." She paused, pensive. "Were you with me in the Recovery Room?"

"For a few minutes," he said, nodding. He wondered how much she remembered.

"Those drugs . . . I couldn't think straight. It was like a dream. I have the strangest memory of your saying something about a scar."

He struggled with himself. Everything was timing, phrasing. And now the time seemed right. He smiled casually and shrugged. "I was just curious about your operation."

She stared at him blankly. "Operation? This operation?"

"No, the one you had before. The other vaginal surgery."

Michelle was totally befuddled. "So you *did* mention a scar. But I never had any other surgery."

He studied her quizzical expression. If she was lying, he'd be damned if he could detect it. She appeared to be telling the complete truth. His smile widened, and he clapped his hand on his thigh. "I *told* Taylor you didn't. It figures. After all those long hours, he can't see straight anymore."

Michelle looked a little piqued. "Did Taylor say I had surgery before?"

"Don't be silly!"

"Craig—"

"He said your laceration was in a spot they often *do* vaginal surgery. He didn't say you *had* vaginal surgery."

"But didn't you just say—"

He stifled her words with a swift kiss on the lips. "No more dope for you, Mike. You have no tolerance for narcotics. They make you sound like you dropped your brain in La Machine."

He left her room to make rounds. Michelle watched him leave, feeling almost content. Yet in the back of her mind, there was the slightest hint of uncertainty.

When he finished rounds, Erikson paged Taylor, hoping to continue their conversation, but the operator told him Taylor was still in Surgery. Poor bastard, he thought. The guy had been up all night. Erikson lunched alone.

He managed to finish the clinics by four. Again he put in a call to Taylor. He spoke with one of the junior residents. It seemed that Taylor was completely wiped out and had just gone to bed. Erikson toyed with the idea of going up to Taylor's room, but he couldn't bring himself to do it. Taylor desperately needed the sleep. He returned to Michelle's room, and found her anxious to go home.

"Hey, you just got out of Surgery."

"That was last night. Anyway, I feel fine. Can you arrange it, Craig? This place gives me the creeps. It's twice in one month. It's getting to be a habit. And I'd like to show up at work on Monday without having to explain my sex life."

"I'll try."

He spoke once more with the junior resident. Michelle's blood count was fine, said the resident, and the nurses said she was doing well. He had no objection to discharging her if someone was responsible for her at her home. Erikson decided who that someone would be. By suppertime, he was driving Michelle back to her apartment under the condition he serve as nurse.

With a smile, she agreed.

CHO RETURNED from his lecture early in the afternoon. Driving to and from Baltimore, he kept thinking about the green object. When he was able to focus down on the individual cells and see the protoplasm and nuclei, he had known it was alive. He had to study it further. That meant keeping it alive, in essentially the same environment that had given it shelter previously.

Back in the lab, he found that he was inundated with work. There were dozens of tissue specimens from the morning surgery, enough to keep him busy for days. Yet he had to spare an hour to study the green object further. Before he left for Baltimore, he'd placed the mass on a blood-agar culture medium and put the petri dish in a small locked incubator. The former would supply nutrient; the latter, a semblance of body heat. He had created an artificial environment that would sustain the object outside the patient's body.

The Pathology slip listed Dr. Taylor as the surgeon. Before he opened the incubator, Cho paged Taylor to get some information. When Taylor rang back, he sounded utterly exhausted. He'd been up all night and was just about to take a nap. Cho promised to be brief. He asked a few questions and let Taylor go.

Now Cho was more confused than ever. Endometriosis was impossible. Taylor admitted that the mass looked peculiar, but his main concern was whether or not it was benign.

"No question," Cho assured him.

"Good. Any idea what it is?"

For a moment, Cho considered telling him the startling

news. But until he had more answers, he decided to keep it to himself. There was enough going on in this hospital. Until he had something more concrete, he wouldn't panic anyone. "I'm working on it. But don't worry about it. It's not malignant."

He removed the object from the incubator and unlocked the door to his office. During the next hour, he analyzed the sphere without disturbing its circuits. Using an operating microscope, he removed a minuscule fragment and subjected it to spectrophotometry and multiphasic chemical screening. He borrowed a protective lead apron from the Radiology department and X-rayed the mass.

He knew he had to get back to his other work. He replaced the petri dish in the incubator and propped his feet on his desk while he tried to organize his thoughts. The concepts were confusing; it was hard to digest what he'd learned. Interspersed between the circuits was a network of tubules and organized sheets of living cells. His analysis had finally proved the green pigment to be chlorophyll, and further investigation had shown that the cells were capable of undergoing photosynthesis. To Cho, that was both astounding and frightening.

The green object was a plant. Definitely a plant.

DURING THE drive to her apartment, Michelle rested comfortably beside him, her eyes closed. Erikson knew exactly what he was going to say about her former surgery: nothing. He doubted she wanted to deceive him. At least, he hoped she didn't. What bothered him most was a nagging suspicion that grew more and more credible with each passing moment: that Michelle was not entirely stable.

He was baffled by their chat in the hospital. He hadn't been at all prepared for her denial, but why would she lie? No, she wasn't capable of that. Unless . . . unless she truly did have a mental imbalance? Should he encourage her to resume her sessions with Dr. Bender? Above all, he had to remain objective, for emotion clouded judgment. Sound judgment was what he needed most. Somehow he had to weave through the cloud that had suddenly obscured their relationship. Though he was a trained observer, what he now knew was utterly baffling. On the one hand was Michelle's sincere and innocent denial; on the other was what Taylor said had obviously happened to her. He simply had to remain patient.

He hadn't realized how tired he was. Once in her apartment, he'd turned on some classical music, out of habit. Still clad in his whites, he lay on the couch, nestled in her lap, and fell asleep.

Later that night, he awakened suddenly.

She combed her fingers through his hair.

"What time is it?"

"Around ten o'clock."

He sat up. "I didn't mean to sleep that long."

"You had a busy day."

"How're you feeling?"

"Good. It doesn't hurt at all anymore."

He nuzzled her neck and winked at her. "That's the best news yet."

She closed her eyes, feeling his lips nearing her ear. Softly, "You're not thinking what I think you're thinking, are you?"

He pulled away abruptly, feigning indignation. Then he smiled. "Well, maybe we'll give it a few more days."

They decided to go to sleep early and slid under the cool sheets in Michelle's bed. Whereas Michelle fell instantly asleep, Erikson lay awake, tossing uncomfortably. He kept thinking about something Taylor had said earlier: about Michelle's prior operation. He wrestled with the recollection. Vaginal surgery? he wondered. Why vaginal surgery? Eventually, fatigue overtook him, and he slept.

They spent the night in each other's arms. Once, in her sleep, she rolled away. He unconsciously reached out for her, as if they had been longtime bedmates. He held her breasts and nestled his face into the warm hollow of her neck. It was the most contented night either of them had spent in years.

In the morning, he awakened her with a kiss. She stretched lazily in bed. When she opened her eyes, he was already dressed for work. He was putting on his tie.

"Hi," she said.

"Good morning. How'd you sleep?"

"Great."

"Me too." He slipped into his shoes and bent over to tie them. There was a snap. "Damn."

"What's wrong?"

"I broke a shoelace, and I'm already late. Do you have any?"

"In the closet, near my track shoes. But they're white."

She closed her eyes, puffed up her pillow, and rolled over again. She heard him rummaging through her clothes, moving among the hangers. Then there was silence. Michelle waited a few moments and wondered what was taking him so long. Then she opened her eyes and propped herself up on an elbow. "Craig, did you find them?"

He didn't answer. But then she heard his footsteps. Michelle rolled to face the door. Erikson walked slowly toward the bed, holding a framed color snapshot.

"This is Trish, isn't it?" he asked.

She took the photo from him. It was her favorite picture. She gazed at it wistfully. She had hidden it in the closet months before when she found remembrances of Trish too unbearable. But now she could look at it with fondness. Trish was smiling in the photo, sitting alongside the trophies in her Georgetown apartment. Michelle had taken the picture herself. Now, she looked up at Erikson and nodded. "That's Trish. My sister."

"When was it taken?"

"It seems like ages ago. But it was just last winter, a few days before she died," she said sadly.

He looked at the picture again and suddenly the color drained from his face. There, amongst the trophies, was a slender vase sitting on the table, just slightly out of focus. Its con-

144

tents would be easily overlooked by most people. But not by Erikson.

The large magenta orchid was identical to the flower he'd seen in Dr. Wolfe's apartment just before the older man's death.

Erikson felt as if he were suffocating. He couldn't talk. He turned away from Michelle before she could see the horror in his eyes. As he wheezed for breath, he had the most sickening feeling that Michelle had never, ever, lied about a thing.

Chapter 12

He knew he was visibly shaken, but he hoped Michelle wouldn't notice. Erikson summoned up an air of nonchalance and slowly walked out of the bedroom, photo in hand. He didn't want her to notice the confusion he felt. His mind raced furiously. It was the orchid. It now linked Sam Wolfe and Trish Van Dyne in death.

No, he thought. It couldn't be. It just couldn't be. For a moment he considered calling the police. Yet he knew, from his medical experience in such matters, that the police would chalk it up to mere coincidence. At any suggestion of a *plant's* playing a role in a crime, they would laugh him out of the station. And who could blame them? And where was Sam's orchid as evidence?

Yet there was no denying the visual evidence he held in his hand. He slipped the photograph into his breast pocket, undetected by Michelle. He dared not tell her his suspicions. At this point in her convalescence, his speculation might have a physical effect on her, perhaps even cause a relapse. He knew how close she'd been with Trish; he couldn't risk it. Calmed, he returned to the bedroom and finished dressing, pretending nonchalance, aware that Michelle was staring at him.

"What's wrong, Craig?"

"I'm a little late."

"Are you worried about something? You seem—well, pre-occupied."

"I am. I have this obsession with punctuality."

The remark was out of character; and why wouldn't he look in her direction? "Craig . . ."

He flashed his cheeriest smile. "Especially when today's guest lecturers are Masters and Johnson."

She wasn't convinced. "Is there something you aren't telling me?"

"Yep. It's a good thing I didn't meet Trish first. From that picture, I suspect I would have spent all my time following her instead of you."

Michelle couldn't say why, but something in Craig's demeanor seemed strange. It frightened her. She decided right there and then to tell him of her fears of being watched, followed . . . of the dark-skinned stranger on the park bench and the man in the rain. She sat on the edge of the bed, one leg beneath her, and blurted it all out.

"Craig, listen to me. Please listen. I know this sounds silly, but there were a couple of times when I thought someone was watching me. Following me."

He sat beside her and put his arm around her. "Why didn't you tell me?"

"I didn't think you'd believe me. I—I'm not sure I really believe it myself."

Erikson studied her face, his concern darkening. Something horrible was happening, something he didn't understand, yet he had the most unshakable feeling that it was all related. Taylor's discovery of a surgery Michelle couldn't remember, and now a question of bizarre circumstances around two deaths. Perhaps, he suddenly thought, Mike's "visions" weren't visions at all. Maybe they weren't what psychiatrists were so quick to call the workings of a repressed mind. Perhaps they were something far, far worse. Something real, a form of recall.

"I'm scared, Craig."

"Mike, Mike," he soothed. His arms went around her,

147

and he hugged her tight. He stroked her hair reassuringly. "Don't be silly."

"What if I'm right?" she said frantically. "What if someone *is* following me?"

"Look," he said firmly. "No one is following you, do you understand?"

"But—"

"No buts," he interrupted, calming her with his steady, even tones. "You're perfectly safe here. You just got out of the hospital, and you're not due back at work until Monday, right?"

"I guess so."

"I *know* so." He kissed her on the cheek and rose to leave. "Just sit tight and don't go anywhere. Let me figure this out."

She got out of bed and ran to him, holding him close. "Call me. Please call me all the time!"

"I will."

He kissed her and left. She watched him leave her building and cross the street. When he was out of sight, she closed the shades in the bedroom. She did the same with the other rooms, checking to see that the windows were locked and the door bolted. Finally she retreated to the bedroom and climbed onto the bed. She pulled the sheets about her knees, her gaze darting from the door to the window. Then she just sat, paralyzed by an irrational fear.

FATIGUED, HANK Cho rubbed his eyes, contemplating his discovery. What in God's name *was* the thing? It was simple, but ingenious. Whoever had constructed it had a tremendously advanced scientific background. Apparently he—or they—had turned the plant into a parasite. Like a Venus'-flytrap, it used protein secretions as a food source for growth. There were many things he didn't know yet, such as how photosynthesis occurred in a human abdomen, without a light source. But in order to survive, the green object must have been feeding off the patient's own protein-rich ovarian secretions.

Everything that was happening seemed to form a pattern, too incredible to be coincidence. The more he thought about it, the more puzzled he became. There were the cancer deaths, always perplexing him with their peculiar floral aroma. Then there was something Dr. Wolfe had once said at a CPC, something about the connection of plants and cancer. And now his incubator contained a botanical wonder straight out of the twenty-first century. Were all of these things even remotely related? Or was he just imagining it?

It was late at night when he finished in the lab. The routine work of pathology was piling up at an unexpected rate; it would take him days to finish, but he'd have to deal with it first before he could resume studying the object. He was exhausted. His mind reeled from the implications of the strange green object. At last he turned off the light and left his office in disarray, forgetting to return the lead X-ray apron, which he left carelessly draped over the incubator.

THE STARS dotting the midnight sky were twinkling gems piercing a shroud of blackness. To the man atop the mountain, their dazzling radiance seemed close enough to touch. He knew they wouldn't have to wait much longer: all was nearly ready. Soon they could put to rest their mounting fears, which now soared like the wind itself in those dark and stormy hours when the clouds precede the tempest.

His attention abruptly shifted to the box beside him. Something was wrong. The phosphorescent glow had vanished: the signal. He quickly got to his feet. Something had interfered with the signal.

His lips formed a tight line. Nothing dared intervene now. He hurriedly leaped onto a narrow granite trail that wound through the rock, immediately knowing what had to be done.

. . .

HANK CHO awoke with a cold that morning. A fit of morning sneezing was soon followed by body aches and a sore throat. He swallowed two aspirin and a decongestant and put a squeeze bottle of nose spray in his pocket. By noon, the bottle was half empty. On his way to lunch, he swallowed some cough syrup with codeine for the sudden spasms that racked his chest. In the coffee shop, he slumped into a secluded corner booth. He would have preferred to eat alone, but he was soon joined by the hospital's Chief of Security.

"You look like shit," the man said.

"Feel like it, too. For two days now I've got this headache that won't quit."

"You ain't the only one," said the Security chief, rubbing his temples. "Have you done the Brewster autopsy yet?"

Brewster, thought Cho. The latest female cancer victim. "No. I'll get to her this afternoon."

"Good. Then I can sic the family on you. They've been driving everyone at the Information desk up a wall."

"About what?"

"Crazy stuff. Some of these people really go off the deep end. Her husband keeps insisting she disappeared about a month ago, and that it had something to do with her getting sick. Like I'm supposed to do something about it now."

"*Did* she disappear?"

"Who knows? He says she was gone for half a day. Hard to check that sort of thing. You know what's funny, though, Doc? I heard another story like that. The Lehman patient."

Cho frowned. He hadn't heard anything about this before. "Did any of those patients say where they had been?"

"No—that's the weirdest part. According to the Brewsters, the woman didn't even remember being gone. Same with Mrs. Lehman."

How curious, Cho thought. "Look," he said to the Security man, "you used to be on the police force. I want you to do me a favor."

150

Cho asked the Security chief to contact his friends still active in the Metropolitan Police. Leaving the coffee shop, he also phoned the head of Medical Records. He asked each of them to try to find out if any of the cancer victims had ever been officially reported missing.

The answer came before he left work that day. The Security man said there were no Missing Person reports on file. So much for that lead.

Yet Cho went home disturbed by the findings. Obviously, neither the press nor medical researchers working on the cancer had heard of those accounts, because no official police reports had been filed. But then he remembered the Security man's saying that such reports weren't made out until after an absence of twenty-four hours. What was starting to occur to him was that someone might be kidnapping the expectant mothers—for short periods of time.

Impossible. This damn cold was making his head swim. He went to bed early that night, achy and feverish. He had a throbbing headache, and it was hard to sleep. He felt truly miserable, shivering under the covers. He rubbed his temples, the back of his neck. And then his eyes opened in concern.

His neck was studded with lumps.

He explored the swollen glands under the angle of his jaw and behind his neck. They were the size of quarters. Rotten virus, he thought. His teeth chattered. God, he felt awful. He rolled onto his side and curled up under the blanket. Huddled under the sheets, he took forever to fall asleep.

The next morning, it was all he could do to drag himself out of bed. Although he felt weak, too ill to work, he decided to take the afternoon off and do some research in the hospital library. He wasn't sure what he expected to find, if anything. He simply wanted to review any known or suspected relationships between pregnancy and plants.

He sank low in his seat, surrounded by heavy medical tomes, leafing through the pages. As he scanned the references on pregnancy, the initial endocrine correlation was between the ovary and the pituitary. The pituitary! Clements had asked him about that recently. The report on the children!

He read on and found a number of references to certain plant extracts and their effects on hormonal function. Some of these herbal derivatives, for example, profoundly influenced the production of breast milk. Various types of ergot fungus were among them, and the bark and leaves of certain tropical trees. And then he stumbled across something else: a handful of obscure herbal drugs, of no known medical value, had been reported by the National Cancer Institute to cause bizarre malignancies in test animals.

Cho's heart raced, partly from anxiety, partly from fever. He was dumbfounded. He vividly recalled what Sam Wolfe had said at the CPC, about a plant fungus—was it from an orchid?—which bore a striking microscopic resemblance to the cancer that was killing pregnant women. They had joked about it then, but perhaps Wolfe had been right.

He scribbled down his disorganized thoughts on a scratch pad. When he reread them they made no real sense. Maybe Clements could make something out of them. Or Erikson; he had a keen mind. It was after six when he shuffled back to the lab. He felt more feverish than ever. En route, he passed a nursing station. On an impulse, he found a thermometer and took his temperature. The reading shocked him: 104 degrees.

One hell of a virus, he thought. Did he have some sort of infection? When he returned to the lab, he bumped into one of the evening lab techs.

"Knocking off early?" he asked her.

"Just going to supper, Dr. Cho. Can I get you anything?"

"No, but you can draw my blood before you go."

"Do you feel okay, Dr. Cho? You don't look so good."

"Only a terrible cold, I'm sure. Just take a CBC to be safe."

Cho sat in a chair, feeling wobbly. The technician put on a tourniquet and took out a lavender-stoppered tube for a complete blood count. She was good; it took her just a second to complete the venipuncture.

"You want me to run this for you?" she asked.

"No, go ahead. I'll run it myself."

She handed him the warm test tube and left. Cho trudged into another room which housed the autoanalyzer. He uncapped the tube and ran a sample of his blood through the machine. The results were processed in seconds. He tore off the paper and looked at the readings. When he saw the white-cell count, his eyes widened in concern. It was astonishingly high.

Could it be something other than a virus? Sweat poured from him. Slowly, laboriously, he made a smear of his blood on a glass slide. When it was dry, he stained it with cytology dye and rinsed it clean. Then he placed the slide under the microscope. Within seconds, he looked up. His jaw dropped, and his heart was pounding.

Thousands of clusters of malignant cells were racing through his bloodstream.

"FREEZE-FRAME Three. Good; now roll it back a few frames and run it again."

The perspective from the Washington minicam had been excellent. The brief footage revealed the stern expression of Dr. Ridley Clements as he waded through the gantlet of reporters, neither volunteering information nor answering questions. It was the look of a man under siege.

The network anchorman reviewed the videotape several more times, trying to decide how and if to use the footage. Clearly the epidemic in the nation's capital deserved priority, but neither he, the producer, nor the writers could agree where to place it in the evening broadcast.

"It's filler, Bob. Technically nice, but just thirty seconds of filler."

The anchorman shook his head, pointing repeatedly at

preview Three. "No way. I'm going with that as tonight's lead. Who cares if he's stonewalling? What's happening with that man in that city is hotter than next week's summit. Any word about the other networks?"

"Still checking," replied a technician, cradling a phone to his ear.

"I still say it's a pass. We couldn't get a word out of him. Cool as a cucumber. Our D.C. feed was really letting him have it, and he wouldn't even give them the finger."

"That's just the point. How many is it now—twenty-two women dead?"

"Twenty-three, as of noon today."

The anchorman nodded his head in emphatic agreement. "That's right. And that's precisely what I'm saying! In the little more than two months since we learned how this thing has gotten out of hand, the whole Eastern Seaboard is counting along with us. I guarantee you that everyone who tunes in tonight knows that number by heart and is scared shitless that we're going to announce number twenty-four!"

The producer shrugged, the expression on his face a silent acknowledgment.

"Look," continued the anchorman, "our job is to report the news. It doesn't have to be gospel truth, but it must be news. Right now we're faced with the fact that the city is terrified, the medics seem to be playing dumb, even the World Health Organization has begun its own inquiry, and yet no one will commit to a goddamned thing on film or in print! You know what I honestly think? I doubt Ridley Clements knows much more than the rest of us. It's not that he's covering up; he doesn't say anything because he has nothing to say. And that, gentlemen, is our story right there: his silence. Call it scientific ignorance, call it medical failure. That doesn't matter. Sure, it might boost our ratings if this hotshot candidate for Surgeon General lost his temper on camera and said 'Go fuck yourself.' But don't hold your breath! I say we go with what we've got. And right now what we've got is a numbers game played by the dead and dying."

The small group of newsmen fell silent, returning to study the tape once more, not daring to admit how personally stunned they were by the news they would so professionally report later that night, forcing themselves to remain calm even when the number of dead would ultimately rise to twenty-five.

"MAGNIFICENT SPECIMEN."

"Of what, Mr. Gleason?" Erikson asked. "I know it's an orchid. I was hoping you could tell me a little more about it, like what kind it is, or where it came from."

"It's a *Lycaste*, of course," he said, as if Erickson were a bumbling idiot. Mr. Gleason studied the photo at arm's length, inspecting it from every angle, as a jeweler might appraise a gem. Every few seconds he would mumble something garbled, in the manner of a man accustomed to muttering to himself. To Erikson, Gleason was positively eccentric. He didn't know whether or not his peculiarities had anything to do with his being president of the local chapter of the American Orchid Society. "Where was this taken?"

"Right here in Washington," Erikson said.

"Out of the question. That's quite impossible."

"Why?"

"Your photographer was obviously in Mexico. More precisely, in Chiapas. That's the only place this particular variety of *Lycaste* could grow."

"But there must be local greenhouses that cultivate them."

"Oh, if only there were! Especially one as lovely as this. But most of the American *Lycastes* are quite common. Twentieth-generation, or more. And they certainly bear little resemblance to this one. You're familiar with the Convention on International Trade in Endangered Species?"

Erikson looked blank.

"Idiotic conclusion. The members voted that all orchid species, except for a few already on the Endangered list, should be placed on the Threatened list. Of course, that meant that the exporting country had to supply additional documentation, which is impossible to obtain. As a result, many species are no longer obtainable through importation. No, I'm sure this photo was taken in Chiapas itself, or somewhere nearby. Now, if your photographer wanted to earn a handsome commission, there are ways—"

"What's so special about this *Lycaste?*" Erikson interrupted.

"Size, for one thing. It's rather large for the species. And the color. A pure deep red like this has never been catalogued to my knowledge."

"Where could I find out for sure?"

"Why, the leading authority on orchids like this is Professor Gutiérrez, in Mexico City. You could write him, of course."

"Couldn't I call him?"

"Heavens, no. I've heard that he absolutely despises Americans. Anyway, you couldn't possibly describe this orchid over the telephone."

Gleason thumbed through several directories and located the professor's address. Erikson thanked him and left, returning to Michelle's apartment. Minutes later she unlatched the double locks and gave him a warm return hug.

"I wish you weren't out so late. I was worried. How was your staff meeting?"

"Tremendous," he said, smiling, as he leaned to peck her on the lips. "Every doctor there agreed on my latest suggestion for increasing patient survival."

"What suggestion?"

"As of next week all nurses will go topless, except in the Coronary Care Unit."

He would go to any length to keep her calm and reassured, to lessen her anxiety, which seemed to grow daily. They played backgammon for hours, during which time he constantly punctuated their play with lighthearted chatter.

Neither of them could sleep that night. They tossed and

turned under the sheets. It was only a white lie, he convinced himself, when he told Michelle he was on call at the hospital the next day, and had to remain there twenty-four hours. Finally she fell into a fitful slumber, unaware that Erikson—still awake—was busy at work on his own separate plan.

Chapter 13

HE LEFT HER apartment at dawn, while she still slept, and quietly returned to his own. It took him ten minutes to pack. With luck, he could make the trip as a quick turnaround and return early the following morning, with sufficient time to check on happenings at the hospital and be back with Michelle for the Sunday brunch she had promised him. He took little except a change of clothes, toiletries, and the photo of the orchid.

He flagged down a cab and went to Dulles Airport. When he had called the airlines earlier from his apartment, the Reservations clerk had told him that the flight he wanted was very popular. Most seats were booked weeks in advance. But if he could manage to get to the airport early, he might get a last-minute cancellation. That morning, luck was with him. He did.

The plane landed at Benito Juárez International Airport just after 2 P.M. Mexico City time. He didn't bother changing his money into pesos; the flight attendant assured him that most merchants preferred dollars anyway. Hoping the professor was still in his office, he caught a taxi and gave the driver the address of a particular branch of the Universidad Nacional de México.

He knew he overtipped the cabbie, but didn't care. It was after three when he stepped inside the Instituto Botánico. There was no room directory at the entrance and no information office. The halls were warm and humid, nearly empty. He started uncertainly down one corridor. Two female students rounded a corner, and Erikson grinned: a piece of cake. He approached them self-assuredly and spoke to them in polite English. He realized immediately that it was a mistake. They looked contemptuously at the handsome *gringo* and sauntered away with casual disdain. He glanced at their bulging hips which strained the fabric of their Levi's. American jeans were good enough for them even if he wasn't. Their loss, he shrugged. They'll never know what a wonderful person I am.

Still, he was frustrated, and he quickly walked in the other direction. He didn't understand why the building was nearly deserted. Farther on, he came upon a man dressed in white peasant garb sweeping an office. This time, Erikson addressed him in his tentative high school Spanish.

The man looked at him indifferently. Erikson began to feel like an idiot, standing there holding a suitcase and wearing an expectant look on his face. He knew his Spanish couldn't be that bad. The man glanced toward Erikson's pockets. Erikson rested his suitcase on the floor and took a dollar from his wallet.

"¿ El profesor Gutiérrez, por favor?" he repeated.

The man took the money without hesitation. He put down his broom and motioned for the American to follow. They went up one flight of stairs and down another corridor to a corner office. The man rapped softly on the door and let himself in, leaving Erikson outside. Moments later, he emerged. He shrugged and slowly shook his head.

"El Doctor no quiere ver al señor."

He hadn't come this far to be turned away. He opened his wallet again and took out five dollars, handing it to the porter along with the picture of the orchid. The man's eyes widened. He returned to the office, closing the door behind him. Erikson

159

heard low conversation inside. Then he came out again and walked past Erikson without saying a word. In seconds, a short man in a linen suit appeared in the doorway.

He had sparse black hair and a pencil-thin mustache. He inspected Erikson indignantly. There was no mistaking the unforbearing scorn in his eyes. Erikson had the impression that were it not for the photo, the man would just as soon have spat on him.

"Where did you get this picture, señor?" he asked in excellent English.

"May I speak with you, Professor?"

"Do you represent the press?"

"No. My only interest is the orchid."

"Follow me," he relented, with consummate haughtiness.

Beyond an anteroom, his rear office was dank but refreshingly cool. Other than a small desk littered with papers, the room was filled with plants. To Erikson's untrained eye, most appeared to be orchids. They hung from the ceiling, the walls, or grew in pots on the floor. Some were in bloom, and their flowers were magnificent. The combination of green leaves and radiant blossoms gave the room a mystical air.

"You were telling me about the orchid, señor?"

There was no place to sit. The Professor eased himself into the only chair in the room, leaving Erikson standing. He felt like a schoolboy in the principal's office. Gutiérrez looked from the American to the photo and back again, waiting for Erikson to speak.

"I have nothing to tell, Professor. I came here to ask."

"The picture, señor."

"I have a friend who's vacationing in Chiapas," he began, recalling what Gleason had said in Washington. "He sent me this photo along with several others. I'm studying at Guadalajara, and I'm going home tomorrow. My folks love orchids. I was hoping you could tell me where I could buy one of these."

"Where did you get my name?"

"In the University library."

"You are lying, señor," he said, glaring at the younger man.

Erikson didn't know whether the Professor was calling his bluff or stalling for more information. After a minute of stony silence, he felt he had no choice but to stand his ground.

"I'm not, Professor. According to the books in the library, you're the leading authority on orchids. Can't you help me out? I can pay you, if you'd like."

He got up from his chair. "I'm not interested in your dollars," he said with resentment. "They have corrupted my country as it is. As for this orchid, I'm sure it's not for sale. The Government wouldn't allow it, so don't think you can bribe some official."

A real winner, thought Erikson. Yet distasteful though the conversation was, he wasn't discouraged. He had the feeling the Professor's contempt was purely political, and had nothing to do with his own lie. He just didn't like Americans. This spurred him on. "I'm not here to bribe anyone. If it's not for sale, I can accept that. I just thought you could tell me where I could find one."

"This is a sacred flower, señor. La Flor del Dios, they have called it. It has been described to me, but I have never seen even a photograph of one, until now. Your friend in Chiapas: where is he, precisely?"

"He's with the Peace Corps. I'm not sure where he is now."

"Probably in Tabasco. Or maybe Campeche," he continued aloud. "I would be very interested in speaking with this friend. Do you know where I can contact him?"

Erikson avoided the question. "Why do you call it a sacred flower?"

"There are many stories about this *Lycaste*, señor. No doubt most of them are rumor. No one has officially verified its existence for centuries. You see, La Flor del Dios was the religious symbol of the Maya."

"The Maya?"

161

"You have never heard of the Maya?"

"Heard of them, yes. I know a little about the Aztecs, and the Incas, but the Mayas . . ."

"Then you know nothing. The Aztecs were barbarians, and the Inca were in Peru."

"Why was this orchid sacred to the Maya?"

He got up and strolled around the desk, inspecting his specimens. "Some say the Maya used La Flor del Dios in their ceremonies. Descendants of the Maya in Yucatán still speak of this flower, though I doubt they have ever seen one. This makes me all the more curious about where your friend took this photograph."

"Would it be possible for me to speak with one of the Maya?"

Gutiérrez laughed. "What do you study, señor? Certainly not history?"

"No."

"There are no more true Maya, as the priesthood once existed. Their civilization collapsed. The last of the real Maya disappeared a thousand years ago."

A thousand years . . . Hadn't he once read something about the Maya and the mystery of their disappearance? "Can I get more information on this flower somewhere?"

"Of course. In any library."

He didn't have time to search through a library. What he wanted was something more relevant than obscure information on the dog-eared pages of a dusty book. He hadn't come this far to go back empty-handed, not when at long last he had a clue about what had happened in the deaths of both Sam Wolfe and Trish Van Dyne.

"But isn't there someone I can talk to? Just give me a lead. A name!"

Gutiérrez seemed to hesitate until Erikson promised to contact his "photographer friend in the Peace Corps." "Perhaps there is one person, señor."

"Who? Tell me!"

162

"His name is Helmsley. Professor Helmsley. He has lived in my country for years."

Helmsley? The name sounded British. "Is he an Englishman?"

"He is an American, like you."

"Where can I find him?" he asked excitedly.

"Right here in Mexico City, close by. But unfortunately, I do not have his address."

"Do you know who does?"

"There is a police station two blocks from here. Go there. They can tell you where to find Professor Helmsley."

Erikson thanked him and left. As he walked down the hall, he thought he could hear raucous laughter reverberating behind him. His face reddened. He despised that man. Professor Helmsley was probably nothing more than a cheap trick Gutiérrez had used to get rid of him. He felt humiliated.

Minutes later, he mounted the steps to the police station. He approached the desk sergeant and spoke in his most polite Spanish.

"I speak some English, señor."

"Thank goodness for that. Sergeant, I'm trying to find a man named Professor Helmsley. I don't know his first name. I was told he lives around here, and I was hoping you could tell me where I can find him."

"Helmsley, the archaeologist?"

Erikson narrowed his eyes. "Probably. He may have been an archaeologist, perhaps specializing in the Maya."

"Yes. Then you are looking for Professor Robert Helmsley. I can tell you where to find him, señor. But I do not think it wise to meet him."

"Why not?"

The policeman pointed to his head. "He is crazy, señor."

Was that why Gutiérrez had laughed? "Is he dangerous?"

"Dangerous? No, he is harmless. A crazy old man."

"Then please help me out. It's important that I speak with him!"

The officer shrugged. "As you wish, señor." He escorted Erikson to the front entrance and gave him directions. "You can find him near the railroad station. It is no more than a kilometer from here. Just ask any of the children. For a few centavos, they will lead you to El Loco."

Erikson started down the steps, then turned. "Why do you say he's crazy?"

"Worms, señor. He has the worms in his brain."

Did he mean that literally? Erikson frowned. He'd read about tropical parasites that could infest the brain, but what was he getting himself into? The stinging memory of Gutiérrez' laughter rang in his ears more loudly than ever. He walked through the dusty streets, following the policeman's directions. Maybe it was a waste of time. What could this Helmsley possibly tell him? And yet, the only other choice was to return home knowing no more about the flower than when he had arrived.

The narrow streets were little more than alleyways, littered with garbage. The dirty roads near the train station were channels that snaked through a slum, lined with stray cats and naked children. Every few blocks a group of street-wise urchins would approach *el turista* and tug at his clothes, begging with palms held open. Erikson brushed them politely away.

Soon he neared the depot. A group of older boys were playing soccer with a frayed rubber ball. He approached the one who appeared to be the oldest. He was also the grimiest.

"¿ *Conoces tu al profesor Helmsley, un norte americano viejo?*"

He eyed Erikson suspiciously. Erikson took a coin from his pocket, and the boy grinned. "¿ *El Loco? Sí, señor.*" He held out his hand and reached for the coin.

Erikson closed his fist around the coin. "*Demuestramelo.*"

The boy spoke to his friends too fast for Erikson to understand, then motioned for him to follow. He led him through the streets to a dirt path that wound through the rubble. At the end of the dusty trail was a stucco shack set apart from the rest. It had no door, and broken tequila bottles lay on the ground near the entrance.

"*Aquí, señor. El Loco.*"

Erikson approached cautiously. Near the doorway, a rancid stench of stale liquor assaulted his nostrils. He hesitated, then composed himself and continued. It was dark inside the entrance. Flies buzzed around his head. He cleared his throat and took a deep breath.

"Professor Helmsley?"

There was no answer. He glanced at the boy, who nodded emphatically up and down.

"Professor Robert Helmsley?" he repeated, louder.

"Who the hell wants to know?" came the hoarse reply.

The boy grinned and tapped on Erikson's arm. He gave the boy the coin, and the child ran away, laughing.

"Professor, may I come in?"

"Go away!"

"Come on, Professor. I've come all the way from Washington to see you. I won't take much of your time."

"Leave me alone."

"I have a picture to show you. A photo of La Flor del Dios."

There was rustling inside, and the scratching of a match. He could make out the dim illumination of a lantern. The light approached.

The Professor came into view. Erikson steeled himself to the older man's appearance, but he wasn't nearly as grotesque as he had anticipated. From what the policeman had said, he had almost expected the Professor to be covered with some sort of larvae. Instead he found a sick old man, a pathetic man. He was much shorter than Erikson and walked hunched over. He carried an old kerosene lantern in one hand and a half-filled tequila bottle in the other. The lantern's glow lit up his face, which was covered with ulcers and oozing sores. Edematous red cheeks showed through the white stubble of his beard. His

lips were dry and cracked, and scaling skin peeled from his ear-
lobes. Yet in spite of his obvious ill health, his eyes gleamed
with surprising awareness. He looked at Erikson suspiciously.

"Well, what is it? I haven't got all day."

Erikson couldn't help feeling pity for him. "May I come
in, Professor?"

"Professor," he muttered. "That's a laugh. All right,
come in if you want. But you can't stay long."

Erikson followed him into the hovel. As his eyes grew
accustomed to the darkness, he was surprised to find that in
contrast to the shack's dilapidated exterior, the inside was com-
paratively neat. The floor was hard-packed clay. It could have
used a good sweeping, but it had none of the debris that clut-
tered the streets. The room was perhaps twenty feet square.
There was a cot in one corner, and a small table with a kerosene stove rested against another wall. And then there were the
artifacts.

There were thousands of them. Arranged in neat piles or
standing alone, a wealth of carved stone greeted his eyes. There
were small figurines and ornate statues, delicate beadwork and
fine pottery, elaborate porcelain vases and large, hand-hewn
stelae that rested against the walls like tombstones. It was a
looter's dream. Erikson wondered how he managed to keep his
collection intact.

"I won't ask you to sit down," he said, "because there's
no place to sit. Who told you about me?"

"There's a Professor Gutiérrez at—"

"Filthy traitor!" Helmsley fired. "What did he tell you?"

"Only that you—"

"You know what that conniving cheat is like?" he interrupted. "I was on a dig near Petén. Fabulous find, untouched.
Before I knew it, he and his men ... Ah, the hell with it.
That's ancient history now." He took a swallow of tequila and
plopped heavily onto the cot.

Erikson studied the little man. He was an obvious alco-
holic, and perhaps he *was* insane. The way he acted, it was no
wonder they called him El Loco. And yet, there was something

about him; something that bespoke a wealth of knowledge, waiting to be tapped. He opened his luggage and took out the picture.

"Do you recognize this orchid, Dr. Helmsley?"

He took the picture and squinted at it. Then he slowly sat up straight—an almost respectful posture. He put down the bottle of tequila and held the photo in both hands under the light. "So it is true," he said softly.

"What is?"

"It's true," he repeated with reverence. "It exists."

"Come on, Professor! What are you talking about?"

He looked up at Erikson, his blue eyes alive with interest. "Where did you find this picture?"

"I didn't find it. It's a picture of my girlfriend's sister. She took it herself."

"But I was sure it was extinct," he continued. He inspected it again, agitated. "If what you're saying is true, this woman could be in danger!"

Erikson frowned. "That picture was taken last winter," he said haltingly. "The girl you see there is dead now."

Helmsley gazed at him. "Hmfff. I'm not surprised. Death follows this flower." He set down the photo and took another swig from the bottle. "Where was this picture taken? Guatemala? In the jungle?"

"It was taken thousands of miles from here. In Washington, D.C."

He appeared genuinely surprised, even animated. "Washington, you say?"

"What's so unusual about that?"

"Washington!" he repeated excitedly. "I knew it! Then the priesthood *did* survive!"

"The *what*?"

Suddenly Helmsley leaped up, eyes ablaze, leering wildly. "Hah, I told them! I told the bastards, and they didn't believe me, called me crazy, laughed at me!" He thrust a clenched fist toward the ceiling. "But by God, I was right! Why, I unearthed the only evidence of their departure from here, and the others were too stubborn to believe it! That was when I came back here to stay. Do you know what else I discovered, last time I was in the States?"

Erikson let the rambling continue uninterrupted.

"It was at an excavation on the James River, looking for Virginia's lost settlement. There were ruins, early-seventeenth-century; a pile of bones from some sort of massacre. But one of the skulls, you see," he said, punctuating his speech with rapid gestures, "wasn't American Indian at all! I took one look and knew the bone structure was Mayan! They just laughed at me. Laughed! And now this! Do you understand what this means?"

"What, Dr. Helmsley?"

"It means the Maya are alive, now, in the twentieth century, somewhere near Washington! Why, with this proof I can go back now, and . . ." He looked at Erikson, who was motionless. "And . . ." His eyes narrowed. "You don't believe me either, do you?"

Calmly, "Of course I do, Professor."

Helmsley's burst of enthusiasm waned, and he returned to the stained cot. "You know nothing about that orchid, do you?"

"No, Dr. Helmsley, I don't," said Erikson, beginning to lose his patience. "That's what I've come to you for! There's a possibility the woman in this picture was murdered, and—"

He held up his hand, indicating for the younger man to stop. "Come here, my boy." He patted the cot beside him. "Sit down."

Erikson slowly sat beside him on the tattered woolen blanket that covered the cot.

"So you want to know about La Flor del Dios, do you?"

Erikson nodded.

"I can tell you what I know; but then you must tell me about the woman in the picture. Agreed?"

"You're on."

"I've been in this country for nearly fifty years," he began.

168

"Most of that time in the jungle. I've seen things no one else has dreamed of. There are priceless ruins out there. Whole temples, completely hidden. And I'll keep their location to myself," he said, cackling as he tapped his head, "so they won't steal it from me."

"You were saying about the orchid."

"Yes, La Flor del Dios. The Maya didn't call it that, of course. That's the Spanish derivative. But it was their most precious flower. A sacred flower. It's in all their paintings. They used it in their sacrifices."

"Sacrifices?"

"Human sacrifices. They might cut the hearts from their victims, or a certain part of the brain, and they would mix it with the petals of this flower as an offering to the gods."

"That's barbaric!"

"It was meant to be. Appeasing the gods was the only way to keep the masses in check. But I'll tell you something," he said, leaning closer as if to share a secret: "to the Mayan priests, it was all for show."

"The sacrifices weren't real?"

"Oh, they were real, all right. But the leaders didn't give a damn about that sort of thing. Come here: I'll show you something." He led Erikson across the room to a group of small statues, no more than six inches high. Helmsley picked one up and handed it to him. "This is what they really cared about."

It was beautifully carved jade, polished until it gleamed. Around its base was the unmistakable marquetry of lush foliage.

"Jade?"

"No, flowers. Plants. Everything green."

"Why was it special?"

"Because it gave them the world. That's another thing I discovered that no one else knows. I tried to tell them, and they laughed at me. But it's true." His eyes gleamed. "The priests learned the secrets of the plants ages ago."

Erikson turned away, wondering if he had made a mistake by wasting his time with this babbling old man. "What secrets, Professor?"

"Strength. Longevity. Special powers. To the uneducated, the Maya were a race of barbarians. But in fact, their priests were just the opposite. During the Mayan Classic Period, which lasted seven hundred years until roughly A.D. 950, the Maya were quite sophisticated, even cosmopolitan. They were masters of astronomy, numerology, and architecture. But their greatest achievement was their understanding of plant life. I'm not simply referring to agriculture, though their irrigation system was centuries before its time. Rather, they lived in perfect harmony with the plants around them. They used the plants. There seemed to be a genuine respect for the species."

Throughout, Erikson had been listening patiently. He could see why Helmsley was considered eccentric, maybe even a little insane, but he spoke to him convincingly. Yet the time had come to get to the point. "You still haven't explained about La Flor del Dios."

"But I have, don't you see? To the priests, care of plants and flowers was everything. And this was the most sacred flower of all."

"What in God's name does it have to do with the death of the woman in the photo?"

"According to their culture," he said solemnly, "it meant she was marked for sacrifice."

Erikson was flustered. "But that's impossible! The Maya have been gone for a thousand years!"

"Have they, young man?" he asked with uplifted eyebrows.

"But you said yourself—"

He held up his hand. "And you're holding a picture of something long extinct."

Erikson spun away, impatient with the old man. Surely he was the *loco* the community had labeled him. Yet . . .

"Come," Helmsley said, beckoning. He squeezed

through a narrow space in the walls. Erikson followed him into a small alcove, a storage chamber for even more of his artifacts. He lit another lamp and searched amidst the piles of dusty books until he found what he wanted. It was a sketch pad, yellowed from the years. On one of its pages, the artist's pen had drawn a flower identical to the orchid in the photo. "You see? I drew this myself, from a mural on a temple wall. And I have more." He thumbed through the pages. The pad was filled with intricate drawings. "Here," he said. "It's the same."

Erikson knew it was, and his head began to swim. A death flower . . . An ancient civilization . . . It seemed too much to comprehend. Helmsley was about to close the pad when Erikson asked him about an old photograph crudely taped to the pages. It was a fading color picture taken in the jungle.

"That's me in the center," he commented. "The Indians around me are all that's left of the Maya. Unless you believe, as I do," he said, raising his clear blue eyes, "that the priesthood survives to this day."

Erikson was no longer listening. He was staring at the Mayan descendants, mesmerized by the features of the people who posed for the camera. Their appearance might have been diluted by the passing centuries, but to him it was unmistakable. The Indians in the photo had an uncanny resemblance to the scout in his Civil War book, the man he had assured Michelle would be well over a hundred and thirty years old. The man she had said she recognized.

WHY DID she feel so apprehensive? Michelle sat upright in bed, unable to sleep, after Erikson departed. She knew the doors were locked, the windows shut; yet she couldn't shake the overwhelming sense of anxiety that seemed to fill the apartment. It wasn't so much what Craig said as what he didn't say. She felt as if he were trying to protect her from something; she had had that feeling before.

Her concern mounted when he didn't answer his hospital

page. She tried calling his apartment, then the hospital again. Could he be tied up in a clinic, or be involved in an emergency? Michelle left word for him to call her as soon as possible.

She got out of bed and paced back and forth on the bedroom rug, replaying their conversations in her mind. When had it happened before? she wondered. Yes, it had been when she awakened from anesthesia; hadn't he mentioned something about a scar—a vaginal operation? Why wouldn't he admit it? And now, when he'd seen the photo of Trish . . . something had upset him, she was certain. Yet in his typical glib manner, he'd covered it up. Damn!

Michelle quickly went to the closet and searched for the photo, worrying even more when she couldn't find it. Had Craig taken it? What did he want with it, for God's sake? Again she phoned the hospital, biting her lip when the page went unanswered. She slammed down the phone in frustration. She knew this had something to do with Trish. But what, dear Lord, what?

She returned to bed and drummed her fingers on the nightstand. Her thoughts immediately strayed to Trish, and the days before her death. Michelle rehashed the supposed suicide, trying to remember all the little things—the subtlest, fuzzy hint that might pass unnoticed by any stranger. Try though she did, she could think of absolutely no reason, no circumstance so horrible that it might make Trish want to jump from a window and kill herself. No, Michelle concluded. It was murder.

Yet there had been moments of idle speculation between them—the casual "what-I-would-do-ifs" so common to the truly close—that might be misinterpreted. Trish had occasionally spoken about injury, and about what it would mean to their athletic careers. She was much more concerned with matters of health than her younger sister. Michelle smiled at the memory and looked upward. Oh, Trish, if you only knew what's happened to me recently!

Other than being injured, the only thing that might ever have worried Trish was being physically ill. Disease had frightened her; it was all the more incentive to keep in superb physical condition. The memory jarred Michelle: Dr. Bender had also asked her about Trish's health, hadn't he? But it was a dead end now, as it had been then. As far as she knew, Trish had never been sick. Since Michelle had come to Washington, the only doctor she remembered her sister's seeing was a gynecologist. What was his name?

She knew she was being impulsive when she leafed through the bedside list of phone numbers for the doctor's card Trish had given her. She had to call, if only to lessen her pangs of guilt. It didn't matter if he wouldn't speak with her. She found the number and dialed.

"Are you a patient of the doctor's?"

"No, my sister was. I'm calling about her."

"I'm afraid the doctor won't be able to speak with you without your sister's permission. The office maintains strict confidentiality, Miss . . ."

"Van Dyne. Michelle Van Dyne."

There was a pause at the other end of the telephone. "Are you Patricia Van Dyne's sister?"

"Yes."

Another pause. "One moment." Then silence, as Michelle was placed on "hold."

Finally there was a click, and a man's voice. "This is Dr. Stern."

"Yes—this is Michelle Van Dyne . . ." So the conversation began.

They spoke briefly, no more than a few minutes. Enough for Michelle to learn that the doctor was a great fan of hers; and that Trish had visited him on several occasions. And enough time to learn that, yes, Trish had had one minor physical problem. But he had admitted too much already; he couldn't possibly discuss the matter over the phone.

Michelle hung up, stunned. She couldn't believe it. Trish

had never kept anything from her before. Was it an older sister's protectiveness? She knew Craig had told her to stay put, but Stern's office wasn't far. Frightened though she was, she knew she had to find out for herself. Anyway, Michelle reasoned, it was broad daylight.

An hour later, the receptionist ushered her into one of several consultation rooms. She had not been waiting long when Dr. Stern entered the room. He was a short man, fiftyish, with a pleasant smile. He extended his hand.

"A pleasure, Miss Van Dyne. I recognize you from your pictures."

"Thanks for seeing me, Dr. Stern. I don't mean to impose on your time when the waiting room is full. But anything you can tell me about Trish is important."

"You understand, it's very irregular to talk like this. But under the circumstances—considering her death—I suppose no harm can be done. Still, I doubt I can tell you anything of consequence." He opened a slender manila folder that bore Trish's name and studied the few pages within. "Hmmm. What exactly are you looking for, anyway?"

"Whatever you can tell me about her health. You see, Dr. Stern, I have never believed that my sister committed suicide."

Stern arched his eyebrows and peered at her over his pince-nez glasses. "Really?"

Michelle shifted uncomfortably. "It's a long story. Just tell me, if you can: was anything physically wrong with Trish?"

Stern's gaze returned to the chart. "Let's see, now . . . Yes, I remember her last visit well. I don't think it was more than a month or two before her death. It was potentially a chronic problem," he said, shaking his head as he read the entry. "Certainly nothing that would make her want to take her own life. And not at all hereditary, if that's worrying you."

"Please, Dr. Stern! What was wrong with her?"

"I thought at that time that your sister had a mild case of pelvic inflammatory disease. In fact, I was certain of it. She'd had it once a year or so before."

"What is that?"

"In her case, nothing more than a mild bellyache, really. It's an inflammation of the tubes and ovaries."

Michelle tried to recall the time frame, but it was a blur. "Does that . . . do anything? Does it have any aftereffects?"

"Depends on your point of view. With proper antibiotics, the symptoms disappeared within days. It would have no effect on her running. There may have been sequelae, though, as we say."

"Such as what?"

"There was a strong possibility your sister was going to be permanently sterile."

MICHELLE LEFT the doctor's office near tears, frightened and confused. Her mind struggled for control. She began running down the street, giving no thought to direction. She simply had to get away from there.

Slowly, she calmed herself, trying to sort out the puzzle. It was difficult, with her chin quivering, her hands shaking. As she continued her quick pace, she felt more guilty than ever, and surprisingly angry—at herself, for not being available when her sister had needed her; and more so, at Trish for not confiding in her. Was it all that terrible, not being able to have children? Why, Trish could have adopted, if need be. They could have worked it out!

No, Michelle concluded, it wasn't the sort of thing to make Trish act rashly, and certainly nothing to make her commit suicide. Yet, she wondered, might Trish's infertility have had significance to someone else? But why? Suddenly her heart began to pound, and her fingers flew to her lips. Michelle quickened her pace.

She should never have left her apartment. Michelle was irrationally frightened by her own speculation. Her imagination was going wild. Breathing deeply, she tried to calm herself. She had to tell Craig everything she had learned from Dr. Stern. Craig would know what to make of it.

Now blocks from the doctor's office, Michelle began

175

looking nervously over her shoulder, scanning the sea of vacant faces. She flew along the sidewalk, searching in vain for an empty cab. Mercifully, a bus appeared, and she immediately boarded it for the short trip to her apartment. Several blocks from her street, the bus stopped at an intersection, waiting for the light to change. Michelle looked nervously out the window.

Something was wrong. She sensed it then, felt it—a primitive instinct that defied logic. Her heart began beating faster as the bus pulled away. Though she was sitting, her legs felt incredibly weak. She bit her lip. Something was out there, again. Waiting.

The bus neared her stop and Michelle quickly struggled to her feet. She had to get across the street and upstairs into the safety of her apartment. She craned her neck and looked up and down the avenue. For some reason her throat was impossibly dry, but she swallowed hard and lowered her head, trying to appear as inconspicuous as possible.

Uncontrollably agitated, she stood on the corner and waited for the bus to pass. Soon it pulled away, kicking up dust and street debris in a blast of hot exhaust fumes. Suddenly a funny sensation tingled at the base of her scalp. With a reflex response, she whirled about. No one was there. Without hesitation, she turned back and dashed across the street. A car screeched, narrowly missing her. The driver cursed at her. Breathing heavily, Michelle frantically skipped around the front fender, oblivious to the danger, wanting only to reach the other side. She skirted traffic and double-parked vehicles and hurried toward the building's entrance.

Her mind struggled desperately for control. For some reason, she was scared witless. Half-running, half-sobbing, she staggered through the front door. She took the elevator, closing her eyes for the short ride up, praying it would go quickly. Finally the elevator door opened and she ran down the hall.

Inside the apartment, her breath came in shuddering spasms. Tears filled her eyes as she collapsed against the closed door. Alone now, she felt so terrified and panic-stricken that she thought she might die.

She walked into the living room, and suddenly it happened again—the tingly prickling of gooseflesh which made her slowly straighten up and look warily across the room. Something loomed up behind her. She gave a little gasp, unable to look around, as her whole body trembled uncontrollably with fright. Her eyes widened in terror and her lower jaw went slack, her mouth forming a silent oval. Then, as if in slow motion, she turned toward the ominous presence behind her.

In that dark moment, in the last dim twilight of her vision, their eyes locked together as his merciless black stare bored right through her.

THE PREDAWN flight from Mexico landed at Dulles Airport at 7 A.M., and Erikson assumed Michelle would still be asleep. He went first to the hospital, planning to check on several patients there before returning to his apartment to change. He wasn't due at Michelle's until ten.

The ward was packed when Erikson arrived; he was glad he wasn't on call. There had been several new admissions during the night; it would take the senior resident on duty all day to catch up on patients' histories and outline their treatment plans with the junior residents. The only good news was there hadn't been a cancer patient for twenty-four hours. Erikson finished his brief business and was about to leave when he was paged by the hospital operator.

"Dr. Erikson, I have a message for you from Dr. Cho. It came in last night, but he said we should give it to you when we heard from you this morning."

"What is it?"

"He left word that he wants you to come to his apartment as soon as you can."

"Now? Is he still there?"

"I don't know, Doctor. But the night operator said he

wanted you to come by even if he didn't answer his telephone."

Erikson hung up, worried. That didn't sound like Hank at all. He dialed Cho's number. Sure enough, there was no answer. Then he called the lab. No one there had heard from Cho. But some of the lab technicians thought he might be ill.

Erikson didn't like it. He knew Hank wouldn't leave a message like that if it weren't important. Fortunately, Hank didn't live far. Erikson reached Cho's building in fifteen minutes. The doorman knew to expect Erikson; he had a message to send Erikson up no matter when he arrived. Puzzled, he got on the elevator.

He walked to the apartment door and knocked twice. There was no reply. He turned the doorknob; the door was unlocked. He let himself in and turned on the hall lights. He listened for the shower, thinking his friend might be bathing. But the apartment was quiet.

"Hank?"

Silence. In the back of his mind, he thought it might be a practical joke. He wouldn't put it beyond Hank. But as he started to walk through the quiet apartment, he knew it wasn't. Hank wasn't in the kitchen, or in the living room. And only some scattered papers were on the desk in the den. Quickly now, he walked to the bedroom and rapped on the door. No answer. He turned the knob and peered inside. In the dim light, he saw Cho lying on the bed.

Erikson thought he was sleeping. As he walked closer, he could see that Hank was clad in a robe. His head rested against the pillow and his eyes were wide open. As Erikson neared the bedside, his heart leaped to his throat.

Cho's hair clung in moist strands to the pillow. His jaw was slack, the mouth open. A stream of bilious mucus had soaked into the sheets, leaving a green ring on the linen. There were flecks of blood in it. Drying bubbles of pink froth were in his nostrils and on his lips. He wasn't breathing.

Oh, Jesus, no! Erikson thought.

178

He leaned over and frantically felt for the carotid pulse. There was none. But Erikson refused to accept the obvious. He shook his friend's shoulders.

"Come on!" he shouted, slapping Cho's cheeks. "Wake up, Hank. Hank!"

Cho's head slumped to the side. His eyelids eased fractionally open. His sightless gaze fixed on the wall beyond.

Erikson was still. Reality took hold. With two trembling fingers, he closed his friend's eyes. Then his whole body started to shake. An involuntary sob escaped him.

ONE OF the hospital's many cleaning women made her weekly tour of the lab area. She preferred this part of the hospital to the on-call rooms, which she hated. There, all she had to do was change the linen and tidy up. But the rooms were often a mess, littered with sandwich wrappers and cigarette butts or beer cans.

In contrast, Dr. Cho's office was almost always clean. She took out her passkey and let herself in. She dusted the shelves and made a neat pile of the magazines on his desk. A large, wilted flower was in a slender vase in the corner. No use for a dying blossom, she thought. She turned over the vase and shook the flower into her garbage bag, where its drying red petals shifted softly amongst the other debris.

Chapter 14

SOFT, SO soft. Unable to awaken, Michelle moaned softly, stretching in her sleep as her body subconsciously savored the luxuriant pliancy of the mattress beneath her. It caressed her back and shoulders, and in her stupor, she did not hear the distant, rainlike sound, gentle drops of falling water. Her eyes remained shut.

Directly above her, ten feet overhead, was a latticework of aerial boughs and stems. It was an intermeshing, fanlike roof of palm and fern, resembling the intricate construction of a botanical garden; yet here the overhead arbor—a trellis that served as the matrix for an overgrowth of vines—had grown together of its own volition.

Beyond her lay a spectacular natural oasis, in the midst of which was a dazzling waterfall which plummeted earthward from a height of five or six stories, misty sheets of rain that tumbled in glistening cascades. The water splashed into a wide, shimmering pool, its surface perfectly clear. One could see through it to a depth of ten feet, as if looking through a glass-bottomed boat.

The setting was part tropical rain forest, part South Seas lagoon. The temperature was a balmy seventy degrees, humid but comfortable. Overhead there was the hint of a patch of blue. Yet not from the azure hue of true sky.

Just beyond the moss was a trail of beaten humus. The plants bordering it were astonishingly lovely—an enchanted forest. Most of the growth was tropical, except for an occasional palm or cedar. Some of the plants were shrubs, some bushes; others, towering trees with beautifully arching branches. They shared one characteristic: they were all magnificent examples of their species.

The trail followed the water line, where the plants grew haphazardly, without rows or furrows. Every shade of green was represented, from the palest pastel to bright emerald. It was a bizarre artist's palette of color, with striking rows of lustrous flowers, in pinks, yellows, and whites.

In her druglike slumber, Michelle rolled onto her side. Her mattress was a perfect sheet of moss, with a velvety green surface. Cool and smooth, it was indentable, yet peculiarly resilient. She was oblivious to the footsteps that came up behind her. On the smooth, rocky bluff above her stood a lean and muscular dark-skinned man, more than six feet in height, whose straight black hair fell to his shoulders. He wore a loose garment, like a tunic. His savage eyes were widely spaced, and his nose had a slight hook to it.

Ten feet beyond him, on either side of her, two more of his kind appeared, arising from the jungle thicket like apparitions.

Their leader looked at Michelle's still form with a jet-black stare as he slowly came down from the rock. He had a smile on his face, a haughty grin, like that of a maleficent child who smiles as he pulls the legs off a live grasshopper. He nodded to the men beside him.

The two Indians seized Michelle roughly by the arms and legs. They carried her limp body along the path by the water's edge, following it around the base of three large trees, whose complex mop of gnarled roots sank deep into the earth. Flat stepping-stones appeared in the path, which proceeded up a hill, the slope leading behind the waterfall. A fine mist sprayed their skin as the trail led under a wide, overhanging eave, half-hidden in a tangle of vines. Beyond it was an entrance that led into the core of the rocky cliff.

They followed the path into the darkness, down a carved limestone staircase. It seemed as if they were entering a tomb. Deeper into the sepulcher, there was a faint light. The steps ended, and they walked across cool, hard rock. Every few feet, built into the cavern's walls, was a glasslike pane. The glass glowed with light as they approached, and then the lanterns grew dim again as they passed. It was an incandescent yellow-green, like light from a hundred fireflies. Yet beneath these panes were plants, plants that pulsated with light.

Proceeding along the passageway, they passed bizarre glyphs and inscriptions along the walls. They were ancient cave paintings. Some were small renderings, embellished in jade; others were wide bas-reliefs in stucco—huge carved panels depicting rituals. They reached another limestone stairway and started upward. From its top, an eerie light streamed down the steps. They carried their captive roughly up the chiseled rock toward the entrance above.

Before them stretched a vast, verdant plain, a mile wide. Scattered throughout were clear pools and fountains. Plants were everywhere, organized in groves, forests, and orchards. It was a sumptuous view of serenity, an unmistakable Eden, made all the more incongruous by the savage demeanor of the men. The plain was enclosed by a crater almost a mile wide. The sidewalls seemed partially man-made, stone tiers and terraced plateaus whose upper facade of rockery slanted backward. The massive structure was surprisingly light and airy. An occasional peculiar stone building, shaped like a pyramid, adapted gracefully to the contour of the land.

They made their way down to the floor of the crater, eventually entering one of the small pyramids. A handful of Indians were seated around a table of polished onyx. Several of the Indians were women, and the coppery hue of their strangely unlined skin gave them an appearance of youth and vigor that belied the fact that they were more than a century old. Their fierce gaze went past Michelle's form to the man who was their leader, the one they called Hanahpú. The two bearers laid Michelle heavily on a rough-hewn plank. Then, in unison, everyone assembled stared at her with the same unemotional curiosity, as if contemplating a trapped animal.

Michelle stirred, and Hanahpú clapped his hands sharply. The first potion was beginning to wear off; they had to prepare her. A woman brought in a serving tray with a pitcher and a single stone mug. Hanahpú filled the cup with a turbid brown liquid. Again he nodded, and two others lifted Michelle to a semireclining position, propping her harshly against the stone wall as they continued to support her beneath her arms.

Her vision was blurry, a dark veil obscuring the dawn as Michelle struggled to open her eyes. Her lids were heavy, and she couldn't quite open them. Then someone yanked her head roughly backward, and she felt as if there were a hand prying open her mouth. A cool liquid filled her throat, some of its droplets spilling out of her lips onto her chin. She coughed and thought she could dimly see people staring at her as she spluttered. The liquid forced her to swallow, and she was only vaguely aware of the bitter beverage that slid down her throat.

She gagged, yet still there was the blurred vision of people staring at her. She tried to blink, but was unable to clear the film in front of her eyes. She was impossibly dizzy, and try though she did to shake her head free of the cobwebs, she couldn't focus.

Michelle struggled to cry out, but couldn't. Her body was swaying. Yet, there before her, she knew she saw a man signaling to others to make ready, preparing to do something to her. She saw the gleam of a knife, the glinting of its blade. And she was horrified. In the last vestige of her awareness, her heart pounded, and her mind shrieked, the mental convulsion before the scream. And then her world went black in a sickening vortex of primal fear.

• • •

As THE ambulance attendants removed Cho's body from the apartment, Erikson spoke succinctly with the police and promised to remain available if they needed him. Then, placing a few discreet calls, he arranged for Cho to be returned to the hospital mortuary rather than the Medical Examiner's office. At least Hank would return, albeit temporarily, to the place of his devotion. Before he left the apartment, he called Michelle to let her know he might be a little late. When there was no answer to his call, he assumed she was in the shower.

He returned to the hospital at nine o'clock and busied himself with the requisite paperwork and death certificate. He was more shaken by Hank's death than he thought he wanted to acknowledge. The shock was a physical jolt that left him limp. In many ways, it was a far harsher blow than the death of Dr. Wolfe. He was infuriated by the unfairness of it. Both those men had been kind and gentle people, but while Wolfe had lived his life to the full, Cho had been in his prime, a gifted man the medical community could ill afford to lose, the kind who kept a level head and keen perspective when most other doctors would panic.

It was nearly 10 A.M. when he dialed Michelle's number again, but there was still no answer to his phone call. Where the hell was she? The night before last, she hadn't said anything about going out. Erikson put down the receiver after the tenth ring, wondering if he was overreacting. No matter; he'd be at her place soon. It was just that he needed her very badly now.

The call from Clements was unexpected.

"What the hell is going on around here, Erikson? I have my hands full enough as it is! Can't I leave for a few days without returning to find one of my best men dead?"

"We're all pretty upset over it, Dr. Clements."

"But you were the one who found him! What happened?"

"I'm not sure. He hadn't been feeling well, but I had no

idea how serious it was. No one did, and the suddenness of it
... I keep thinking about Dr. Wolfe."

"I want an autopsy, and I want it now! You were his
friend. Arrange it!" Clements hung up abruptly.

Cho's only relatives in America were a sister in Philadelphia and a brother in New York. Earlier, Erikson had taken it
upon himself to break the news to the family while waiting for
the ambulance. He had found their numbers in a small phone
book in Hank's apartment. He had placed the calls and tried to
prepare himself for a response of shock and grief. From the
tone of their voices, he could feel their immense sorrow; and
yet they had accepted Hank's passing with Zen-like equanim-
ity.

He wished he had written their numbers down. He'd have
to briefly return to Hank's apartment. Before he left the hospital, he called Michelle again, frowning when she didn't
answer.

He drove quickly across town. The doorman let him into
Hank's apartment. Erikson found the phone book and went
into the den to make the calls. As clearly as possible, he explained the need for the autopsy. Hank's death was an enigma
that raised many questions; only a postmortem could supply
the answers. The family members listened patiently. But with
the same sense of calm with which they accepted Cho's death,
they politely refused Erikson's request for an autopsy. They
wanted their brother buried as quickly and as peacefully as
possible. In fact, the interment was already scheduled for the
morning after next in Philadelphia.

Reluctantly, Erikson phoned Clements with the news of
the family's refusal. Clements listened in stony silence. Then
he hung up without further comment. Erikson was about to
leave when his eyes fell on a loose pile of papers on the corner
desk. He leafed through the pages and could see they were a
series of handwritten notes, a kind of diary. He picked them up
and started reading. Hank's writing was jerky, but legible. It
would take him a while to digest the information, and he had

to return to Michelle's place first. He put Hank's notes into his pocket and went back to his car.

He unlocked the door to her apartment with the key she had given him and tiptoed in. He eased open the bedroom door and peered inside. The room was empty, the bed still made. He switched on the light and looked around. "Mike?"

He walked through the apartment, growing concerned. Where could she have gone? The earlier unanswered phone calls were vivid in his memory. He returned to the tidy bedroom. It simply was not possible that she had gone somewhere without letting him know.

"Goddammit, Mike!" He searched for a note, found none. She knew he would worry if he found her gone. Hadn't he told her to stay put? Calm down, he told himself. There had to be a logical explanation. He plopped onto the sofa to wait.

Half an hour later, he was beginning to seriously worry. He kept walking to the window, at any minute expecting to see her jogging back toward the apartment after a morning run. Yet she was nowhere in sight. Finally he opened the telephone directory by her night table and started to call the friends he had come to learn were close to her. Perhaps she had spent the night with one of them while he was in Mexico? But none of the friends recalled seeing Michelle in days. He slammed down the phone.

"Damn it to hell!" he cursed. Michelle had absolutely *no* right to leave the apartment. Why, a few days before, she had been terrified that a man had been following her. And from what he had learned in Mexico, he was beginning to believe that she might be right. Jesus! Why, then, had she gone out?

By dark, Erikson was frantic. Where was she? During the day he visited the nearby parks and tracks, questioning the joggers he met en route. No one recalled seeing her. He called her apartment every hour, but there was still no answer. He paced up and down the banks of the Potomac, from Key Bridge to the Lincoln Memorial. Nowhere.

He'd returned to her apartment again at three and six. The notes he had left for her were untouched. Twice he tried his own apartment, and called her friends once more. By evening, he was desperate.

At midnight, he had a sudden inspiration and phoned the Emergency Room clerk at the hospital. He asked her to call all the ERs in the city to see if Michelle was on one of their sign-in sheets. She told him she'd need at least an hour to find out. He gave her more, calling back at one thirty. He didn't know whether he wanted to find Michelle in one of the hospitals or not. But when the clerk told him the negative results of her search, Erikson was utterly disconsolate. He sank onto his bed, trying to rest. He managed, at last, to fall into a fitful slumber.

"IT SIMPLY isn't done, Dr. Clements. We have no signed consents."

"Damn the consents, man! You're the Medical Examiner—you don't need consents!"

"But it would look downright suspicious if I suddenly showed up in the middle of the night, temporarily removed the body for an hour, and—"

"It would look a lot more suspicious if a certain young doctor leaked unsubstantiated rumor and speculation to the press! Must I keep reminding you that I am largely responsible for your appointment?"

The hours passed. It was now 5 A.M. In the first light of dawn, the two men talked outside the hospital driveway as the Medical Examiner's van returned its cargo, their work done.

"Remember, Dr. Greenberg: not a word of this to anyone."

"How long do you expect to keep it a secret?"

"Forever, if necessary. I fail to understand how revealing the truth about Dr. Cho would foster our understanding of this disease, not to mention the adverse political effect it would have on me!"

"And the doctor you mentioned?"
"Leave him to me."

MICHELLE LAY in the small room, its confines
dank and cloying in spite of the profusion of plants everywhere. Asleep though she was, her wrists were tied to the sides
of the hemp bed with braided restraints. Only her legs were
free. A white cloth lay under her hips like a bandage.

Michelle's chest heaved in sleep, and she was hideously
exposed. Her bare breasts lay cold and open. At her bedside
stood Hanahpú and the three Indians with him. One steadied
a cart containing assorted bottles, dials, and rubberlike tubing.
Two pencil-thin clear tubes went through a stopper capping a
quart-sized container. Each flexible tube was a yard long; their
free ends were attached to what looked like funnels. Hanahpú
motioned for them to tie her, and the first two Indians
strapped Michelle's feet and hips to the mattress. He knew it
was an unnecessary gesture. Once in the sanctuary, none of the
women had ever awakened.

Satisfied that all connections were secure, one of them
turned on the apparatus. The muted motorlike sound filled the
silence as the dial on the pressure gauge began to climb. Another adjusted the uppermost portion of the mattress, elevat-
ing Michelle to a near-sitting position. The man at the cart
carefully put the funnels onto her breasts. Then they all circled
about her, a coven of priests.

A steady suction increased about her breasts. In the
room's cool air, Michelle's nipples involuntarily hardened. The
pressurized suction was continuous, the clear funnels sticking
to her like leeches. All the Indians watched expectantly. Then,
slowly, Hanahpú began to smile; and soon all in the room
seemed pleased. The four of them departed, closing the door
behind them.

The whitish substance that was suctioned up by the vac-
uum bottle reflected dimly in the room's dark shadows. The

droplets of milk, wet and sticky on Michelle's chest, were whisked away in a steady, even stream.

ERIKSON AWAKENED at first light, unable to sleep anymore. He made a cup of coffee and sat in the living room. As he sat on the sofa, uneasy and shaken, he remembered the pages he had folded into his pocket yesterday and began to read them. In an instant, he was wide-eyed and alert.

Michelle Van Dyne. Everywhere there were notations about Michelle. What in the world . . . ? Hank's writing was fragmented, disjointed. It was some sort of chronology, but it might take Erikson hours to make sense of it. He read through everything once, quickly; then he began to reread more carefully. Hank kept referring to some sort of parasite, totally green in color, plant-based, an object that had thrived in the body of Michelle Van Dyne.

Erikson felt as if he were suffocating. All Michelle's suspicions now compounded with his own, and the dizzying replaying of Helmsley's claims made matters worse still. A thousand-year-old civilization that still lived, coexisting with mystical plants; a curious green object that might hold the key to Michelle's disappearance. It was too much for him to handle alone. Though the hour was early, there was only one person he could speak with who might help him.

Clements answered the phone gruffly. "I presume your call is of earth-shattering importance, Dr. Erikson."

"I wouldn't disturb you if it weren't, Dr. Clements. What I'm about to say may sound strange. Fantastic, even. But please hear me out."

"Go on."

"Yesterday I stumbled across some notes in Dr. Cho's apartment. I've been going over them for hours, and I can't quite make sense of them. Hank kept referring to some sort of green sphere, a parasite, and its relationship to Michelle."

"Michelle?"

189

"Michelle Van Dyne, a girl I've been seeing. She was the botulism patient at the hospital a while back, and I got the impression from what Hank wrote that this green thing might have something to do with her most recent hospitalization. I was hoping you might know more about it."

"Get to the point, Erikson."

"This is the hard part, Dr. Clements," he said, taking a deep breath. "You see, Michelle is missing. I don't know where she is, and I'm worried stiff. What's more, I have reason to believe that a secret . . . society . . . may be living among us, and that they may have been responsible for her disappearance. I also suspect they played a role in Dr. Wolfe's death. And Hank's too, for that matter. For all we know, Hank may have died of the cancer."

There was a long pause. "Are you feeling all right, Erikson?"

"*Please*, Dr. Clements. I know this sounds peculiar, but I'm desperate to find Michelle."

At the other end of the line, Clements was frowning. Erikson was obviously delirious. The only part of his wild story that concerned him was his suggestion about Cho's death— uncannily accurate. He couldn't risk letting that sort of speculation leak out to an already panic-stricken public. Not when his reputation was at stake. "Sometimes, Erikson, it's possible to lose one's perspective. Especially when one is searching so hard for a solution."

"Do you mean me?"

"I know what a strain this must be for you. First Sam, and now Dr. Cho. Both were dear colleagues and friends who earned my respect. But I see no basis for your conclusion that Dr. Cho died from the same malignancy that somehow claimed Dr. Wolfe."

"I agree that only an autopsy would confirm it, and you know we couldn't get one."

Again Clements paused; but when he spoke, his tone rang with authority. "What if I were to tell you that we do have an autopsy? Would that make you change your opinion?"

Erikson was dumbfounded. "But—"

"Would it, Dr. Erikson?"

"Yes, I suppose. But how—"

"There are ways, Dr. Erikson. Not that you are to mention this to anyone. But there is one thing I can assure you of: Dr. Cho did not die of cancer."

Erikson was incredulous, unable to speak.

"But secret societies? Green objects?" Clements continued, making Erikson squirm. "You'd better get a grip on yourself, Doctor."

Clements hung up.

The minutes passed. Erikson was frustrated, feeling utterly helpless.

He dialed Taylor's apartment next.

"Taylor, you operated on Mike. Does some sort of a 'green object' mean anything to you?"

"A what?"

"Hank made some notes about a green object that might be related to Michelle. I found them in his apartment. Does that ring a bell?"

"Maybe he was referring to the cyst. Didn't I tell you about it?"

"No, but I wish you had."

"It was so damn small, I didn't make much of it."

"Was it green? Is a cyst ever green?"

"Usually not. But this one was. Green as grass; a tiny little thing. But don't worry, Hank thought it was benign. And he also mentioned he was still working on it."

Erikson felt a sudden rush of encouragement. The green object might even still be in the lab, he thought. "Thanks, Taylor. Catch you later."

Soon Erikson was walking through the hospital lobby. He felt for his hip pocket, and his fingers wandered across the heavy ring of keys that had belonged to Hank. The various keys to the lab would be there, along with the key to Hank's office. He wound his way through the hospital corridors until he reached the lab. The few technicians on duty paid no attention as he brazenly walked into the lab. Cho's office was in the rear, hidden from the goings-on up front. Erikson got out the key and let himself in.

The office was as neat as Hank always left it. He switched on the fluorescent light and gazed around, not certain what he was looking for. The room was dominated by a massive desk, atop which rested Hank's microscope. Erikson pulled back the chair and sat down.

Where to begin? The obvious place would be the surgical-specimen index. But the secretary who typed the pathology reports handled that locked file, and she wasn't in today. A green object that Hank was still working on . . . Had he possibly kept some sort of log for items that were still pending? Erikson opened the desk drawers and searched through the assorted files and folders. In the middle right-hand drawer, he found a fat folder simply marked "AWAITING FINAL MICRO." He pulled it out and quickly leafed through the pages. They were light blue papers, typewriter-sized, capped with the patient's name and file number. In the middle of the folder, he came across it: Michelle Van Dyne, A-307.

Beneath it was typed the visual, or "gross," description of the object. "The specimen consists of a single oval mass," it said. "It is symmetrical and smooth, 9 millimeters high and 5 millimeters in depth. It is firm but resilient, perfectly green in color, and weighs exactly 1 gram."

That description meant little right now. It couldn't help him. What Erikson needed was A-307. He replaced the folder and looked around the room. Several file cabinets stood against the far wall. He walked toward them and scanned the drawer labels. He opened the first one, marked A–E, and thumbed through the numbers. In seconds, he found it. He pulled out the folder. It was Michelle's hospital chart.

Opening it, he returned to the desk to read. Hank's longhand notes were filed neatly inside, in front of the face sheet that chronicled Michelle's official hospital record. Erikson read through Cho's observations slowly. He was incredulous. The spectrophotometry reports, the pigment analysis, the microscopic appearance . . . He blanched. Then he slowly turned and peered through the doorway, gazing in white-faced horror at the incubator that rested fifteen feet away.

A plant. The small green object was a living plant.

The chart grew heavy in Erikson's fingers, and he replaced it in the file. He couldn't believe what he had just read. The green object was something botanical and had been kept alive by the warmth of Michelle's body. It was a parasite. The device was a living, thriving, half-plant, half-electrical horror that had nursed on Michelle's body fluids. She didn't even know it had been there.

He found the key to the incubator and unlocked it, first removing an X-ray apron someone had left on its lid, and placed the petri dish on the desk. Lying there in front of him, the small green mass seemed harmless. He stared at it blankly. Who in God's name had inserted it on Michelle's ovary? And how? And why? He concluded that this was why Michelle's previous surgery had been performed. The surgery she insisted she hadn't undergone.

He couldn't seem to grasp all the stupefying information. He turned on the radio on Hank's desk, hoping the classical music would soothe him, help him think. He leaned over the desk and tried to concentrate, but the radio crackled with static. Erikson slapped the casing, but the audio seemed to be on the blink.

He got up to return the green sphere to the incubator.

No sooner did he reenter Hank's office than the radio was functioning perfectly. The music was sharp and clear. Erikson frowned. He looked at the radio, and then at the incubator. On impulse, he carried the large portable radio out to the incubator. The sound again began to whine, and the reception became brittle. When he returned the radio to the office, the musical quality corrected itself. He was astonished. The plant was generating some sort of signal that interfered with radio reception.

193

What the hell was this thing? he wondered. And what kind of signals did it generate? Obviously, the impulses interfered with the FM band. Erikson was thoroughly stumped. And then, after many minutes of concentration, he kicked himself for being so obtuse. Determining what he needed to know would be simple. He had all the tools he needed right in his own apartment. He locked the lab and hurried outside.

As the taxi wound through traffic, Erikson tried to recall where he had stored the gadget. Over the years, his apartment had become loaded with electronic devices, some of them fine equipment, others outright junk. He'd gotten interested in ham radio while still in college. A prankster even then, he had extended his interest, in graduate school, into electronic surveillance. He would bug his friends' rooms, tape the sounds of a couple making love, then play the tape back to them through a hidden speaker.

In his bedroom closet, he rummaged through numerous woofers, tweeters, and microphones before he found it. The field-strength meter was in the very back. He took it out of its carton, dusted it off, and plugged it in. The circuits glowed; it still worked.

Encouraged, Erikson carried the field-strength meter under his arm and returned to the lab.

THEY NOW had nearly everything they needed. The disastrous blunder earlier in the year had been rectified, and they were well on their way toward keeping their civilization alive. He looked at the breast pump, temporarily satisfied that there was almost a quart of milk in the container. Yet it wasn't nearly enough. They needed more, much more, a larger quantity to sustain the life that would be spawned months hence.

Once more the woman moaned, stirring in her sleep. It was time to nourish her again. Hanahpú motioned to the man at his side. The Indian went to the top of the bed and steadied

Michelle's face in his hands while Hanahpú removed a plastic stomach tube from his garment. He lubricated the tip, then placed it in one of her nostrils and fed the tubing through her nose. It was imperative that she remain asleep, lest she waken and witness the wonder of the plants, the mystical qualities to which the priests alone had been privy.

She was the perfect specimen. Yet, she was a burden. Still, there would be no reason to kill her in the manner in which they had dealt with her sister. In their haste, they hadn't realized that one was flawed. It had been necessary to dispose of her.

Hanahpú watched the woman, whose breath came in shuddering spasms. When he finished passing the tube, she relaxed. He taped the tubing firmly in place. With a nod from Hanahpú, the other Indian released Michelle's head.

Hanahpú took the syringe and filled it with a thick liquid. He attached the syringe tip to the tubing and squeezed slowly. The fluid went through the conduit to her stomach. He knew it would work quickly; not only would it provide nourishment, but she would soon return to her deep slumber. After checking to see that the funnels were secure, the two men left the room.

The Indians returned to Michelle's room every four hours, simulating nursing as closely as possible. They had nearly finished now—a matter of a few more days. This woman had been their salvation. She was the last outsider they would be forced to deal with. They would return her to her home, after she received the final herbal brew, to await the same fate that had befallen the others.

ERIKSON LOCKED Hank's office and pulled down the shades. He removed the culture dish from the incubator and set it on the desk. Then he turned on the field-strength meter and adjusted the dials. In less than a minute, numbers lit up on the meter's screen. Erikson had discovered what he wanted to know.

The green object was a *transmitter.*

He swallowed hard. It was time for the second part of his plan. He replaced the petri dish in the incubator and went to his car.

Once in the parking lot, he placed the field-strength meter on the seat beside him. He plugged its auto adapter into the cigarette lighter. Most of the electronic bugs he had previously encountered had had a very limited range. He turned on the meter and homed in on the signal frequency. The numbers suddenly blinked to life. The green object was transmitting on the FM band; once the frequency was adjusted, the digital display on his meter would indicate the exact distance from the transmitted signal source. The numbers revealed that in the hospital lot, he was precisely 110 meters from the incubator. Erikson was amazed. He shook his head in fascination, started the engine, and slowly drove away to test the signal's range.

The tiny green object was nothing more than a complex bioelectric bug. A tracking device.

As he weaved into traffic, the signal remained sharp and clear. Over the next half-hour, he drove approximately twenty miles before returning to the hospital. During that time, the signal strength showed no sign of diminution. It became apparent that this particular transmitter could be tracked over a very long range; perhaps its range was potentially unlimited. Someone had been using it for tracking Michelle since it had been planted within her. Following her. But why? Craig Erikson had pulled into the hospital lot when it suddenly hit him.

Because he might want her back.

He walked toward the hospital's entrance, breathing deeply. The answer to Michelle's disappearance was horrifyingly simple. The logic was crystal-clear. Days lost from Michelle's life; her memory impairment; the tampering with her ova; and now the transmitter—like the banding of an animal to permit an observer to watch its movements in the wild.

He now knew they had reclaimed her.

Chapter 15

THEY MET IN the middle of the night. Clements listened to Erikson's recitation without saying a word. Seated behind his desk, he looked across the smooth mahogany surface at the two young doctors before him, glaring at them, tight-lipped.

"Are you finished, Dr. Erikson?"

"I think that about covers it."

Clements rose from his chair. His face was livid with barely restrained anger. "I should fire both of you on the spot!" he snapped.

"But Dr. Clements—" Taylor protested.

"Goddammit, man, twenty-five women are dead from this disease!" He pounded the desk for emphasis as he glowered at them. "While everyone else is in the dark, you two stumble onto some incredibly valuable information, and you decide to keep it to yourselves! Did it ever occur to you to let other people in on your discoveries?"

"I didn't know it was important," Taylor apologized. "I figured it was a cyst. All I saw was this green mass next to her ovary, and I didn't think—"

"Precisely; you didn't think! Did you believe you could solve all of this alone?"

Erikson stood his ground. "But when I called you about the notes from Hank's apartment, you didn't seem interested."

"That was before I knew what this green object was, before you decided to mention this transmitter! I should have been notified days ago, when Dr. Taylor first extracted the object! Even Cho should have known better."

Erikson was still too intensely concerned about Michelle to be shamed by Clements. "Then you *do* think it's all related?"

"Of course it is. Any idiot can see that! Now get out of my office, both of you!"

Taylor rose swiftly, but Erikson hesitated. "What about Michelle?"

"Ten minutes," Clements replied icily. "You have the only key to that incubator, Dr. Erikson. I expect you to return with the object, along with Michelle Van Dyne's folder and that meter of yours, no later than four-ten."

Erikson saw that further discussion was futile. He had come to Clements in desperation, dragging Taylor along with him, and had laid his cards on the table in the hope that Clements would have some solution or plan of action. Yet now he was being dismissed.

The young doctors left.

Clements ignored the closing door and leafed through the pile of papers on his desk—Hank Cho's handwritten notes. The puzzling entries that had mystified him before seemed much clearer now, having become so the instant Erikson mentioned the transmitter. That was the missing link. For months he had been trying to put it together. Taylor wasn't alone in his speculation about intent; Clements himself had suspected as much long before. What had been lacking was the evidence.

In the beginning, there had been only the incessant cancer deaths, all linked by a peculiar floral aroma. Sam Wolfe had hinted about the association of plants and cancer. Though he hadn't admitted it then, Clements had thought the observation was keen, and probably significant. Then there had been the baffling cases of infantile pituitary disease; but they too appeared to fit Clements' theory, for even a first-year medical student knew that a newborn's pituitary was one of the richest sources of hormones that could accelerate growth. Most interesting were the references in Cho's notes, overlooked by Erikson, about the disappearances of the women; but most *disturbing* was what happened to those who got too close to the truth. Wolfe and then Cho.

Clements got up and paced. Outside his window, the late-night sky was still dark. Women who had disappeared, he thought, with no memory of their absence. He had been stunned when Erikson mentioned Michelle Van Dyne's memory loss: a missing piece that fitted the puzzle so well—even more so because she was the only nonpregnant woman among the lot. Compared with that, the discovery of the biotransmitter seemed anticlimactic.

The key lay with the Van Dyne woman; she had to be found. He was convinced that everything that was occurring centered on her. It didn't really matter that a rationale for precisely what was happening was lacking, that the sequence of events linking Van Dyne with the pregnant women wasn't clear. Plants, pituitary glands, pregnant women, cancer . . . all related hormonally; confusing bits of endocrinology which meant nothing separately, but which, when viewed together, horrified even him.

ERIKSON LEFT Clements' office disheartened. He had no choice but to comply with Clements' orders; in fact, it was his only hope. Back in his car in the hospital lot, the meter, adjusted to the proper frequency, was still hooked up as he had left it. The dial lit up in metric distance, and now showed 106.9 meters, the precise distance from his car to the incubator.

But as he reached to unplug the electronic device, he saw movement. The number on the screen had changed: it now read 108.4 meters. As he stared at it in surprise, it changed again, to 112.0. He knew instantly what that meant.

The transmitter was moving.

The numbers blinked more rapidly now. Erikson sat upright in his seat, heart pounding. The change in the display indicated movement at a slow pace, like a walk. But soon it became more like a run. If the numbers were correct, the object was moving due south, away from the hospital. Had Clements taken it? he wondered. Impossible; he had the only key in his pocket. That meant someone else had taken it.

Clements would be furious, but he had to keep up with the signal. It was his one link with Michelle. He gunned the engine and sped out of the lot, following the blinking numbers. Whoever had stolen the transmitter had retrieved the only thing that might incriminate him. Erikson raced through traffic, narrowing the distance between his car and the transmitter.

FAINT PINK streaks of first dawn lighted the sky. Erikson allowed his car to slow. He was drawing nearer to the signal, which was now only blocks away. The morning traffic became increasingly congested. He ignored safety and weaved from lane to lane. Finally he was only a hundred meters away. He maintained that distance, scanning the cars in front of him. There were dozens of vehicles; it could be any one of them. But then, the signal veered sharply left. Moments later, Erikson also turned left and followed it—a nondescript white van.

He eased off a bit, not wanting to be seen. He knew that the field-strength meter had a range of at least twenty miles. If he lagged a mile or two behind, they shouldn't spot him.

He followed the signal down Massachusetts Avenue and swung west on 11th Street, staying several lights behind. He crossed the 11th Street Bridge, turning south. The first sign for U.S. 295 appeared. When he saw the van follow its arrow, he was more content to widen the gap.

He stayed three kilometers behind as the van headed in the direction of Route 495 and crossed the Woodrow Wilson Bridge into Alexandria. Soon he turned west again on Route 66, for what now looked like a lengthy journey.

The van continued west, into farm country. He was beginning to wonder if he hadn't made a mistake. Suppose their destination was Cleveland, or beyond? If it was going to be a long trip, he couldn't stay awake forever. He had been up most of the night and was already exhausted. Sooner or later, he would have to rest.

He continued west, into the Blue Ridge Mountains. If the person or people in the van knew someone was behind them, they gave no indication. Erikson saw from the meter that the van had turned south on to I-81. Thank God he had a full tank of gas.

The highway entered the natural trough of the Shenandoah Valley. The scenery was magificent now, as autumn approached; the foliage was at the height of its color change. The Massanutten Mountains rose steeply to the highway's left, speckled with orange and gold. Mindful of the three-kilometer marking on his field-strength meter, Erikson tried to relax and take in the breathtaking view—the kind of view that was intended to be taken with someone special, an experience to be shared.

Outside Roanoke, the signal changed direction so sharply that Erikson didn't see it at first. The numbers on his meter plummeted, falling to 0 as he passed the exit the van must have taken. He hadn't been paying close enough attention. He quickly backtracked, turning his car around until he found the signal again. He homed in on it. Soon, he was going south on Virginia's Blue Ridge Parkway.

The smooth ribbon of the interstate contrasted with the narrow, winding parkway. Erikson kept the signal steady in front of him. They were traveling more slowly, and he tried to look at the endless patchwork of fields and farms amidst the mountains. To either side he saw the awesomely craggy overhangs of rock that roofed in underground caverns, girded by rushing mountain streams and wild flowers spread out like a carpet.

The road wound gently upward, steadily into the mountains. The Highlands, Virginia's southwest corner, was a land of tall peaks, great pine forests, and peaceful mountain lakes. Every few miles the paved surface would curve around a rocky overhang hundreds of feet high. The endless stretch of mountain greenery, dappled with rich tones of autumn, concealed well-worn trails and bridle paths. But then, near the small town of Willis, the signal abruptly changed direction again. Forty miles south of Roanoke, the van left the parkway and headed up a rural mountain road.

There were fewer and fewer farms with land under cultivation. The expanse of wilderness was relentless. Erikson rounded a bend in the road and then jolted to a stop. Before him was dust rising from a completely hidden unpaved road. Erikson pulled over to the shoulder and parked. His was the only car on the road. He took out the binoculars he always stored in his glove compartment and tried to catch a glimpse of the van's ascent up the remote mountain. Through breaks in the pine, all he could see was a faint streak of dust that inched upward. To judge by the signals coming from his meter, the van was slowing. Then it stopped. Completely. He waited ten minutes. There was no further movement.

It could be a trap. But suddenly the signals on his meter began to fade. In seconds, they were gone. End of the road. He had lost her.

Chapter 16

SHE WAS UNDERWATER. She could see the light at the surface and struggled toward it. It was strange how easily she could breathe beneath the waves; she had never been able to do that before. Almost there now. With a final push, she broke through the surface and found herself awakening from a dream. Michelle looked about her.

Her vision was blurred, her lips thick and rubbery. She shook her head, forcing herself to focus. Something tugged at the corner of her mouth, and irritated her throat. She tried to lift her arms but couldn't. There was a peculiar ache in her lower abdomen, and something held fast to her chest.

She gazed about stunned, in a terrifying moment of shock. Where, in God's name, had they brought her? She looked around in her terror, still dazed, growing damp with perspiration. She was in some sort of room, a room filled with plants. Her gaze darted through the exotic growth. She had never seen such a profusion of plant life before. Michelle looked everywhere in her panic, inexplicably fascinated by the splendor about her.

She had to stay awake. She sensed that these people, whoever they were, intended that she remain asleep, so that they might . . . what? Did they mean to kill her?

She heard the sound of footsteps nearing the room. She

took a deep, shuddering breath and closed her eyes, knowing that they must think she still slept. There was the sound of a door opening, and the footsteps came nearer. Something like tubing brushed against her cheek as it was lifted up, and Michelle fought the tug in her throat that nearly made her gag. Soon the tube grew cool as something passed through it. Her mind trembled at the thought of what might happen next. But then her fear began to wane as she succumbed into blackness.

HOURS, MAYBE days, passed. Michelle kept drifting into and out of consciousness. She was never fully alert, though the amount of time she was awake seemed to steadily grow, as if she were becoming immune to what they were giving her. She was rigid with fear and repulsion over what they had done to her body.

The two funnels on her breasts weren't painful, and yet they caused a sensation of steady suction. The appliances mortified her. Michelle wrenched her body violently about. But no matter how she twisted, she couldn't shake the cups free. She knew she wasn't pregnant; the milk that trickled from her breasts defied the laws of nature. What else had they done to her? And what else might they do?

She was determined to survive. What kept her sane was her observation of the plants. The room was vibrant with communication, an extraordinary dialogue. Each time she awakened, though her vision was never quite clear, she studied them as if through a thin veil. Initially, there was the slightest of movements. But as she watched, she could have sworn the plants began to sway toward her. She thought at first there was a breeze in the room, yet there wasn't. And then there was the sound. It was a susurrant, lyrical whistling; a faint, faraway siren. Petals seemed to curl to its call, folding and opening like scrolls. Green leaves wafted imperceptibly up and down, eagle wings flapping in slow motion. Like a sea breeze across a marsh, stalk and stem waved in unison, a choreography of botanical dancers that swayed together.

The ballet would continue for many minutes, and Michelle felt drawn to it. She had the most halcyon sense of tranquillity watching it, as if they were . . . performing for her. The timeless, regal quality of their motion calmed her, gave her a feeling of serenity.

She heard them returning, and once again she closed her eyes. They adjusted the tubes, instilling the cool substance that filled her stomach. Soon her consciousness drifted, and the footsteps departed. This time, however, she didn't quite fall fully asleep. Her body was sluggish, caught in a dreamlike slumber, yet her mind held fast to the slender thread of consciousness.

She willed her eyes to open. They were leaden, and it was incredibly difficult. Michelle was vaguely aware that her straps were loose, looser than they had ever been before. With every ounce of strength she could muster, she began to tug at her restraints. Though still dazed, she began to realize for the first time that she might have a single opportunity to escape.

Her surprise gave her strength. Ever so slowly, she began to pull at her straps. Her muscles were heavy, her motions clumsy. She quietly worked at the straps, chafing her skin, twisting her arms to and fro. The leather abraded her wrists, but she was making progress.

She sweated from the strain, and the sweat aided her. Her body grew slick with perspiration. It ran down her forearms to her wrists, sliding in droplets under the restraints. She was dimly aware that it was burning her cuts, but the stinging kept her from drifting back into somnolence. She managed to pull one hand out to where the knuckle caught against the strap. Then, with one final burst of energy, she pulled her right hand loose.

Her vision was still blurred, her thoughts clouded. She clumsily untied herself and ripped the loathsome funnels away. Milk ran down her belly in white rivulets. Michelle tried to get up, but lost her balance. Like a drunk, she toppled from the mattress.

For minutes she lay on the cold stone, her cheek against

the floor. It was all she could do to open her eyes again. Slowly she struggled to her knees, conscious of the racing of her heart and the heaving of her lungs. She crawled to the door, willing herself into a semblance of calm, commanding the tremor that shook her body to cease. It was an imposition of mind and spirit she hadn't summoned since her days in competition. With the greatest of effort, she pulled herself up and crouched against the doorframe. Eyes closed, she was suddenly fearful that the slightest additional sound might give her away. She listened for movement outside the room; heard none; then eased open the door and stepped outside.

The stone corridor was long and dark. There was no sound, and little light. Michelle had no idea where she was, or where she might go. A voice within her compelled her to move and slowly begin to stumble ahead, reeling from wall to wall.

She tried to walk slowly, on the balls of her bare feet, but it was impossible. She fumbled with the buttons of her blouse, but her fingers were too heavy to close them. The rocky floor was smooth and cool. There was a kind of faint light throughout the passageway, a pale glow overhead that seemed to come from within the rock itself. Even in her daze, Michelle had the impression that the passageway was hewn out of solid rock, as if the entire complex were an enormous granite sponge honeycombed with a labyrinth of interconnecting channels. The hard stone wall, though its surface was not jagged, was slightly irregular to the touch; its contour helped her hand slide forward as she groped for support.

She wasn't quite aware what she was doing, but she knew she had to keep moving, straining to hear any sound. Still nothing; only the beating of her heart, and the throbbing of the arteries in her neck. She staggered forward into the darkness. Her legs wobbled. Once again she clutched the wall for support. Soon she came to a bend in the corridor, and she went around it. There was slightly more light ahead. She slowed to a crawl.

The curving path led to the mouth of a cave. She was inside it, looking dizzily out to the light beyond. In front of her lay a wide, shimmering pool. The increased radiance reflected toward her off its glistening surface. The pool was a lake within a cavern. Michelle squinted above toward the rows of silvery stalactites that hung like tinsel, moist and shining. Every few seconds a drop of condensation would break loose and strike the lake with a hollow plunk, sending tiny wavelets across the surface of the water.

She followed the narrow path leading out of the cave. The trail skirted the edge of the water, and Michelle struggled to maintain her balance. Beyond the gleaming lake lay another dark passage. Bewildered and terrified, she forged on.

Inside the second cave, her back melted into the rock as she slithered around a curve. She thought she heard a noise, and her heart leaped. Nearing panic, she hurried forward, pawing the area before her like a blind woman.

The corridor ended in a widening passageway that was the cave's border. A path led into bushes beyond, like a winding trail on a rain-forest floor. Not far away was an abundance of greenery, a mixture of trees and shrubs and vines dense as a jungle. Michelle held her breath as she stepped out onto the path.

Her heart beat faster as she walked into the luxuriant, sylvan wilderness. The rich earth was moist and springy underfoot, and dark green fronds with viny tendrils brushed about her head and shoulders. The thicket was black and forbidding; and yet she had the greatest sense of tranquillity as she pushed through the foliage.

Soon she emerged from the heavy growth. Compared with the darkness behind her, the light ahead glared like the sun. She slowed and looked frantically about, unable to get her bearings. She sensed a change in the footing underneath. Before, all of her steps had been on solid rock, as if she were walking on ground made smooth by millions of footsteps. Now the earth seemed rough, and it led toward a field of tall, reed-like stalks topped by dazzling silver plumes. The earth grew moist, then mushy. Michelle couldn't be sure, but the reeds seemed to be moving, swaying, blown by a zephyr. At the base of the tall grass she saw a bright splash of color. In that instant of recognition, the magenta hue screamed at her senses. Before her lay row upon row of blood-red orchids.

She heard the shouts to her rear, and she stumbled and fell. She lifted herself in desperation, exhausted and confused. Though still in a daze, Michelle headed toward the orchids. She felt drawn to them, yielding to an overwhelming sense of tranquillity. And she smelled it as she proceeded: fruity and herbal, an exotic fragrance. The delightful aroma beckoned her, promising serenity. The voices behind her grew louder. She knew she had to escape.

She broke into a run, and her eyes searched for a path in the onrushing tall grass. The rustling of the stalks called to her, and the fragrance filled her lungs. She was sprinting now, still dizzy but feeling the spring return to her step. She ran in a blind frenzy as fear of recapture infused strength into her wobbly legs.

Hanahpú and four others emerged from the passage. They found her footprints there, leading toward the swampy marsh. He and the others slowed to a halt. The anger and surprise at her awakening and escape began to wane. They now had everything they needed from this woman, and she was saving them the need to recapture her. The fool was scurrying toward her death.

Michelle plunged forward, feeling cool water about her feet. She charged through the orchids, feeling their multitude of green stalks brush against her like bamboo. She moved headlong through the smooth stems. The water splashed into the air as she ran. It fell on her skin in a shower of droplets as fresh and pure as rain. A gasping sound of joy and relief escaped her. The rustling of the reeds sang to her, and she lunged forward, gracefully now, watching the gentle weaving of stalk and stem. The reeds almost seemed to part before her.

Hanahpú smiled at the ever-fainter splashing that grew muffled in the distance. He grinned and nodded to his comrades. They turned and reentered the inner sanctuary, knowing there was to be no escape from the nursery of death.

Chapter 17

IT CAME AS a flash, the slightest blur of movement. He slammed on the brakes and felt the skidding of his tires on pine needles. He killed the engine, quickly rolled down the window, and stared through the wooded thicket. A deer? Quietly, Erikson opened the car door and stepped onto the spongy earth. All his senses were taut as he paced, slowly and silently, toward what he thought he'd seen. And then he gasped. Suddenly he was running, bounding uncontrollably through the forest.

She appeared like a ghost, arising from nowhere. As he neared her, his heart rose in his throat; for though he was making a frightful racket, she was oblivious of him, staring vacantly ahead as she glided down the mountainside.

"Mike! Can you hear me? *Mike!*"

Still she gazed ahead through eyes of glass. Erikson took in her appearance as he skidded to a halt. Her clothes were in tatters, the shreds of her blouse damp and sticky. Her skin, paler than he remembered, was streaked with dirt, smudged with random cuts and scrapes. Was she in shock? He grabbed her by the arms and looked into the dullness of her eyes, shaking her roughly.

"Mike!" He slapped her cheeks, pleading. "For God's sake, snap out of it!"

It seemed like an eternity before her eyes focused on his. But once they did, they welled with tears. Her whole body shuddered in his grasp, and her chin began to quiver. She was struggling desperately to talk. Her trembling jaw fell open, and the tears rolled down her cheeks, as she began, "They . . . they . . ."

Erikson couldn't bear it anymore, and his arms circled her protectively, drawing her tighter than he had ever held her before. "Baby, baby," he soothed, stroking her hair, hoping the warmth of his arms would quell the violent shaking that racked her body. Then his eyes wandered up the hillside, tracing the direction she had come from. There was nothing but open woods, yet he knew they weren't safe.

Calmly, "Come on, Mike." He led her back toward the car, slowly at first, then more quickly. Every few paces he would glance over his shoulder, up the mountain toward the source of her shock and panic. They're out there, he thought.

By the time they reached the car, her initial limpness had changed into clinging terror. She refused to let him go. Firmly, he eased her into the seat beside him. Then he slammed the door and gunned the engine. Bits of leaf and earthen debris erupted from the rear tires as the car sped away. Soon he was racing down the mountainside, careening wildly, scraping against trees and branches and jarring into unseen ruts that nearly sent them flying from their seats. It was a nightmarish eternity before they reached the highway below. Erikson floored the accelerator and kept his foot pressed down until the mounting speed and distance covered persuaded him to slow.

Still shaken and pale, Michelle didn't speak at first, and Erikson decided not to press her. But when they reached the parkway, she broke down completely. She leaned against him and clutched his arm tightly, her hysterical sobbing mixed with nonsensical mumblings he couldn't decipher. It was a long time before her tears ceased. He gently eased his arm free and put it around her shoulders. Michelle drifted into a fitful sleep, and he drove in silence for more than an hour. It wasn't until they neared the District line that she awakened. She composed herself and tried to talk.

She spoke haltingly at first, but then her words spilled out in gushes. Erikson listened without interrupting; questioning her now would invite a return of panic. What she was saying seemed positively incredible. If he hadn't spoken with Helmsley about the Maya, and the orchid in the photograph, and if he hadn't known about the transmitter, he would have believed she had gone totally insane.

Still unclear was what they had done to her, and why. Taking Michelle's breast milk . . . to what end? Michelle's earlier discovery of her sister's infertility had to be another key factor. Yet the answer to it all eluded him. He decided, for now, not to tell her what he knew of "the Indians," as she had referred to them. There would be time later when she was calmer.

She hesitated, realizing her own words sounded ridiculous. "I know it's hard to believe. But I saw it," she said, her voice rising. "I really saw it. It's the place I dreamed of over and over. But this time it wasn't a dream."

"Mike, Mike . . ." He pulled her close, kissed her forehead. "It's okay. It's going to be okay."

"Do you believe me, Craig?"

"Of course I do." He wouldn't pursue it now, knowing that what he personally believed was of little consequence. What mattered was what *they* believed, he thought, as he drove through the first outskirts of the capital.

An hour later, she was safely tucked into bed. He knew that what she needed most now was rest. Every few moments he checked that she slept. He sipped a cup of tea, wondering how he would ever broach the subject with Clements. Deep in thought, he was suddenly startled by a soft moan from the bedroom. He dropped his cup with a clatter and rushed to her side.

Michelle was curled up in bed, still asleep. She had rolled over, throwing off the covers in the process. At first he was reassured by the steady, even tempo of her breathing. But then his eyes widened in fear, and the color drained from his face as he noted the crimson stain on the mattress.

She was hemorrhaging again.

CLEMENTS FINISHED the vaginal suturing, utterly perplexed. The bleeding area he had just resutured was from a fresh incision not more than a day or two old, its appearance hardly consistent with the operation Taylor had done a while before. He thought about the cystlike structure Erikson had discovered to be a transmitter. After a moment's hesitation, he tore off his gloves and asked for a new surgical gown. He had to look into her abdomen for himself.

"Nearly finished, Dr. Clements?" asked the anesthesiologist.

"No, I'm going to do a laparoscopy."

The nurse was startled. "But we only have consent for—"

"She may have internal bleeding!" he barked, knowing that his slightest objection demanded compliance. "Just prep her belly for me."

Minutes later, with Michelle still anesthetized, Clements made a small incision beneath her navel and inserted the surgical telescope. He had a perfect view of Michelle's pelvic organs through the laparoscope. He inspected the area where Taylor had removed the "cyst," but he saw nothing. Then he narrowed his field of view to the ovaries.

The normal-sized ovary had a corrugated surface, somewhat like cauliflower. In its crevices were tiny fluid-filled spaces, the follicles that contained ova. Yet now, in a dozen places on both ovaries, there were punctate red dots.

"What the hell?" he murmured to himself. "Turn up the light intensity."

The nurse did as bidden, and the laparoscopic field of view grew brighter. Clements studied the ovaries closely. The scarlet specks appeared to be healing hemorrhages. He looked up, stunned. In a far corner of his brain, there was a steady, ever-louder drumming of comprehension.

To his trained eye, it appeared without doubt that the follicles had been drained. Someone had removed Michelle Van Dyne's ova.

THEY LOOKED in on Michelle, saw that she still slept, and quietly closed the door to her hospital room. Dr. Clements paused to remind the security man that Miss Van Dyne was to have absolutely no visitors; then he motioned for Erikson to follow him. A spacious solarium was at the end of the hall. Clements halted in front of a long window and surveyed the busy traffic in a city once again at peace with itself.

"You can't expect me to keep that from her!" Erikson snapped.

"Keep your voice down, Erikson. 'Expect' it? No, I demand it. As her doctor!"

"She has a right to know, Dr. Clements."

"To know what? You said yourself that she remembers no such operation. What possible good could come from your telling her that a handful of ova have been removed? Given what she's been through, that sort of information might damage her irrevocably."

What good, indeed? thought Erikson. The woman he loved was safe now, on the road to physical recovery. Her emotional health was another matter. He hadn't yet told her of his knowledge of the orchid in Trish's photograph, nor anything about the Maya. Did he have the right to tamper with her precarious psychological balance, simply that the truth be known? Knowing about all of it might very well drive her insane, as Clements implied. Still, Erikson wasn't satisfied.

"You don't believe a word either of us said, do you?"

"On the contrary, I believe quite a bit. There are just some aspects of both your stories that strike me as . . . fanciful."

"We didn't imagine it, Dr. Clements. Or make it up, if that's what you're implying."

Clements turned to him, still the commanding image of authority, but his expression had softened. "I'm not suggesting you did. It's just that in times of stress, certain things can be misremembered."

Erikson shook his head, annoyed. "You're incredible."

"Am I, Dr. Erikson? It strikes me that the 'incredible' elements are coming from your mouth, not mine."

Erikson lost his patience. "Just what *is* it you believe, anyway?"

Clements, unruffled, gazed through the window. "Think of the people out there, Erikson. More than a million. They go to and from work with little knowledge of what really occurs in this city. Over there," he said, pointing toward the Capitol, "or right here, within these very walls. They have no idea of the tremendous advances in medical technology. What do you suppose they would think—those civil servants, those housewives—of your theory of a primitive society?"

"Then you *do* believe me?"

Clements continued, ignoring him. "Probably the most remarkable progress has been in the field of fertility. Out there, all they hear is about test-tube babies. Yet that concept alone staggers their imagination. But there is more—so much more. We have nearly reached the point where we can take a single cell and make it reproduce an entire human being. We can manipulate its genes, alter its life-span. Up until now, the real race had been to see who would do it first."

"What do you mean, 'up to now'?"

"The race is over, Erikson. It's been done. I believe they did it with Michelle Van Dyne."

"The Maya?"

"Oh, Erikson, please. Of course not. Don't you realize you're deluded with this Indian nonsense? There are dozens of possibilities, each far more logical than what you suggest: billionaire industrialists, anxious to clone themselves; genetic-engineering firms; private medical enterprises. Whoever they are, they're ingenious. Clearly they were interested in Trish Van Dyne, the perfect female specimen. And perhaps she was murdered, as you believe. That left the younger Van Dyne as the obvious choice. So they took her ova and have probably fertilized them by now. No doubt they intend to enhance their growth with infantile pituitary extracts. My speculation is the only plausible answer."

"What were they doing with the pregnant women?"

"Taking their placental lactogen, of course. That substance is produced in the afterbirth; it's a placental form of growth hormone. No doubt it will also be used to accelerate the growth of the fertilized ova. And what better source of placental lactogen than the human placenta? What surprises me most is why none of us in the field ever thought of it before. But their true genius, Erikson, must lie in their discovery that the amount of placental lactogen can be dramatically increased by giving the woman particular herbal derivatives. I'd wager on it. Unfortunately, those derivatives caused a rather lethal side effect."

"What does this have to do with Michelle's breast milk? You can't deny she was lactating!"

"I *don't* deny it," Clements replied, unruffled. "These children, her children, that will be spawned, perhaps months from now—they'll need ideal nourishment. What better than an endless supply of breast milk taken from the natural mother?"

Erikson wasn't convinced. "I don't see what this has to do with Michelle's first disappearance."

"Nor do I. Yet if, as Miss Van Dyne alleges, her sister was sterile—then the people who now wanted Michelle's ova would probably want to convince themselves that she had no such fertility problem. No doubt they would want to inspect her 'plumbing' firsthand."

"But if you don't believe the Maya were responsible, how can you account for the fact that the epidemic has apparently stopped?"

"Mainly because we're aware of this group's activities,

215

whoever they are. It's too dangerous for them to continue. Anyway, they now have what they want."

Erikson could only shake his head. Here was a publicly acclaimed medical hero, the man who some of the media speculated had spearheaded the cure for the cancer epidemic, still refusing to believe the truth of their story. "So what's the bottom line, Dr. Clements? Are you simply going to write me and Michelle off as a couple of crazies?"

"No, you're far too intelligent for that. But what would you think if you were in my place? There's no trace of the transmitter you describe, and not even the National Park Service can locate Miss Van Dyne's "secret paradise"; not to mention the fact that, going by your orchid theory, the orchids she says she encountered should have killed her by now! Your Dr. Helmsley is reputed to be unbalanced. Yet the power of his suggestion is too strong to allow you to isolate the truth. Miss Van Dyne, on the other hand, could have been hallucinating because of their drugs or something more sinister. She has been deliberately confused about her environment during the operation."

Over the next few days, the endless questioning took its toll on Michelle. She became withdrawn and sullen. Erikson tried to spare her the worst, but the psychiatrists interrogated him too for hours. Everything had to be cleared through Clements. The older man truly believed what he'd confided to Erikson, and no evidence arose to dissuade him from that belief.

Erikson's explanation was given no credence. Clements scoffed at Michelle's preposterous tale and forbade them to repeat it to anyone. Then she was subjected to deep, intensive hypnosis. And finally she was left alone, for the story that kept emerging was so ludicrous that Clements ultimately insisted that everyone involved had been brainwashed.

In the end, Erikson was relieved that the interrogations were curtailed. His reputation at the hospital was already jeopardized, and Michelle had little to gain from the burden of proving her story to be true. His hope was that they would both forget the whole thing—awaken as if from a bad dream.

Chapter 18

THERE WAS LITTLE traffic on the Pennsylvania Turnpike as they drove toward Cleveland. An unseasonably early chill dusted the Adirondacks with flurries that swept out into the Atlantic. Now the snow had stopped. A patina of frost hugged the roadway's shoulders, and eddies of white flakes gusted across the concrete like tiny ghosts skittering over the highway.

Michelle looked out the window. The pine-studded hills were dark and deep, and she lost her thoughts in their depths, content to let her gaze wander through acre after acre of wind-whipped boughs. The view calmed her. Now, many weeks after her ordeal, she still needed that comfort.

Though the cancers had stopped, she had only recently grown convinced she was safe. They rarely mentioned Clements or the more popular speculation in the media; but they talked endlessly about what had happened in the crater—he doing most of the listening as Michelle rambled on for hours of repetitive, often confusing description. Her narrative bewildered him, but he never interrupted. Most perplexing was her description of the magenta orchids, the death flower. He would never understand how she had escaped the doom they bore. Deep down, he was worried that the frightening tribulation she had experienced might have induced an intermittent psychosis. But his psychiatric colleagues reassured him that such disorders were always temporary in nature, and that the best remedy would be companionship and support, until her catharsis eventually spent itself and she returned to full normality.

There was no longer a question of telling her about the surgery, or the missing ova. With his prompting, Michelle now believed that her bleeding had been caused by some accident she couldn't accurately recall. He would protect her from the facts forever, if need be, for he was now convinced that whatever had truly been done to her had left no residual damage. She had resumed running, and Clements convinced him that her physical and reproductive health would be completely normal. There was no reason she need ever know.

At times she still thought she could feel them following her. Tracking her. She lost count of the instants when she sensed a sudden chill and looked over her shoulder, only to see nothing; or the times she would wake screaming in her sleep, seeking the warmth of his arms to dispel the horror of her dreams.

Now, Erikson followed her gaze to the distant hills, the trees bare except for scattered dark patches of fir and pine that covered the slopes like a tattered green blanket. And he was nearly satisfied. Their relationship was secure, enough for them to think of making it permanent. With his urging, she had agreed to a brief trip home. He and her family had arranged a small celebration—an engagement party, of sorts.

The gray sky had cleared, giving way to streaks of wispy white cloud against a backdrop of blue. To Michelle it seemed surpassingly fresh and pure. As she gazed up toward the blue sky above a neighboring mountain, her expression softened. The summit was ringed by a halo of mist, and a rainbow of color streamed downward when the sun struck the fog.

"Stop here," she said suddenly.

"You want me to pull over?"

"Just for a moment."

He slowed on the shoulder of the road, and they got out

of the car. Wordlessly she started up the slope, as if she knew precisely where she was going. He followed her in bewilderment. They had gone several hundred yards when she stopped at the edge of the forest, a look of serene contentment on her face. A rising breeze gusted down the mountain.

"Do you hear it?" she asked.

"The breeze?"

She just smiled at him, kissed him on the cheek. He would never understand the message. She alone had seen their swaying, heard them cry out to one another. She heard the sound of their very existence. And she knew. In that moment of her understanding, a sense of peace enveloped her like a warm blanket, quieting her fears once and forever.

"I remember a riddle," she said. "If a tree falls in the forest, or if a twig snaps, and no one is there to hear it—what sound does it make?"

"I remember the answer. No sound."

She smiled at him again, then looked away. The wind blew harder, and gusts ruffled their clothing. A low howling sailed on the currents that swept the air. The wind caught Michelle's fine hair and sent it across her face like a veil. There was whistling in her ears.

An icy breeze danced through the trees in invisible circles, and he was chilled. But Michelle just stood there, her placid gaze sifting through the deep forest. He gently tugged on her elbow.

"Let's go, Mike."

Still she was motionless, head cocked to one side as if she were listening to something, a smile on her face. What, in God's name? he thought. Finally she yielded to his urging. Grim-faced, he turned and led her down the mountain as quickly as possible.

SHE SLEPT on Erikson's shoulder, adrift in a sea of dreams. It was a long drive back to Washington. Jarred awake by a bump in the road, she stretched in her seat and yawned. Erikson noted that her fatigue of recent months finally seemed gone.

"How're you feeling?" he asked.

"Great. Better than ever."

"I still can't believe your parents had separate bedrooms for us. We'll have to make up for that as soon as we get back," he said playfully, tracing his fingertips against her soft neck.

"Hmmm," she sighed, rubbing her cheek to the warmth of his touch. "I suppose they are a little old-fashioned."

"And those flowers!" he laughed. "I can't believe they bought out the florist shop for such a small party."

"They didn't," said Michelle, gazing out the window. "I did."

Chapter 19

MICHELLE RETURNED TO WORK as if nothing had happened. Within weeks she was once again the energetic young executive her colleagues had come to know and love. She had started to run again, and the papers were abuzz when, after a scant few weeks of training, she led the local heats with a blistering pace. At the hospital, the incident of Erikson's short absence now forgotten, he resumed his own briefly precarious career, quickly regaining his former prestige and stature through his characteristic admixture of wit and hard work. Over the weeks, Michelle refurbished her apartment, adorning it with the masculine touches that made him feel at home.

He had an unusually busy day at work. He was exhausted when he returned to her apartment; after giving her a warm kiss, he had to lie down. She brought him a drink as he loosened his tie.

"Did you work out tonight?"

"As always." She smiled. "And listen to this: They want me to run at the Pan-American Invitational in April!"

"That's great, Mike. Where is it held?"

"In Mexico City."

He had a sudden glimpse of the past, of a squalid hut and a dust-filled street, an old man in a ghetto. . . . Don't be ridiculous, he thought. "How long will you be gone?"

"Four or five days. The meet itself is on a Saturday, but I need a few days to acclimatize to the altitude."

"Do you want me to go with you?"

"No, silly, you're busy enough as it is."

He turned on the living-room TV while she undressed in the bedroom. He stretched out sleepily on the couch. The late-night news was on. He leaned against the cushions and watched without watching, dulled by the flickering images. He reached for the TV's remote control, about to turn the set off when the figure of Ridley Clements flashed on the screen. Erikson closed his eyes and listened.

"Have you concluded that the women of Washington can finally feel safe?" asked the reporter.

"I think so. It's been over three months since the last cancer death. Not one new case has been reported since then."

"I suppose this virtually ensures Senate approval of your nomination as Surgeon General."

"That would be flattering, Miss Bernard. But my main concern has always been with this disease, not politics."

"Are you still working under the assumption that it was caused by a virus?"

"Yes. We still haven't identified the precise strain, though I imagine we'll pin it down in a few weeks."

"How do you account for its sudden disappearance, Dr. Clements? During the summer, we all had the impression that it was an epidemic, out of control."

"I presume it was the development of natural immunity. An organism as virulent as this probably infected the entire Washington area. Most people responded the way the body intended, with the development of antibodies that neutralized the virus. Some pregnant women, for reasons we're not sure, simply didn't manufacture those antibodies. And for them, unfortunately, the infection proved fatal."

Brilliant, Dr. Clements, Erikson thought, as he was overtaken by sleepiness. He buried his face in a cushion and surrendered to fatigue. He slept, no longer hearing the newsman's

222

voice, or Michelle's soft footsteps as she tiptoed into the living room. Her eyes fixed on the TV for a moment and then she shut it off.

She disliked lying to Craig. The altitude would have no effect on her; her physical condition was excellent. Yet she wanted those extra days. There was someone there, she knew; she sensed it in her soul. The presence of the one person who might blindly stumble onto secrets that only she must know. She dared not let that happen.

She glided to the living-room window, where the bulbs she had planted for winter bloom were just beginning to blossom in a clay pot filled with paper-white narcissi. Michelle stroked their petals. Then she gently wagged her finger in front of them before she held it still. The thin flower stems slowly inclined toward her finger until they touched it. Finally she looked up, her blue eyes glowing radiantly as she peered out across the capital's nighttime panorama. Her piercing gaze fixed intently on the once-magnificent spruce adorning her neighbor's lawn. Its drooping branches, bedecked with thousands of glistening Christmas lights, slowly inclined forward as if to touch her living-room window.